DEATH

runs

ADRIFT

ALSO BY KAREN MACINERNEY

"Mixes a pinch ~~...~~ ᴀᴛʜ ~~...~~ in island divided by environmental issues and, of course, murder. Add Karen MacInerney to your list of favorite Maine mystery authors."—Lea Wait, author of the Antique Print Mystery Series

"Just what's needed for a cozy evening in front of the fire."—Cynthia Riggs, author of the Martha's Vineyard Mystery Series

"Karen MacInerney has a winning recipe for a great series."—Julie Obermiller, Mystericale.com

"Clever plotting, charming characters—and of course, decadent recipes—will leave you hungry for more."—Michele Scott, author of the Wine Lover's Mystery Series

Berried to the Hilt

"The fourth in this pleasant cozy series highlights the glories of Maine, which this time include several recipes chock-full of cranberries."—*Kirkus Reviews*

"The satisfying conclusion will whet the reader's appetite for Natalie's next adventure."—*Publishers Weekly*

"MacInerney is at her whimsical best in her fourth visit to the charming Gray Whale Inn on Cranberry Island, Maine."—*Mystery Scene Magazine*

Murder Most Maine

"All thumbs up for *Murder Most Maine*, another in the engaging series of Cranberry Island mysteries. Karen MacInerney writes with verve and vitality, and her Natalie Barnes is a Maine original. I'm ready to book a room at the Gray Whale Inn!"—Susan Wittig Albert, bestselling author of *Nightshade* and other China Bayles Herbal Mysteries

"MacInerney adds a dash of the supernatural, throws in some touristy tidbits, and finishes with some tasty diet-right recipes."—*Publishers Weekly*

Dead and Berried

"I love this series. I wish I could go stay at the Gray Whale Inn. The descriptions of the island and the Inn are so wonderful. It sounds like a place you could go to get away from everything. Natalie is a great character as well. She's well-rounded and naturally inquisitive. The recipes and food descriptions will make you hungry! . . . The author has created plenty of twists and turns to keep the reader guessing. I highly recommend this book and *Murder on the Rocks*, the first in this series."—Dawn Dowdle, www.mysteryloverscorner.com

"A delicious sequel to *Murder on the Rocks*. A developer wants to destroy a cranberry bog on the island but that's not the only problem as a murderer strikes and Natalie's best friend becomes the prime suspect."— *Mystery Scene*

"A truly smart and gripping cozy mystery."—OnceUponARomance.net

"Deliciously clever plot. Juicy characters. Karen MacInerney has cooked up a winning recipe for murder. Don't miss this mystery!"—Maggie Sefton, author of *Knit One, Kill Two*; *Needled to Death*; and *A Deadly Yarn*

Murder on the Rocks

"MacInerney's debut is an agreeable entry into the crowded field of culinary cozies, complete with the obligatory complement of artery-clogging recipes."—*Kirkus Reviews*

"Sure to please cozy readers."—*Library Journal*

"[An] appealing debut—this is a new cozy author worth investigating." —*Publishers Weekly*

"… It may be old-fashioned to describe a book as charming, but MacInerney's writing is evocative of the most delightful, comfortable cozies of old, with just a soupçon of modern wit. *Murder on the Rocks* is a delightful escape for mystery fans. Check in for a stay at the Gray Whale Inn and you'll want to return often."—*Bed and Breakfast America*

"Karen serves up intrigue as effortlessly as her heroine whips up oatmeal chocolate cookies. This debut novel is a whale of a great read."—Deb Baker, author of *Murder Talks Turkey*

Karen MacInerney

DEATH

runs

ADRIFT

— *A* —
Gray Whale Inn
Mystery

MIDNIGHT INK
WOODBURY, MINNESOTA

FIRST EDITION
First Printing, 2014

Book design by Donna Burch-Brown
Cover design by Ellen Lawson
Cover illustration: Chris O'Leary/Lindgren & Smith
Edited by Connie Hill

Midnight Ink, an imprint of Llewellyn Worldwide Ltd.

This is a work of fiction. Names, characters, places, and incidents are either the product of the author's imagination or are used fictitiously, and any resemblance to actual persons, living or dead, business establishments, events, or locales is entirely coincidental.

Library of Congress Cataloging-in-Publication Data

MacInerney, Karen, 1970–
  Death runs adrift / Karen MacInerney. — First edition.
    pages ; cm. — (A Gray Whale Inn mystery ; 6)
  ISBN 978-0-7387-3460-6
1. Hotelkeepers—Maine—Fiction. 2. Bed and breakfast accommodations—Maine—Fiction. 3. Murder—Investigation—Fiction. 4. Cranberry Isles (Me. : Islands)—Fiction. 5. Mystery fiction. I. Title.
  PS3613.A27254D435   2014
  813'.6—dc23   2014006542

Midnight Ink
Llewellyn Worldwide Ltd.
2143 Wooddale Drive
Woodbury, MN 55125-2989
www.midnightinkbooks.com

Printed in the United States of America

Dedicated to my passionate, funny, and inventive son Ian,
who never ceases to surprise me and make me laugh.
I love you!

ACKNOWLEDGMENTS

Thank yous, as always, go first to my family—Eric, Abby, and Ian—for all their love and support; also to Dave and Carol Swartz and Ed and Dorothy MacInerney. I am so lucky to have my extended family so close! Thanks also to Bethann and Beau Eccles, my adopted family; my wonderful nieces and nephews on both sides; to my sister, Lisa, and her family; and to my fabulous grandmother, Marian Quinton (and Nora Bestwick). Thanks as always to Clovis and Maryann Heimsath, who introduced me to this beautiful corner of the world and inspired Cranberry Island. Thanks also to the ongoing support of my many writing buddies, including Mary Chipley, Kathy Waller, Jason Brenizer, Boye Nagle, Graham Smith, Rie Sheridan Rose, Skyler White, Emily McKay, and Jackie Hinson. It is a blessing to have such a wonderful circle of creative friends!

Many thanks go to my agent, Jessica Faust, and I cannot say enough good things about the fabulous Midnight Ink team—particularly the patient, kind, and always helpful Terri Bischoff, and Connie Hill, editor extraordinaire, for finding my mistakes and making me look good, and Ellen Dahl, whose cover concepts rock.

And a big thank you to all those supportive friends out there—particularly my wonderful Facebook community, who offer recipes and encouragement, along with all my friends at the Westbank Library and my local coffee haunts. A special thank you to all of the kind readers who take the time to tell me you enjoyed the books; I couldn't do it without you!

ONE

"DID YOU TRY THAT bouquet garni I tossed in for you the other day?"

I smiled at the young farmer, who was a recent—and very welcome—addition to Cranberry Island. "We made soup with it," I said, gathering my basket of fresh leaf lettuce, brilliant orange carrots, and red and white French Breakfast radishes that glowed like jewels. "It was fabulous."

"I tossed in some shallots this week." Zeke Forester adjusted his ball cap above his bright blue eyes. "They should be terrific in salad."

"I'm so glad you decided to start a farm here," I said, looking past him at the verdant fields of lettuce and dark green plants he'd told me were potatoes. After years of making do with produce that had traveled farther than any vegetable should, it was a treat to make salads with crisp, fresh greens and shortcake with locally grown strawberries. The guests at the Gray Whale Inn had been raving over the food, and I'd recently gotten a terrific write-up in the Portland paper, in part due to Zeke's gorgeous produce.

"I'm just continuing an old tradition," he said. "According to Matilda, there used to be two farms on the island. You can see the old stable there, next to the greenhouses." He pointed to a falling-down wooden structure near the tree line; beside it were three greenhouses cloaked in opaque plastic sheeting. "If things go well and I can talk Murray into renting me some more land, I might think about having a few cows, too."

"That would be amazing," I said, thinking of how lovely it would be to have fresh milk. "Good luck with Murray Selfridge, though." Murray, the local real estate mogul who had tried to develop large swathes of Cranberry Island in the past, was motivated by one thing only: money. He was not, to say the least, one of my favorite people.

Zeke shrugged and grinned optimistically. "From what I hear, he can't do anything else with that land. The board of selectmen won't let him. Why not rent it to me and make a few extra bucks?"

"That's the kind of argument Murray will understand," I said. "I'm glad to hear the farm is doing well. Your produce is absolutely gorgeous." And with my slightly plump, late-thirties figure, I was hoping the influx of fresh vegetables would help me stave off further poundage. I would never be thin, but hopefully I could at least avoid moving into muumuu territory. Fortunately, unlike my former career working for the Texas Department of Parks and Wildlife, I didn't need to wear business suits, and could get away with jeans and loose button-down shirts most of the time. A few years ago, I'd quit my job, sold my house, and plowed my savings into starting the Gray Whale Inn on Cranberry Island. It had been scary, but the move had resulted in a life that was both enchanting and deeply satisfying. It was wonderful seeing that excitement mirrored in the face of another entrepreneur. I pushed a strand of my bobbed brown hair behind one ear and smiled at the young farmer.

"It's gone better than I expected, to be honest," he told me. "I was worried I wouldn't survive." He let out a long breath. "I still have winter to contend with, but I've picked up a few restaurant contracts on the mainland, and that's a huge help. If I had a dairy, it would help with the winter." He glanced over his shoulder toward a short, smiling man who was humming to himself as he pulled up weeds. "My brother has never been happier. Moving here has been great for him."

"He's a nice young man," I said, smiling at Brad. The young man had been born with Down's syndrome, and I knew his love of being outdoors was a large part of Zeke's decision to move to the island. Here, Zeke knew that Brad could wander safely, and would be looked after by everyone in the community. Both of their parents had passed away young, and Zeke had been taking care of his brother for years. From all accounts, it had been a good move, and one I hoped would be a lasting one. "I'll be rooting for you. It was tough the first few years when I opened the inn, but it seems to be smoothing out."

"Thanks," he said as I fished my checkbook and a pen from my back pocket. I hoped Zeke would find a way to make it through. With the long Maine winters, he would need some extra income to tide him over to the short growing season. Most islanders did a variety of jobs to make ends meet; with luck, Zeke would figure something out.

"Aren't you planning on doing a project with the school this fall?" I asked.

"Yeah," he said. "I was going to help them build a greenhouse … but that depends on whether the school remains open."

I bit my lip. "Are they really thinking of closing it?"

"Three more kids are moving off-island this summer." He shook his head. "Lobster prices have been down."

"And Murray Selfridge is tired of paying high taxes, so he's leading the charge to close it." Murray envisioned quaint Cranberry Island as a future tony resort, and seemed to waste no opportunity to try and turn our small community into a jet-setting destination. He'd recently begun a campaign to close the school—a move that was almost guaranteed to decimate the year-round population of our island community. I sighed. "He's a piece of work, isn't he?"

"He is," he said as I handed him the check. "Maybe your future mother-in-law can persuade him to stop petitioning to have the school closed—and to let me rent that land."

"Catherine?" I asked, surprised. My fiancé's Bostonian mother had come to live with us after her finances collapsed; now, she was helping me with the rooms, but not the cooking. Like my niece Gwen, who had headed back to California for a year to finish her degree, Catherine was helpful with the cleaning, but a liability in the kitchen. Her last attempt at chocolate chip muffins had involved egg whites, olive oil, and Splenda. They were not, to put it mildly, delicious. "Why would she have any influence over Murray Selfridge?"

Zeke blinked at me. "You don't know? Apparently Murray's after her."

I almost dropped my basket of vegetables. "You mean … romantically?"

"Charlene hasn't filled you in?"

Charlene, island postmistress, gossip hub, and my primary source of information, had been visiting her cousin in Portland over the last week. "It must have started after she left," I said. "So … are his feelings reciprocal?"

"I have no idea." He tucked the check into the cashbox and closed it. "I just heard it from George McLeod that there was a rose order coming over on the mail boat, and that Murray had ordered it."

"Hard to keep secrets on this island, isn't it?" I asked.

Zeke gave an uncomfortable chuckle that made me wonder, for a brief moment, what secrets he was keeping. Whatever they were, Charlene would doubtless ferret them out soon enough. I grinned, thinking of the news I'd have when she returned. As distasteful as the thought was of having Murray hanging around the inn, it would be nice to have a piece of gossip to share with Charlene for a change of pace. Usually it was the other way around.

"You hear anything about those bones they dug up?" he asked, changing the subject.

Murray had decided to put in a pool behind his sprawling mansion, and the workers had made a grisly discovery as they dug a hole.

"No, but I've got a guest who thinks the bones might be her grandfather's."

Zeke blinked. "How does she know?"

"They found an unusual cross with the body," I said. "Her grandfather was an Episcopal priest on the island—he disappeared suddenly when her mother was very young. She's got a photo of him wearing a crucifix that looks a lot like it, and she's hoping to compare the two and see if it's a match."

"Weird," he said.

"I know. And I've got another guest who's trying to write a mystery, so it's pretty much all they talk about down at the inn." The two had checked in earlier in the week, and the mystery of the bones had drawn them together immediately. In fact, they were both on the mainland today, trying to get a look at the crucifix that was found with the bones.

"Did he disappear or something?" Zeke asked.

"Apparently he vanished in the 1920s, which looks to be about the age of the bones. He was a priest on the island; his family was in Bangor."

"And wasn't the old rectory on Selfridge's land?"

"It's the building he uses as a storage shed," I said. "He's thinking of tearing it down."

Zeke shook his head. "Lots of secrets on this old island, aren't there?"

I smiled. "That's what makes it interesting. You'd think everything would have already been discovered, but something new keeps turning up!" I hefted the bag to my shoulder. "I'd better get back to the inn. Good luck with the cows—and with Murray," I said. "I don't know if it'll help, but I'll ask Catherine to put a good word in for you."

"Thanks," he said, his bright smile back. "See you in a couple of days? We should have green beans soon."

"Looking forward to it!" I called over my shoulder. I waved to Brad as I headed down the lane toward home. The young man looked up from his weeding, and his face split into a sunny smile as he vigorously waved back, weeds still clutched in his hand.

———

Catherine wasn't in the kitchen when I arrived back at the inn, and there was no sign of the roses Zeke had mentioned, but I knew she'd been here; there was a smell of lemon cleaner in the air, and the countertops sparkled. I stowed the vegetables in the crisper and headed down to the carriage house, where my future mother-in-law had been staying since moving to the island a few months earlier.

When financial difficulties struck John's mother the previous winter, we had offered the carriage house to her, but both of us had had misgivings. When John and I had visited her in Boston, Catherine had been very concerned with appearances, and we both worried our relatively rural life would pose some problems for her. John had always told me she hated Cranberry Island, where they had spent summers when he was a child; would that have changed in the intervening years?

Our worries had been assuaged, fortunately. Although she still dressed largely as she had when she lived in Boston—primarily cashmere, pearls, and twinsets—she seemed to be adjusting nicely to the small community, even volunteering at the local historical society. The biggest surprise of all, however, had been her willingness to pitch in around the inn when Gwen decided to take a leave of absence to finish her degree. Her high standards for decor and cleanliness had turned out to be a real asset—not only had she added several tasteful touches to the inn, but her help eased the burden of taking care of the rooms every single day.

My relationship with my future mother-in-law hadn't been my only concern, though. I had also been worried about John's moving from the carriage house, which he'd lived in for years, to the rooms above the kitchen of the gray-shingled Cape where I'd made my home since investing my life savings in the inn a few years back. Although we were engaged to be married, we had always lived separately, and I was worried about how we would do living in the same space. Again, I had been pleasantly surprised at how congenial it

7

was—I enjoyed the company, and between John's workshop and the inn, we found we had more than enough room. Together with my niece, my future husband, and my future mother-in-law, I had built not just a life, but a wonderful family in this beautiful part of the world. And after living for fifteen years in Texas, the views out my white-curtained windows, with dizzying tall pine trees, craggy pink granite, and the ice-cold Atlantic foaming against the rocky coast, still made me want to pinch myself.

A cool breeze riffled the blue water as I walked down to the carriage house, wafting the sharp, briny scent of low tide with the sweet scent of the beach roses that lined the path. The purr of a lobster boat mingled with the sound of the surf hitting the rocky shore as the tide began to turn, and I glanced over toward Smuggler's Cove, where a boat with a buoy I didn't recognize was idling. The turquoise and fluorescent orange buoy was unfamiliar; I made a note to ask Charlene about it when she got back. Although officially the waters around the island were fair game to anyone with a lobstering license, in reality they were divided up into closely guarded territories. If a boat from elsewhere was hoping to ply these waters, its captain would soon find him- or herself warned off—and not just verbally. More than one murder had occurred over fishing territories.

My eyes were still on the unfamiliar boat as I knocked on the carriage house door. Catherine opened the door on the third knock, looking lovely in a pink silk blouse and white Capri pants. I turned and smiled at her and caught a glimpse of red roses on the kitchen table. "Wow," I said. "You look nice!"

"Thank you," she said, her pale cheeks coloring slightly. "I was on my way out to catch the mail boat."

"Oh?" I asked. "Do you need a ride?"

"Actually, a friend is picking me up." She reached up to touch the back of her upswept blonde hair. "We're having afternoon tea at Jordan Pond House."

"My favorite place on Mount Desert Island," I said. And it was. There was nothing like sitting on the lawn overlooking Jordan Pond and its twin mountains, the Bubbles, while sipping chai and buttering their enormous popovers. The lobster stew was amazing, too.

I was about to ask who her "friend" was when the sound of a car descending the hill reached my ears, and I turned to see Murray's Jaguar rolling down my driveway. Zeke had been right.

"Your friend has arrived, it seems." I watched as the car disappeared behind the gray-shingled inn. Then I turned and grinned at Catherine. "He didn't pick you up in the yacht?"

"It's low tide," she answered solemnly. "The water by the dock is too shallow."

I had been kidding, but limited myself to wishing her a good time and exhorting her to eat a popover for me.

"Oh, I won't be eating popovers," she said. "Way too many carbs!"

I shook my head. Not eating popovers at Jordan Pond House was practically a sin. On the other hand, based on the pink flush in her cheeks, the company might be pleasure enough. "To each her own," I said, thinking not only of popovers, but of the prospect of a few hours in the company of Murray Selfridge and his ego.

It wasn't until I'd said a brief hello to Murray and retreated to the safety of the inn's kitchen that I realized I'd forgotten to ask Catherine to put in a good word for the school—and for Zeke. On the other hand, I thought as I watched him escort her up the walk, his meaty hand cradling her elbow as if it were a wounded bird, it looked like there would be plenty of opportunities to come.

There was no accounting for taste.

———

Neither of my guests was staying for dinner—they were planning to grab dinner on the mainland—so it was just John, Catherine, and me, providing John's mother wasn't swept away by Murray in his yacht. As much as I enjoyed having a night off from cooking, I'd miss chatting with my guests. Beryl told me stories about her family that made me laugh—apparently she hadn't always been the strait-laced, serious woman she was now—and Agnes, the mystery writer, was curious about everything on the island. I was planning on frying up some trout fillets John had brought home the day before, and trying out a new lemon blueberry pudding cake recipe for dessert. I had assembled almost all of the ingredients for the dessert, lining up lemons on my white countertop, when I realized I'd forgotten to pick up blueberries.

For a moment I considered heading back to the farm. Then I glanced out the window and changed my mind. The weather was perfect; it was 70 degrees, there was only a light breeze, and the sky was a blue porcelain bowl over the island. I stowed the ingredients in the fridge, grabbed a windbreaker and a lidded coffee can I reserved for berry picking, and headed out the back door toward the dock.

The *Little Marian* started on the first try, and in no time at all I had cast off and was motoring away from the little dock behind the inn, admiring the beautiful Cape-style house I'd sunk my savings into a few years ago. Although I would never be rich, my risky business venture had made it possible to live the life I'd once only dreamed of. The inn's blue shutters contrasted beautifully against the weathered shingles, and the coral geraniums and blue lobelia I'd planted in the window boxes glowed in the afternoon sunshine. Moon jellies blossomed in the water around me, their rings pale white against the murky water.

I was headed to an out-of-the-way blueberry patch that was a long way by foot, but easy on the water. Normally I'd pick berries on the path next to the inn, but my guests had been searching for blueberries there several times in the last week, and it was likely picked over. If I picked enough, I thought, I might make a steamed pudding for breakfast the next day. Although it was traditionally served as a dessert, I found my grandmother's recipe for blueberry steamed pudding (served with Lyle's Golden Syrup) vanished every time I put it out on the breakfast buffet. And with the tiny, sweet-tart native Maine blueberries...

By the time I pulled the *Little Marian* up on shore near the blueberry patch, I was wishing I had a nice slice of steamed pudding on hand, but contented myself instead with eating the first few handfuls of berries I picked. It was pleasurable work, moving from one lime-green-leaved low bush to the next, popping a blueberry into my mouth from time to time and wondering why John and I had decided to get married in Florida when we lived in the most beautiful place on earth. Still, at least we wouldn't have to cater it, and it would be good to spend some time together near water that was warm enough to swim in.

I was thinking about sand beaches and wedding rings when I heard a whimpering sound from the wooded area next to the field. I stopped picking and scanned the trees. A thin young woman stepped out from the underbrush, eyes red and puffy and tears on her face. I had seen her in the store a few times, but we'd never met.

"Hello?" I called. "Are you okay?"

She looked up, startled, then turned and hurtled back into the trees. I watched her go, wondering what was so upsetting, and resolved to ask Charlene about it later. As postmistress of the island and keeper of the store, she knew all the gossip. As I put my can of berries into the skiff and pushed it back into the water, I accidentally dipped one sneakered foot into the cold surf.

It was a short trip back to the inn. The multicolored lobster buoys were everywhere; festive red and green, a deep navy blue and black I knew belonged to Adam Thrackton, Gwen's boyfriend, and several others I recognized. No orange and turquoise, though. Had someone cut the foreign boat's trap lines, I wondered, or was the lobster boat near the island for another reason?

I rounded Cranberry Point and the slender spire of the lighthouse, disturbing a flock of gulls that were foraging in the rocks. A few visitors were leaving the building the island had renovated just a few years earlier—a building with a checkered past, we'd discovered when the renovation turned up a skeleton in a subterranean chamber. I'd gotten a few more bookings from the new tourist attraction, but most of the visitors were just day-trippers.

As I ruminated over the number of tragic stories our small, quaint island had spawned over the centuries, I noticed a skiff bobbing in the waves. I squinted at the inn's dock in the distance; John's skiff *Mooncatcher* was still there, and we were far from the town dock. Someone must have mistied a knot, setting their skiff adrift.

I turned toward the little boat, planning to tow it back to the inn and tie it up next to *Mooncatcher* until I could figure out whose it was. I slowed the engine as I approached, and suddenly the hairs stood up on the back of my neck. As I grew closer, I caught a glimpse of red flannel, and then the tip of a rubber boot.

A wave rocked the skiff as I turned the *Little Marian* to come up alongside, and I gasped.

A dead man lay in the bottom of the skiff.

TWO

My gorge rose, and I looked away, but the image was already emblazoned on my mind. His face was pale and waxy, dark stubble like a shadow, his mouth slack and ajar. The water in the bottom of the boat was tinged red with blood, and had soaked into the red flannel shirt, staining it almost black. There was a jagged, blood-soaked hole in his chest that made my stomach churn.

I turned back and forced myself to watch his chest, but there was no sign of breath. Swallowing hard, I reached over and touched the back of his hand. It was stiff and cold, but there was a crumpled piece of paper in it.

I tugged at the paper. *Meet me at 10. The usual place. T.* I tucked it back into his hand, then dipped my own into the water, as if that could somehow purify it, and swallowed back bile.

As I struggled to master my stomach, the wind turned the skiff, pushing it away from the island and out to sea. I took a few deep breaths, then reached for the rope and maneuvered the *Little Marian* in front of the skiff. I tied the two boats together, trying not to look directly at the corpse—it was a young man, probably not more than twenty—and wishing for a working cell phone, so I could contact the authorities. I usually loved the island-out-of-time feel of my home, but there were moments when I wished it were a bit more up-to-date, and this was one of them. When I'd tied the skiff to the back of the *Little Marian*, I checked my watch and approximated my location, then motored back to the inn, hoping my fiancé—who was, conveniently, the island deputy—had made it home from Island Artists.

The short trip back to the inn seemed to take days, and my fingers fumbled on the ropes as I tied both skiffs up, wishing I had a tarp or a length of canvas to cover the poor man. When I was sure both the *Little Marian* and the other skiff were secure, I hurried first to John's workshop. I have never been so relieved to hear the sound of a power saw.

My goggled fiancé stood over a plank of wood, sending a blizzard of sawdust to the floor as I stepped inside the barn. I waited until he was done, admiring his competence as he maneuvered the whirring blade, but as soon as the end of the plank hit the floor and he powered down the saw, I caught his attention.

"What's wrong?" He lifted his goggles and stepped toward me, away from the saw.

"I found a body in a boat," I said, the words tumbling out of my mouth. Just saying the words made it horribly real. "It's down at the dock."

"Who is it?"

"A young man," I said. "I don't know him. There's blood in the water, and he's ... he's definitely dead. I think he's been shot in the chest." An involuntary shudder passed through me.

John closed the distance between us and put his work-roughened hands on my shoulders. His green eyes were steady on mine. "Are you all right? You're pale."

"Just … it was a nasty shock," I said. "Will you go down and take a look?"

"Of course," he said, pulling off his goggles and tossing them onto his worktable. "Why don't you call the police on Mount Desert Island; the number's next to the phone in the kitchen. I'll go down and take a look, then keep watch so the birds don't get to him before the investigators arrive."

I shuddered. "Gross," I said.

"It's nature." He shrugged, then studied my face. "You're sure you're okay?"

"I've found bodies before." My voice shook a little.

He reached out and touched my face. "It doesn't make it any easier, does it?"

I shook my head.

"Go call the authorities and put on a pot of tea. I think you should bake something, too—take your mind off things. Too bad Charlene isn't back yet, or I'd tell you to have her over." He paused for a moment. "On second thought, maybe I wouldn't. News will travel fast enough as it is."

As I headed up the path from John's workshop to the inn, I realized I'd left my can of berries in the *Little Marian*. I briefly considered heading down to retrieve them, then decided against it.

Lemon bars would be just fine for now.

———

Despite John's efforts to keep things quiet, the police launch got the grapevine humming; I had barely squeezed the first lemon before the phone started ringing. It probably shouldn't have surprised me that Charlene was on the line.

"Where are you?" I asked.

"I got back this morning," she said. "Came over on the first mail boat. What's this I hear about a police launch over at the inn?"

I reached for another lemon and told her what I'd found on my way back from picking blueberries.

"You're kidding me."

"I wish I were."

Charlene sighed. "You're a regular Jessica Fletcher, you know that? If you don't watch out, Cranberry Island is going to take the place of Cabot Cove. You're sure he was murdered?"

"There was blood in the boat," I said, shivering at the memory of that strange dark water. "I guess it's possible he fell and hit his head," I added, not sounding very convincing even to myself.

She was quiet for a moment. "Wait a moment. Was he young?"

"Late twenties I'd say. I didn't recognize him."

"Dark hair? Kind of skinny?"

"Yeah," I said.

"Uh oh."

"What?"

"I hope it's not Derek Morton."

"Who's that?" It was a name I didn't recognize, which was unusual; I knew, or at least had heard of, almost everyone on the island.

"He's from Ellsworth originally. He's been working as a sternman for Adam Thrackton," Charlene said. "Derek is kind of flaky. My niece has gone out with him a few times."

"Why do you think it might be him?"

"He was supposed to take her over to Mount Desert Island last night, but didn't show up—and didn't call, either. Tania was in a fine mood when I got to the store this morning."

I felt a shiver of foreboding. "I hope it's not him. He was wearing rubber boots and a red flannel shirt—ring any bells?"

"Same outfit as half the lobstermen on Cranberry Island." Charlene gave a rueful laugh; she often complained about the wardrobes of her male neighbors. "Was there a name painted on the skiff?"

I thought back to the white-painted dinghy bobbing in the waves. I hadn't seen any identifying marks at all. "Not that I saw."

"So nothing there, either. I'll ask around and see if anyone's missing a skiff—or if they know where Derek is."

I squeezed the last lemon and glanced out the window toward the dock, then wished I hadn't. Two officers were transporting a black body bag from the skiff to the launch—a difficult task with the small craft bobbing in the water. Who was his mother? I wondered, thinking of how I'd feel if I learned my niece had died. The thought was unbearable, and I pushed it away. "How close were Derek and Tania?" I asked Charlene.

"She had a huge crush on him, but I don't know how he felt about her." She paused for a moment. "Feels, I mean. I'm talking like he's dead already, aren't I?"

I sighed. "I should probably go down and ask John if they've identified him."

"Let me know what you find out, okay?"

"As soon as I'm able," I told my best friend. Which meant as soon as I knew the victim's family had been notified. Whoever that young man was, I thought as I poured the lemon juice and zest into a mixing bowl, his family was in for a terrible shock.

———

The bright smell of lemon bars baking filled the kitchen when John and a burly detective came up from the dock a little while later. My fiancé introduced me to Detective Johnson, a transplant from Long Island. He and John had met at a continuing education class in Portland not too long ago. I invited him to have a cup of coffee.

"That sounds terrific," the detective said, settling down at the big pine farm table and leaning back into his chair. In my cozy yellow kitchen, with its clean white curtains and the scent of lemon, it was hard to imagine that a dead man had been zipped into a bag just a few minutes earlier. "No matter how long you do this, it's always a shock. Particularly when they're young."

"I know," I said as I scooped coffee into the grinder, inhaling the comforting aroma. Already I liked him about a billion times better than Sergeant Grimes, the incompetent and surly detective who had haunted the island when I first got here. "Any idea who it is yet?" I felt my heart catch as I asked.

"Looks like it's Adam's sternman, Derek Morton," John said.

"I knew it," I whispered as I scooped the last of the coffee in.

I sensed the detective perk up at the table. "What do you mean by that?" John, too, was giving me a questioning look.

"My friend Charlene—she's the postmistress and runs the island store—said that he was supposed to take her niece to the mainland last night, but he didn't show up. When I told her I'd found a young man, she was worried that's who it might be."

"You didn't know the victim?"

19

I shook my head. "I knew Adam had hired someone not long ago, but I hadn't met him."

Detective Johnson whipped out a steno pad and began writing. "The victim was dating a young woman on the island?"

"Apparently they'd gone out a few times," I said, then pushed the button on the grinder. When the beans had been turned to fragrant powder, I released it and added, "I don't know if they were officially a couple."

"Her name?"

"Tania Kean. She helps out at the store." I tapped the coffee into the filter. "Any idea what happened to him?"

"We'll have to wait for the autopsy." He scribbled something else down on the lined page.

"Whatever it was, it didn't look like natural causes."

He looked up sharply. "Please don't repeat the details to anyone."

I shuddered. "I won't."

As the coffee brewed, Detective Johnson gestured to the seat across from him. "Please, sit down. I'd like to ask you a few questions."

I sighed and slid into the chair next to John, who put his hand on mine under the table as I told the detective everything about my afternoon. "And after all that," I concluded, "I left the berries down in the skiff."

"What time exactly did you find the skiff?"

"The tide was just starting to come in," I said, standing up to retrieve a few mugs and pour the freshly brewed coffee. "I got back to the inn around one-thirty, so I'd say it was about one o'clock."

"And where was it, exactly?"

As I distributed coffee and set a pitcher of cream and a bowl of sugar cubes on the table, John reached for the framed map of the island he'd bought me for my birthday. It had been painted in bright blues and greens by one of our local artists, and I'd hung it in the kitchen next to the door to the porch. "Right here," I said, pointing to a spot in the blue water just off the coast.

John's work-roughened finger drew a short line to the cliffs a short way from the inn. "About halfway between Smuggler's Cove and the lighthouse."

"Wait," I said. "I saw a lobster boat there earlier, not too far from the cove. It had a buoy I didn't recognize."

"What colors?" Detective Johnson asked, his spoon suspended in midair.

"Turquoise and orange," I said. "I looked for traps, but I didn't see any—figured maybe they'd already been cut."

"Have you heard of any gear wars in the area?" the detective asked John as he dumped the cubes into his coffee and gave it a quick stir. He might be from Long Island, I thought, but he certainly knew about the issues in our part of the world.

My fiancé shook his head. "Not recently. Then again, I'm not down in the co-op that often. I'll ask Adam if he's heard any rumblings lately."

"And we'll see if we can find out who's got turquoise and orange buoys." The detective took a sip of his coffee, then turned a page in his notebook and looked at me hopefully. "Did you see a name on the boat?"

"No, just the buoy. And I can't remember the pattern—just the colors."

"Well, the colors narrow it down, at least. If it's connected at all. Still, a lead is a lead." He put down his pen and cradled the mug in his large, square hands, then glanced at the oven.

"I've got a few scones left over from breakfast, if you'd like," I said. "Maple walnut."

He brightened immediately. "I'd love one, but only if it's not too much trouble."

"None at all," I said. "You, too, John?"

My fiancé grinned at me in the way he had that made me feel as if I were the only woman in the world. "How can I say no?"

I plated three scones and sat down with the two men. Detective Johnson had just taken a big, crumbly bite of maple-frosted pastry when a knock came at the door.

"What's up?" the detective asked the young woman who appeared at the door.

"Found a note in his hand." She held up a plastic evidence bag.

"Umm…" I felt myself color.

Both officers—and John—turned to me. "Yes?"

"My fingerprints are on that note," I said. "I just grabbed it without thinking."

John shook his head, and Detective Johnson looked suddenly weary. "Why did you handle it?" the officer asked. "You contaminated the evidence."

"Sorry," I said. "I was trying to figure out who he was, I guess."

He stood up, his mouth a thin line. "Excuse me," he said, giving me a frosty look as he abandoned his scone to join the officer on the porch.

When he'd closed the door behind him, John looked at me. "Really, Nat?"

"I know," I said.

He sighed. "So, what did it say?"

"Something about a meeting with someone named T," I said, a sinking feeling in my stomach.

"Tania starts with T," he said in a quiet voice.

"Even if it does, it doesn't mean she… well, that Tania had anything to do with his death."

"No, there are other possibilities," John said. "Like Adam."

I felt as if he had punched me. "Adam? What do you mean?"

"Derek was in his dinghy," John said quietly. "I recognize it."

I broke off a corner of my scone, feeling miserable. "So Adam's on the hook, along with Tania. Charlene wanted me to let her know if it turned out to be Derek. And now there's this note… What do I do?"

John ran a hand through his sandy hair. "We can't say anything until the family's been notified."

"I know." I sipped my coffee without tasting it, wishing I could erase the image of the young man's pale face, his hair floating in the bloody water. "He was from Ellsworth, apparently."

"I imagine he has family there, then. They'll probably send an officer this afternoon." John grimaced. "I'll ask Johnson to let me know when we can talk to Charlene. I hope Tania wasn't too serious about him."

"I hope so too." My eyes strayed to Detective Johnson, who was conferring with the officer. *Please, please, please don't arrest my friends*, I prayed.

"We should ask who else Derek was involved with," I said, feeling the need to take some action—beyond prayer—to help my friends.

"I think Detective Johnson will probably take care of that."

"It doesn't hurt to ask around, though. Sometimes locals know more than the police," I protested. "As islanders, we might be able to help. You know that."

"So, you're a local now?" He gave me a strained grin. "Fred Penney know that?" Fred was an island lobsterman who didn't believe you were a "local" unless you'd not only lived here, but had at least three generations of islanders in your family. The only reason he spoke to me was that he was sweet on Charlene, and knew she was my best friend. John winked at me, but I whacked him on the arm anyway.

"You know what I mean."

"Yes, I do." His voice had a familiar grim tone. "And I think you should stay out of it."

"Why?" I asked, even though we'd been through this conversation at least a dozen times.

He gave me a look that made me all warm inside. "Because if something happens to you, who's going to bake all those muffins every morning?"

"You're pretty handy with a muffin pan," I pointed out.

"Okay," he said, lowering his voice to a rough growl. "Who's going to warm my bed on cold winter nights?" He pulled me into an embrace that made my heart thump under my T-shirt. And unfortunately was disturbed only ten seconds later by the opening of the door to the porch. We jumped back like high schoolers caught under the bleachers as Detective Johnson stepped back into the kitchen.

"Am I interrupting?" he asked with grin playing around the corners of his mouth.

"Not at all, officer," I said, feeling my face warm, and plunked down gracelessly in my chair.

"I think we're about done here anyway," he said. "One of my colleagues is informing the family right now." He cleared his throat. "I don't like to impose, but could I ask for a ride? I have a few stops to make on the island, and without a vehicle or a map ..."

"We'd be happy to," John said.

"Thanks," the detective said. "Sorry to trouble you."

"No trouble at all," I told him, thankful we weren't still on the subject of the note I shouldn't have touched. "Not quite as many homicides here as in New York, I imagine," I said.

"Not so far," he said. "Hope it stays that way."

"Me too," I said with a shiver.

THREE

WHEN THE CALL CAME a few minutes later to confirm that the immediate family had been told, I grimaced. "I feel so bad for them. Did both parents live in Ellsworth?"

"Single mom," he told me. "Dad is long gone, apparently. He was the youngest of three."

"Does she have any idea who would have wanted him dead?"

The sturdy detective shook his head. "They haven't questioned her yet; she's still too upset."

John grimaced. "But now we have news to deliver."

"I understand he's got relatives on the island—an aunt and uncle. I'm going to have to break the news to them and ask a few questions."

In case they were involved, I knew he was thinking, but didn't say. Everyone related to the murder victim is a suspect ... a fact I knew from personal experience.

"I need to talk to his aunt and uncle, as well as the young woman he was dating. I'd also like to talk with the lobsterman he worked for. Can you point me in the right direction?"

"We can take you where you need to go," I said. "I want to head down to the store myself, to offer Tania moral support. Adam might be out on the water, though."

"I do need to talk to him. If he isn't there, is there some way to get a hold of him?"

"If he's not there, we'll tell him you need to get in touch with him," I said. "He's practically family."

The detective nodded. "Small island, eh?"

"Yup." I finished cutting up the lemon bars, which were the perfect mix of buttery shortbread and tangy lemon curd, the tartness cut by the blanket of powdered sugar, then put about a dozen into a plastic container to take with me. It was bitter news we had to share, and although it wasn't much, I was hoping my offering would bring at least a smidgeon of comfort.

Murray Selfridge's Jaguar was purring down the lane as John and I stepped out of the inn. Detective Johnson had told us he would join us in a moment, then headed down to the dock to check with the team on the police launch.

John was surprised to see Murray, and I realized I hadn't ever mentioned Catherine's date to him. "What's he doing here?"

"With the ... the hullabaloo this afternoon, I guess I forgot to tell you. He took your mom out to lunch."

John blinked. "He what?"

"I know. I found out from Zeke Forester. Apparently Murray wanted to pick her up in the yacht, but our dock is too shallow." The sudden urge for a lemon bar gripped me at the sight of the familiar Jaguar, but I ignored it.

We both watched as the car rolled to a halt in front of the inn. Murray got out, his blue seersucker pants slightly wrinkled, and hurried around to open Catherine's door. He murmured something to her as he helped her out of the Jaguar, and she laughed like a schoolgirl.

John and I exchanged an ominous glance.

"How was lunch?" I asked. Both looked up, startled; they hadn't noticed us.

"Oh, it was divine," Catherine said, beaming. "They have the most wonderful little salads, and Murray here is quite the raconteur."

"You're the one with the stories," he said, touching her on the arm. There was a look on his face that I'd never seen before: total adoration. Zeke was right, I realized. If you wanted something from Murray, you'd be wise to ask my future mother-in-law to put in a good word for you.

"Thank you for a wonderful afternoon, Murray." She played with the small string of pearls around her thin neck.

"Can I tempt you to dinner on the yacht tomorrow?"

"I can't see why not. Natalie, you'll be fine on your own tomorrow evening, won't you?" There was an excitement in her eyes I'd never seen before. I was going to be seeing a lot more of Murray Selfridge in the near future, I realized with a sinking feeling.

"Of course," I said.

She turned to Murray. "Well, then, I'd be delighted."

"*Bon soir, ma chérie*," he said, the *chérie* coming out with a distinct Maine twang.

"*Á demain!*" she replied. "I'm just going to go inside and freshen up," she told us. Her eyes registered Detective Johnson, and she gave him an appraising glance. "I don't believe we've met."

"Detective Johnson," he said, extending a hand, which she took uncertainly.

"You're a police detective?"

"There's been a bit of an incident," I said.

She blinked. "Is everyone okay?"

"Natalie found a young man dead in a dinghy this afternoon." John's voice was neutral. "There may have been foul play involved. Detective Johnson is here to investigate, and there's a police launch down at the dock."

"An islander?" Murray's tone was strained.

"No," John said. "A young man from Ellsworth. He was working as Adam's sternman."

Murray let out a deep breath. "Well, that's good. I'd hate for it to be one of our own."

"Murray." Catherine drew herself up, and her eyes flashed. "Just because he wasn't from here doesn't mean it isn't a tragedy."

"I know, dear," he said, his voice patronizing. *Dear?* I thought. They must be getting along very well indeed.

Murray smiled broadly, exposing a line of yellowed teeth. "It's no less a tragedy. It's just … well, islanders are like family."

I almost choked, remembering how he'd tried to manipulate many "family" members to enable him to make big profits over the years.

But the argument seemed to appease Catherine. She turned to me. "That must have been an awful shock. Did you know the young man?"

"No," I said. "But he was dating Charlene's niece Tania, apparently."

"Poor lamb," she said. "If there's anything I can do to help, let me know. Such a tragedy."

"Yes," Murray said, shaking his head. "Terrible thing."

"Well, I'm going to head inside and change. Thanks for a lovely afternoon, Murray." She smiled at Murray, then swept by us in a cloud of tuberose perfume and disappeared into the inn.

"We should be going too," I added as Murray stared after the door through which she'd disappeared, then slowly turned back to his Jag. "Have a good evening."

"Oh." Murray turned to us as if he'd forgotten we were there. "John, I had no idea your mother was such a charmer. Where have you been hiding her?"

"Boston. She always hated it here," my fiancé volunteered.

"Well, she doesn't seem to now. I'm glad you brought her up here to visit. She's a corker!" With that, he got back into his car like a man in a dream, and John and I watched as his car disappeared up the hill.

"A corker," John repeated. "I've heard many words used to describe my mother, but that is not one of them."

I grinned. "Nice of you to let him know how much she enjoys the island." As we climbed into the van, I found myself shaking my head. "He's really smitten, isn't he? I've never seen him look like that before."

"Murray Selfridge," John said quietly as we backed out of the driveway and followed him up the lane. "I can't imagine anyone would find him attractive, much less my mother."

"He … well, he seems nice enough." I remembered his take-no-prisoners approach to development on the island and revised my statement. "To Catherine, at least."

"For the moment," John said. "You and I both know what he's like, though."

"Not your favorite person, eh?" Detective Johnson said from the back seat of the van.

"You can say that again," John replied.

"Your mother seems to have him well in hand," I pointed out. "It must be fun, going out to lunch at Jordan Pond House and having someone invite you to dinner on his yacht."

John shook his head. "I don't trust him."

"She's a grown woman," I reminded him. "And it's not like they're planning to be married, or anything."

"I certainly hope not," John said darkly.

———

It took almost no time at all, it seemed, to get to the store, which was commonly known as Cranberry Island's living room. The small wooden building had a broad front porch and big, wavy-glass windows posted with local notices; inside, I knew, were worn couches and armchairs where locals sat and caught up on the news, along with grocery aisles packed with essentials and a bank of post office boxes into which my best friend sorted the mail each day— taking special note of the postcards and the return addresses of handwritten envelopes, I knew. I often supplied the store with extra baked goods from the inn; they always disappeared quickly, and not just because of the day-trippers who wandered into the store looking for a snack.

As we walked up the steps to the front porch, I could see through the mullioned windows that Tania was at the counter of the cozy island store, her young face pale and wan. She wore a black miniskirt that covered approximately 5 percent of her long legs, and a sparkly pink camisole clung to her bony chest. Her aunt Charlene sat across the counter from her with a worried expression on her beautiful, impeccably made-up face.

Unfortunately, they weren't alone; Charlene's most ardent admirer, Fred Penney, was parked at his habitual spot at the counter. Although my friend had told him repeatedly that she wasn't interested, he appeared to favor the Chinese water torture approach to courting. He'd tried to give her a pair of tourmaline earrings the previous week, and seemed to spend more time in the store than on his lobster boat.

Charlene looked up as the bell above the door jangled, announcing our arrival. Our faces told her everything she needed to know. My friend's pink-frosted lips thinned into a line, and she shook her head slowly, her normal effervescent energy dulled.

Tania turned on her stool, a fearful look on her thin face. She had her aunt's terrific cheekbones and bright green eyes, but not her bulk; where Charlene's avowed chocolate addiction gave her a curvy, well-padded figure, Tania looked like she hadn't eaten in a month.

She turned her haunted eyes toward us. "Who's this?"

"Detective Johnson," the policeman said, handing her a card.

Fred's eyes widened; I could almost see his ears perk up.

"You know something." Her young voice was high and reedy. I glanced at John, but before any of us could speak, she said, "It was him, wasn't it."

It wasn't a question.

"Miss Barnes found a young man named Derek Morton today," Detective Johnson said.

She flinched as if he'd hit her. "Dead?" she whispered.

"I'm afraid so," the burly policeman said, compassion in his eyes. "I understand you two were close. I'm very sorry for your loss."

"Oh, honey." Charlene reached across the counter to touch her niece's shoulder. Tania's face crumpled, her hair swinging down like a curtain, and her narrow frame heaved with silent sobs.

I crossed the wooden floor of the store quickly, setting the container of lemon bars on the counter and putting my arms around her bony frame. She didn't resist, and I cradled her in my arms until Charlene rounded the counter.

"How did it happen?" she wailed. "I knew he was going to get into trouble. I knew it!"

I glanced at Detective Johnson, who looked like a hunting dog on a scent. I gave him an inquisitive look, and he nodded. "What made you think he was going to get into trouble, Tania?"

"Just … just … I don't know! I can't talk about this right now. Derek." She gave a long, low moan. "I can't believe he's gone!"

She broke down in my arms. Charlene stroked her hair, and I rocked her back and forth. It seemed like forever before her sobs subsided and she pulled away, swiping at her mascara-smeared eyes with the back of her hand.

"I know it's a difficult time, miss, but I'd like to ask you some questions," Detective Johnson said gently. "We're hoping you can help us figure out what happened."

"I don't know anything," she said.

"You might be surprised," Detective Johnson told her. "Even the tiniest detail can sometimes help. I'd like to ask you a few questions now, while your memory's still fresh."

She took a deep, shuddering breath and leaned against the counter, hugging herself tightly. "Okay," she said. "But not right here."

"You're welcome to use the back room if you'd like," Charlene offered the detective.

Detective Johnson smiled, his eyes crinkling at the corners, and again I found myself thankful that he wasn't Sergeant Grimes. "It'll only be a few minutes."

Charlene sighed, and she gave her niece a squeeze. "We'll be right here, honey."

Tania shrugged, then glanced up at the detective with swollen eyes. "I still can't believe it."

"I know," he said gently. "I know."

When they'd disappeared into the back room, Charlene popped the top off the lemon bars. "I can't believe Derek died. I hope Tania didn't get the Kean curse."

John reached for a lemon bar and pulled up a stool at the counter. "What curse?"

My friend blinked at him. "The boyfriend curse," she said. "The men I date either turn out to be scoundrels, or they …" She shrugged. "You know. Something happens to them." She glanced at Fred, who was still staring at her like she was a triple-layer chocolate cake, and thrust a lemon bar into her mouth.

"I'd take the risk," he said in a rough voice I suspect he thought was sexy, but reminded me of an outboard motor that needed a tune-up.

"I'm sure it's just a coincidence," I said, although Charlene did have a less-than-stellar track record with the men she'd been interested in since I'd known her. The mortality rate had been rather high.

"I can't believe someone left him floating in a dinghy," Charlene said.

"A dinghy?" Fred perked up. "I was just down at the co-op this morning. Young Adam Thrackton was looking for his; had to borrow someone's to get out to his boat."

My stomach clenched. "When did it go missing?"

"Last night sometime. He's going to borrow one from old Eli White."

"I'm sure it's a coincidence," Charlene said, echoing what I'd said a moment earlier, but like me, she didn't sound completely convinced.

I decided to change the subject. "Did either of you know Derek well?"

"Only saw him working with Adam," Fred said. "Expect the police will want to talk to that young man before long. For all his high-and-mighty degree, he used some pretty colorful language last week."

"What do you mean?" I asked.

"Found out the kid had been borrowing the boat on the sly." Fred's mouth turned up in a slight smile. "I heard Adam threatened to kill him if he caught him at it again."

I groaned. "When was this?"

"Last week," he said. "I always said that young man would get into trouble. He's not from here. Got his head filled with all kinds of rubbish at that fancy Ivy League school of his."

"Adam's a fine young man," I said sharply.

Fred grunted. "That'll be for the cops to decide, I expect."

"Don't you have some lobster to catch?" Charlene asked tartly.

"Why go chasing mermaids when I can sit here and be served coffee by one?" he said in that so-not-seductive growl.

"Fred, I need some time alone with my friend," Charlene said, rather bluntly. "Why don't you go do some fishing?"

He gave her a pleading look, but she held firm, and a moment later he swaggered to the door. "Let me know if you want me to take you out this weekend, darlin'. I know how to show a woman a good time."

"I'll keep it in mind," she said shortly, still giving him a hard look. "Bye."

When the door shut behind him with a jangle, Charlene brushed a bit of confectioners' sugar from her chin and shook herself. "I can't stand that man," she said.

"I can see why," I agreed. "Is what he said about Adam true?"

She shrugged. "I heard Adam fired him, but I didn't hear about the death threat."

"What about the missing dinghy?" John asked.

"Even if it is missing, that doesn't mean anything. Anyone could have taken it."

"Without the key?" John asked.

"Who said there was a key in it?" Charlene pointed out. "Besides, all anyone needed to do is untie it, not run it, and every person on this island knows how to untie a knot."

"I guess we'll find out soon enough," I said, feeling dread coil in my stomach. "How well did you know Derek?"

"Enough to know he wasn't good boyfriend material—although Tania didn't believe me." My friend frowned, her lipsticked lips making a pink upside-down crescent. "I hate that he died, but I don't think he was a good influence on her."

"Why?" John asked when he'd polished off his lemon bar. Already the container was half-empty; apparently the recipe was a winner. I reached for one myself. The sweet-tart flavor of the lemon curd mixed with the buttery shortbread crust was divine; I could see why the bars were disappearing so fast.

My friend licked a stray bit of powdered sugar off her index finger before answering. "She was always waiting for him to call, and he wasn't very good about showing up on time. I heard he wasn't a particularly good sternman, either. Showing up late, lazy on the job. I never heard anything about him taking out Adam's boat, though."

John leaned forward on his stool. "Did you talk with him at all?"

She shook her head. "I didn't see him around the store much; he just waited outside for Tania. He never wanted to come inside."

Never a good sign, I thought, wondering why he didn't want to talk to Charlene. Was it because he was shy, or because he had something to hide?

"Did he have any friends on the island that you know of?" John asked.

"He was friendly with Ingrid Sorenson's son Evan," she said.

"That's not necessarily a vote of confidence," John said. The selectwoman's son had had drug problems a few years back, and had been in and out of rehab several times.

"That's not fair," I said to John. "I know he's been in and out of trouble in the past, but he's been clean for a couple of years, now."

"True," John admitted. "Anyone else he was close to?"

"As far as I know, he just worked with Adam. And Tania liked him, of course."

As our eyes strayed to the closed door in the back of the store, the bell over the front door jingled, and we all jumped.

It was Matilda Jenkins, the town historian. "Goodness," she said, adjusting her glasses. Her cropped white hair looked slightly wild, as usual. "You all look as if you'd just seen a ghost!"

"It's been a long day," I told her. "Have a lemon bar."

"Ooh, don't mind if I do." As she crossed to the counter and inspected the few remaining bars, she said, "I heard about the police launch, and I came here figuring Charlene could fill me in. What's going on?"

Charlene gave a weary sigh. "Adam's sternman died. Natalie found him drifting in a dinghy."

"The young man Tania was seeing? That's terrible." She shuddered. "Boats can be so dangerous. Did he fall and hit his head? Or get tangled in a line?"

I shivered at the thought. "We don't know." The detective had told me not to share details of what I'd found—not that I had much to share, anyway—so I didn't mention the blood.

"Another mystery." Matilda adjusted the strap of her cloth bag and selected a powdered-sugar-covered square. "So much death. It's especially bad when they're young. I didn't know him except in passing, but still…" She took a bite of the lemon bar. "These are delicious, Nat."

"Thanks."

She turned to my friend. "How recent is the coffee, Charlene?"

"Just made it twenty minutes ago," Charlene said. "Want a cup?"

"That would be lovely," she said, pulling up a stool at the bar. "I still can't get over that young man. What do the police say?"

"They're not saying anything, at least not yet." I thought of the bullet hole in Derek's chest and suppressed a shudder. "But it looks like homicide."

"How do you know?"

"I found the body."

Matilda reached over and squeezed my hand. "You poor, poor dear. Are the detectives working on the case already?"

Charlene nodded toward the closed door in the back of the store. "Detective Johnson is talking with Tania now, in the back room."

"Oh, that's so awful. I hope they're wrong and decide it was an accident. I don't want to have to worry about a murderer running around the island. Although it seems to be a perennial problem." She bit her lip. "Any word from Agnes and Beryl on the crucifix?"

"Nothing yet," I told her, "but I don't expect them back until later."

"I wish I could have gone with them," she said, "but I had to staff the museum. I would love to get into that old rectory."

"Any luck convincing Murray to let you in?"

She sighed. "Unfortunately not, but I'm dying to get in there. There could be some indication as to what happened to the poor man. The police decided the bones were too old to pursue, but that doesn't mean we can't figure out what happened!"

"I like your spirit," I said with a smile.

"Thanks. I can't wait to hear back from Beryl and Agnes."

"I'm sure they'll let you know as soon as they hear anything," I said. The two had become fast friends with the island's historian since arriving at the island. Old bones seemed to be a great way to bring people together, as it turned out.

"If it was the priest," Matilda said, pursing her lips, "and he didn't die of natural causes, it's a real puzzle."

"Being buried out of the graveyard kind of indicates foul play," Charlene pointed out. "Kind of hard to dig a hole, throw yourself in, and cover yourself up if you're dead."

"But why on earth would anyone want to kill a priest?" Matilda's brow furrowed.

I shrugged and darted a glance at Charlene. It had happened before on the island, I knew. Another of Charlene's ill-fated romances.

"Stranger things have happened," Charlene said lightly, and busied herself pouring Matilda a cup of coffee.

The historian shook herself as if to rid her mind of the thought, and turned to my fiancé. "Enough about tragedies," she said. "Too many of them on this island, it seems. How are things with your mother, John?" she asked.

Speaking of tragedies, I thought. I glanced at John, wondering how he would react.

"She and Murray seem to be hitting it off surprisingly well," he said stiffly.

"I know. She's been working with him on his family's genealogy; we've been going through the Selfridge papers." Matilda grinned at John. "They think one of his relatives might have been involved in rum running; he frequently went to Canada. Even married a young woman up there."

"Doesn't surprise me," I said. "The Selfridges like their profits."

Matilda poured two packets of sugar into her coffee and stirred it. "Many islanders have family who got involved in the business during Prohibition. There was lots of that going on off the coast of Maine; ships would come down from Canada and sit three miles out from shore, just outside U.S. territorial waters. It was a good way to make money from something other than fishing." She took a sip of the hot brew before continuing. "William McCoy was one of the most famous rum runners. He brought liquor down from Canada, and he was often off the coast here. Ever heard the phrase 'The Real McCoy'?"

"Of course."

"Some people say it's a reference to his liquor; he only smuggled good stuff, not moonshine."

"Why was Cranberry Island involved?" I asked.

"That's what Smuggler's Cove was all about." Her eyes gleamed, and she chuckled. "It was a great place to stash things. Hard to get to, off the mainland, and only accessible by water. Cranberry Island supplied a lot of those grand summer cottages on Mount Desert in those days."

She was referring to the huge mansions on the mainland that had been built by the industrial barons, I knew. Many of them had burned in the fire of 1947, but a few of the sprawling "cottages" still stood.

I was about to ask her more about rum running when the door to the back room opened, and Tania emerged with a pale, tear-streaked face.

"Poor sweetheart," Matilda said as Charlene put an arm around her and escorted her to one of the couches in the front of the store. Detective Johnson thanked her quietly, then headed for the door of the store with us in his wake.

FOUR

OUR FIRST STOP WAS Derek's aunt and uncle's house, which was not far from the cranberry bog from which the island had gotten its name.

"Do you want us to come with you?" John asked the detective as we pulled up outside the gray-shingled house on Kitchen Lane. Red geraniums bloomed from white-painted window boxes, and marigolds and petunias mixed with beans and tomato plants in a small garden plot in the side yard.

"Do you know them well?" the detective asked as John set the parking brake.

"Not really, I'm afraid." I knew Jeff Abingdon worked on the mail boat sometimes, but we'd never really talked, and I'd never met his wife. The couple didn't mingle much. One of them, however, was obviously a gifted gardener. A few beautiful rose bushes bloomed a gorgeous crimson on the side of the house.

"Why don't you just stay here, then," Detective Johnson said. "I probably won't be too long. I may have to stay until victim services arrives if they're too upset; if so, I'll let you know."

John reached for my hand as we watched him mount the steps to the front door. A burly man answered the door, and his face turned grim as the detective shared the news. A moment later, the detective was inside the house, and the front door was shutting behind them.

"That's got to be the worst part of the job," I told John.

"I imagine so," he said. "I'm glad it's not down to me."

"Nice little house, though," I said as we sat and waited for the detective to finish. "One of them is quite a gardener. Do you know if Derek was staying here?"

"I don't know," he said. "I know almost nothing about the young man, unfortunately."

I studied the clean windowpanes and the small but swept front porch. "It looks bright and cheerful, but you never know what goes on behind closed doors."

John gave me a look. "You thinking they may be suspects?"

"I don't know enough to say, but don't the police look at family first?"

He nodded, and both of us stared at the little house, wondering what was going on inside—and if the grim-faced man at the door might have been responsible for his nephew's death.

It was twenty minutes before Detective Johnson emerged, looking solemn. The bright sun and cheerful flowers seemed too gay, somehow, considering the tragic news he'd had to deliver.

"No victim services?" John asked as he reclaimed his seat in the van.

"I gave them a card in case they need it, but I doubt they'll call. The wife was quite upset; she left the room almost immediately. She looked pretty shaken up to me, but her husband seemed to think she'll be all right."

"Any potential leads?" John asked.

"It doesn't look like it," he said. "He wasn't staying with them, either. Which reminds me, I have a quick call to make." Detective Johnson picked up his cell phone and called his team, directing them to a small house not far from the pier where Derek had apparently bunked while he was on the island. If his aunt and uncle were close with him, I thought as John steered the van toward the co-op, it didn't extend to opening their home to their nephew. After a moment, the officer put away his phone and asked about Adam.

"He's been dating my niece for two years," I told the detective as the van bumped down the narrow road toward the town pier. The gardens in front of the small, clapboard houses were filled with the purples of tall delphiniums and bright pink roses, with the occasional burst of yellow from Black-Eyed Susans. A line of tomato plants bore little yellow blossoms. The arrival of the farm, I thought to myself, had inspired the vegetable gardener in more than one islander—and revealed a few green thumbs.

We passed by the school, a two-story building painted bright blue, with a small playground in front of it, on the way to the co-op. Two elementary-aged girls swung lazily on the swings, heads bent in toward one another as they chatted. The new teacher in town had brought a fresh jolt of excitement to the school; she and her lobsterman partner had moved to the island only six months before. I hoped she was able to fight Murray's bid to close it down successfully. Much of what kept the island vital was the young families who lived here and raised their children—and without the school, many of them would be forced to leave. In the shadow of a lilac bush beside the building, I noticed a trio of teens slouching against the wall. I caught the eye of the tallest, and the three seemed to dissolve into the bushes.

"Thrackton is his last name, right?" Detective Johnson asked as he wrote the name down, drawing me back to more immediate concerns. "Tell me more about him."

I turned away from the school and focused on the road—and the detective's question. "He graduated from Princeton, then decided he'd rather be a lobsterman than a banker. I think he visited here once and fell in love with the place."

The detective let out a low whistle. "Heck of a lot of money for a useless degree."

"Maybe," I agreed, "but he seems happy with his decision."

"You said he was almost like family. Has he said anything about Derek to you?"

I shook my head. "I knew he'd taken on a new sternman, but we haven't talked much; he's been out on the boat almost every day. And with Gwen in California for a few months, he hasn't been by the inn as much."

"I understand things weren't going very well between them," the detective suggested.

I kept my voice cool, despite the tightness I felt in my throat. "Adam and Gwen?"

"No." I glanced back at him, and he shook his head. "The victim and Adam."

A little kernel of ice formed in my stomach, and I looked over at John, who was behind the wheel. His face was impassive, but I could tell by the tension in his jaw that he was concerned. "Why do you say that?" I asked.

"A few people have mentioned it." He leaned back in his seat and looked out the window. "It may not mean anything—it's just worth exploring."

We drove the rest of the short way in silence, pulling up outside the low-slung building that functioned as the Lobster Co-op. The islanders brought their catch here, and the co-op sold it to restaurants and wholesalers across the country. Tom Lockhart, the tall, affable man who was in charge of the operation, was stepping out the door as we pulled up outside.

"Tom!" I hailed him as I opened the van door and stepped out.

"Natalie." He gave me a subdued wave, and I could tell by his face he'd heard the news.

"Is Adam here?" I asked.

He jabbed his thumb toward the door. "Inside," he said as the policeman slid the van door open and stepped out onto the cracked pavement. "Who's this?" he asked.

"Detective Johnson," the policeman said, stepping forward and proffering a meaty hand.

"Is this about Derek Morton?" Tom asked.

"You knew the young man?"

Tom nodded. "Not well—he hadn't been on the island long—but it's a tragedy all the same."

"Who told you?" the policeman said.

"Got a phone call from a friend in Ellsworth who knows his mom. Word travels fast around here."

Detective Johnson whipped out his notebook. "What was your name again, sir?"

Tom told him.

"How long had Derek Morton been working with Adam?"

"A month or two, I think. He was working for Zeke Forester, too, on the side."

The policeman jotted something down. "Who's that?"

"He's a farmer from the mainland. Just moved to the island a few months ago, and started a farm."

"How was the relationship between him and Derek?"

Tom shrugged. "I have no idea. Have to ask Zeke, I'm afraid."

The New York cop scribbled that down. "Was there anything unusual about Derek? Did he seem worried about anything—or afraid?"

"Afraid?" Tom laughed. "He was full of himself. Swaggered around like he was the cat's meow—kept talking about how he wasn't going to be filling traps with dead herring for long. Although with his work ethic, I can't imagine him going very far."

"Did he ever say anything specific about what his new job was going to be?"

"Said he knew some important people. They were going to take care of him."

"Maybe they did," I murmured, thinking of the blood in the dinghy. John shot me a look and I clammed up.

Detective Johnson plucked a card out of his pocket. "Thanks for your time, Mr. Lockhart. If you think of anything, please give me a call."

Tom took the card and smiled. "Anything I can do to help, officer."

The inside of the co-op smelled of gasoline, herring, and men, three of whom were gathered at a table at the end of the long room, listening to the crackle of the radio.

Adam rose as he saw us, his usually smiling face grim. He was a handsome young man, tall and dark, with a quick wit and a kind heart. "I heard about Derek," he said solemnly.

"As has everyone on this island, apparently," the policeman murmured dryly. Detective Johnson introduced himself to Adam and the other two lobstermen, both of whom knew Derek, as well. He asked the same questions he had of Tom. Although they agreed that Derek had been unreliable and rather full of himself, no one had anything new to add to the conversation.

"I understand you fired Derek Morton," the burly policeman said to Adam.

"I let him go last week," Adam said.

The detective made a noncommittal noise. "Did you see him at all after that?"

Adam shook his head. "He didn't come back to the co-op. I don't think anyone else would hire him."

"Did you have any communication with him after you terminated his employment?"

"I paid him a week's severance, and that was it," he said. "I assumed he'd gone back to Ellsworth."

"Can we talk in private for a moment?" he asked. Adam shot me a questioning glance, then shrugged. "Sure," he said, and followed the detective out the door.

"I knew he was bad news," volunteered Ernie when they left.

"Does that cop think Adam did him in?" asked the other.

"I think he's just doing his job," John said, then turned his attention to Ernie. "What did you mean about Derek being bad news?"

Ernie shifted in his chair. "Just a feeling," he said. "He was the kind to get into trouble."

"Did you ever see anything suspicious?" John asked.

"He got to work late a lot," Ernie said. "I think he might have been a drinker; his eyes were always bloodshot, and he was kind of out to lunch sometimes."

"Who did he hang out with?"

"Tania Kean, mostly," he said. "And Evan Sorenson."

Ingrid's son again. "How long has Evan been back on the island?" John asked.

"A month or two. He's living with his parents, and working out at that new farm."

"Really? I heard Derek worked there, too."

He shrugged a flannel-clad shoulder. "I don't know. I can't imagine Derek Morton doing much in the way of weeding. Too lazy."

I glanced at the door. "I heard Derek took out Adam's boat sometimes."

"That's what Adam said," Ernie replied.

"How did he find out?" John asked.

"Boat was tied up wrong a few times, and the gas seemed to be going down awful fast, so Adam stayed back and watched one night. Caught him red-handed."

Before I could ask more, Detective Johnson and Adam returned.

"Thank you for your time," the policeman said, giving Adam a card. "And I'd like you to come and take a look at that dinghy later on today."

Adam seemed paler than usual, and my heart sank a few notches. Even though the dinghy was his, I told myself, anyone could have accessed it. Still, after the way the two men had parted company ... it didn't look good.

The detective handed additional cards to the three young lobstermen. "If any of you know or happen to hear anything regarding Derek's death, please give me a call."

Something about the question sparked my memory. "While I'm thinking of it," I asked the lobstermen, "have any of you noticed a boat with a turquoise and orange buoy around lately?"

"I've seen her a few times," said Ernie, "but I haven't seen any of the buoys on the water. And I've been watching."

"What's her name?" John asked.

"I never get close enough to see," Ernie said. "She's not a boat I've seen before. She's usually pretty quick off the mark when she spots me."

"Think she's putting out traps?" I asked.

"If she is, she's using someone else's buoys to do it," he answered. Each lobsterman in Maine was assigned a specific buoy; it was illegal to be seen picking up a trap whose buoy didn't match the one tacked to your boat. "I'll ask around, see if anyone's seen any funny business."

"What else would a lobster boat be doing hanging around the island?" I asked.

"I don't know, but I aim to find out," Ernie said darkly.

"Don't go taking the law into your own hands, now," Detective Johnson said mildly. "If you see any 'funny business,' I want to know about it. It might be related to what happened to that young sternman."

"I've got your number," Ernie said with a steely smile that told me he planned on handling suspected poachers all by himself, thank you very much.

Detective Johnson gave the young man a long, searching look, then turned to Adam. "I'll be in touch."

The three men watched as we followed him out of the dim, fish-scented co-op, and I found myself glad I was an innkeeper and not a lobsterman.

"Do you want us to run you down to Zeke's farm?" John asked as we got back into the van.

"Thanks, but you've driven me around the island enough already for one day," he said. "The house is over there, right?" he asked, pointing toward a patch of woods not far from the pier.

"I think so," I said. "If you need a ride back, let me know."

"Thanks," he said. "I've got the inn's number right here." He patted his shirt pocket. "Where's the farm located, by the way? Is it within walking distance?"

I gave him directions, then said, "It sounds like Derek might have been getting mixed up with something dangerous."

"Maybe," Detective Johnson said. "Maybe not. Lots of young men talk big."

"He did end up dead, though," I pointed out.

"There is that," Detective Johnson said. "There is that."

———

The police launch had pulled away from the inn's dock, towing the dinghy with it, and was docking at the town pier, near the house where Derek Morton had apparently lived for a few weeks before his death. We'd left the detective near the pier—he was planning on walking to meet his team at the house.

John and I got back to the inn, where the Cape Anne building sat serene above the soft blue waves. I looked out at the blue water lapping peacefully against the rocks, seaweed washing back and forth in the gentle waves. If I didn't know better, I would have thought that nothing unusual had happened. It had, though—and I couldn't get the image of that young man's pale face out of my mind.

Catherine had finished tidying the rooms and gone down to the carriage house after her outing with Murray. John had headed down to his workshop to put the finishing touches on a sculpture for the show he was preparing for—his gorgeous driftwood pieces were starting to get some notice in the art world—while I dusted a pizza peel with cornmeal, dug a grapefruit-sized ball of dough from a plastic container in the fridge, and formed it into a rough round. I'd learned the recipe for no-knead artisan bread from Kathleen Flinn's *Kitchen Counter Cooking School*, and now I always kept a tub of dough on hand for bread. In an hour, I'd score the top with a sharp knife and toss it into the oven with a cup of hot water, and the kitchen would fill with the homey, yeasty scent of fresh bread.

As the loaf sat to rise, I began cutting parchment for fish *en papillote*. The recipe sounded sophisticated and tasted out of this world, but was quick and easy to assemble—perfect for a distracted chef.

I laid the fillets on top of the parchment squares, ignoring Biscuit, who was winding between my legs and meowing pitifully, then drizzled them with olive oil and sea salt before tossing in some minced shallots, summer squash, and a few spears of asparagus. I sealed the packets and tucked the pan into the fridge; I'd slide it into the oven when the bread came out. Catherine would be delighted, I thought; a dish that was low fat *and* featured vegetables! Served with a salad and some crusty bread (which I knew she wouldn't touch), it would be a summer feast.

My eyes drifted to the window, and the placid blue water beyond. Young Derek Morton would never enjoy another summer feast again. Who had taken his life?

Biscuit meowed again, and I reached down to pet her smooth ginger fur. Normally I'd take pity on her and open a can of tuna, but the vet had told me she was getting a bit on the chunky side, and that I needed to cut back. Biscuit wasn't the only one who needed to cut back, I thought, adjusting my T-shirt over my middle and opening the back door so she could go out and get some exercise. She gave me a disdainful look and padded over to the radiator under the window, where she curled up for an afternoon nap. So much for regular exercise.

I pulled my recipe file out and flipped through to my grandmother's steamed pudding recipe. John had brought up my coffee can of fresh blueberries; I knew Catherine wouldn't share it with us, but I suspected both John and I could use some comfort food after the day's grisly discovery. As I glanced over the list of ingredients, my thoughts strayed back to Derek. He had evidently been "talking big" recently. Had he told someone more than he was supposed to?

And if his death *was* a warning, who was it for?

I pulled out the metal pudding steamer my grandmother had given me—it looked like a little Bundt cake pan with a lid—and buttered it, then prepared the pot in which the pudding would cook. Like Boston Brown Bread, what made the pudding so moist and delicious was the steam treatment it received.

While the pot of water was heating on the stove, I lined up the ingredients on the counter, including the rinsed berries I had picked that morning. As I creamed the butter, sugar, and eggs together in a mixer, I cast my mind back to the image of Derek, trying to remember the details. He'd been lying almost straight up-and-down in the bottom of the boat, with his feet toward the bow; if he'd fallen into that position, that meant he would have been standing in the bow, which is not usually where you stood in a skiff. I was guessing some-one had placed him there.

As I mixed the butter and sugar together, I found myself wonder-ing how Tania was doing—and if she had some information that would point to why Derek had died. Adam evidently wasn't the only one Detective Johnson was questioning, but it made me nervous that there was a link between Adam and Derek. I was also worried about having a murderer running loose on Cranberry Island. I poured the dry ingredients into a smaller bowl and stirred them with a whisk, then added them to the creamy butter and sugar in the mixing bowl and reached for the berries.

When the blueberries had been folded into the creamy batter and I had poured it all into the pudding mold, I picked up the phone and called my best friend. She answered on the first ring, sounding less like her cheery self than normal.

"How's Tania holding up?" I asked as I fitted the lid onto the mold and slipped it into the pot on the stove, then added water to create a "bath" for the pudding.

"Not great," Charlene said. "But that's to be expected."

"It's hard to lose someone you care for." I put the lid on the pot and adjusted the heat. "How long had they been seeing each other, again?"

"Only a month or two. She was pretty into him, though." She sighed. "You remember young love."

I much preferred older love, I thought as I flipped through my book until I found the recipe for foamy sauce. It was much more rational, and at least at the moment, very satisfying.

"I wonder who would have wanted him dead?" I mused.

"They've confirmed that, then?"

"No," I said, running my finger down the list of ingredients for foamy sauce. Lyle's Golden Syrup, an English import my grandmother had introduced me to, was easy and good with steamed puddings, but I was out at the moment. Besides, foamy sauce, a sweet concoction made with butter, eggs, and cream, was even better. "Still, obviously they think someone did him in. Did Tania say anything about who she thinks might have killed him?"

"No, but she told me the detective wanted to know a lot about Adam. I guess he's the only one they have to go on."

"I hope his name is cleared quickly." I tucked the phone between my shoulder and my chin as I opened the fridge and checked to be sure I had enough eggs. Although the sauce wouldn't be made until the last minute, I wanted to be sure I wouldn't be caught short. "Shouldn't be hard. I can't imagine Adam hurting anyone."

"I wouldn't think so, either," Charlene said, "but apparently things aren't looking too good."

I almost dropped the eggs. "What do you mean?"

"Tania said Derek and Adam had a run-in about a week back."

I wasn't sure I wanted to know, but I had to ask. "What did he say?"

"Adam seemed to think Derek had been taking out his boat without asking permission."

Just what Fred had said down at the store. "Did Tania confirm that?"

Charlene sighed. "Tania didn't know for sure, but she does know he left to do 'errands' at night a couple of times and wouldn't say where he was going."

"Adam must have had some pretty solid evidence to lose his temper like that. He's usually so easy-going."

"Derek was reportedly running the lobster boat with its lights off, and had almost run over someone on a skiff."

"How did he know it was Derek?" I asked.

"One of the lobstermen saw him rowing a dinghy back to shore the night it happened, and whoever he tried to run over said he saw the boat's name—it was the *Carpe Diem*."

Adam's boat, I thought, feeling sick.

"They tracked Adam down and filed a complaint with the police in Southwest Harbor," Charlene continued.

"No wonder Adam fired Derek."

"He didn't just fire him." I didn't like the foreboding sound of Charlene's voice.

I remembered what Fred had told me down at the store, and cringed. "What else did he do?"

"He threatened to kill him if he set foot on the *Carpe Diem* again."

FIVE

I TIGHTENED BOTH HANDS and realized I was still standing in the middle of the kitchen with a carton of eggs in my hands. I set them down before I damaged them, and groaned. If Adam was going to threaten somebody, why did he have to do it in front of half the island?

"I hope he has an alibi," Charlene said. "Does anyone know when Derek died, yet?"

"Not that I know of. And even if they did, I'm guessing they wouldn't tell me."

"Maybe we're worrying too much," Charlene suggested. "After all, they didn't arrest him."

"They haven't even finished the autopsy yet, Charlene."

"That's right," she mused. "Maybe he died of natural causes after all."

"He didn't," I said, looking out at the mountains beyond the serene blue water and wishing I felt as calm as the scene outside looked.

"How do you know?"

"I'm not supposed to say anything, but it was pretty obvious what had happened." I told her how I'd found him.

"Did you notice anything else?"

"There was a note in his hand. He was supposed to be meeting someone named 'T.'"

"Tania?"

"I don't know," I said. "I've been asking myself that question all afternoon." As I gripped the phone, I glanced out the window toward the island. Beryl and Agnes were walking down the road toward the inn. "My guests are back from the mail boat," I told Charlene. "I've got to run."

"Now you have me worried."

"I'm sorry. I didn't mean to do that."

She sighed. "Call me if you hear anything."

"Of course," I said, hanging up the phone and reaching for a bottle of wine and a box of crackers. Murder or no murder, I still had guests to feed.

———

"How did your trip go?" I asked as I walked into the parlor carrying a tray laden with Irish cheddar, water crackers, and a bottle of Merlot. The room was cozy, with big windows facing the water, overstuffed couches, and a thick peach-and-blue Oriental rug. On cold nights, I laid a fire in the big river stone fireplace, but tonight was perfect even with the windows open. An early evening breeze ruffled the curtains as I set the tray down on the coffee table.

Agnes, the mystery writer, sat up eagerly, adjusting her chambray shirt over her ample middle as she reached for the cheese knife. "This looks fabulous. I'm absolutely starved," she told me.

"I've got dinner going in the kitchen," I said. "Tell me about the trip. Was the crucifix a match?"

Beryl answered, eyes shining with excitement. "It's not a hundred percent, but they're pretty sure it's the same one. They're doing DNA testing to confirm his identity; I had to give them a swab."

"When will they know?"

"They're going to test it this week." She shivered. "It's weird to think of my grandfather being murdered, but it's looking like that's what happened."

"How can they tell?"

"Well, the unmarked grave is suspicious," she said. "He wasn't in a cemetery, and as a man of the cloth, he would have wanted to be buried on hallowed ground."

"Makes sense," I agreed.

"But beyond that, it appears someone put a bullet through his skull." Beryl shuddered. "They even found the bullet."

"You're kidding me," I said.

"It didn't pass all the way through his skull, so they buried him with it still in his head." She grimaced. "He was a country priest. Who could have wanted him dead?"

"Maybe there were other things going on in his life," I suggested, thinking of a murder that had happened on the island a few years back. "Even priests have private lives. Maybe Matilda can shed some light on what might have happened."

"Oh, that's right … we were going to call her!"

"Tell her she's welcome to join us," I said. "I've got enough to add a plate."

Beryl stood up, smoothing out her cotton dress. "Can I borrow your phone?"

"Of course," I said, pointing her to the desk in the front hall.

As Beryl hurried off, Agnes poured herself a glass of wine and sat back in her wing chair. "Speaking of death or possible murders," she said in a low voice, "I heard there was a bit of excitement here this morning, too."

"How did you know?"

"George McLeod told us you found a body in a dinghy." She shivered.

"It's true, unfortunately," I told her.

"How terrifying," Agnes breathed, but her eyes were gleaming with interest. "Was he murdered?"

"We're still waiting to hear the official word," I replied, "but from what I saw, I can't think what else it would have been."

"Was the victim local?"

"He lived here with his aunt and uncle for a bit, but he came from Ellsworth. He was dating a young woman I know, though."

"You wouldn't think something like that would happen on an island like this," Agnes said, taking a sip of her wine.

"It is surprising," I agreed. "But it does happen."

Beryl walked back in and told us Matilda was on her way. When she arrived a few minutes later, Agnes wasted no time filling her in on what she had missed, and the plump woman's eyes grew round. "Do you think we're safe?" she asked, pushing a salt-and-pepper curl behind one ear.

"I think we'll be just fine. Besides, you should be safer here than anywhere else on the island; my fiancé is a deputy."

"That handsome man with the green eyes?" Beryl asked.

I nodded, feeling a surge of pride. "He's really good looking," Agnes said, taking another sip of wine. "Are there more like him around here?"

"If there were, my friend Charlene would call first dibs," I joked.

"Is she the pretty woman who runs the store?"

"That's the one." I grinned. "She's been on the hunt for eligible bachelors for years. She's not a fan of the smell of herring, though, so her local options are limited."

"I'm sure she'll find her Prince Charming someday." Agnes reached for another cracker and cut off a wedge of cheese. "She's too cute not to!"

"And you're engaged," Beryl said. "How did you two meet?"

"John was my tenant, actually," I said, smiling. I told her how he'd been renting the carriage house when I bought the inn, and that the relationship had developed as we'd gotten to know each other. It hadn't been without hiccups, but I was excited to be sharing my life with such a wonderful man. "When are you getting married?" Beryl asked.

"In September," I told her. "We booked a resort on the beach in Florida, and they're taking care of everything. I sent in the rest of the deposit a few weeks ago; I should probably call and confirm that they got it."

"How romantic." Beryl gazed out at the water beyond the parlor window. "A beachside wedding."

"It sounds lovely … but I'm still curious about this body you found," Agnes said, pulling the conversation back to poor Derek. "I heard he was in a boat. Was he just lying there? Had he hit his head or something?"

"I did find him in a dinghy, but I don't think I'm supposed to talk about it," I said, glancing up at the clock. "I'd better get back in the kitchen and get dinner going. There are wine glasses in the buffet in the dining room if you need another for Matilda."

"Thanks, Natalie," Agnes said. "Keep me posted on the case; it might be excellent source material for my book!"

"Will do," I said, and escaped to the kitchen before she could pepper me with unanswerable questions.

The kitchen smelled deliciously of steaming pudding, and I inhaled the comforting scent as I cleaned new potatoes for the pot and whipped up a quick vinaigrette for the salad. The fish was already in little packets; I arranged them on a tray, then checked the timer on the pudding; it only had a few minutes to go. I'd make the foamy sauce at the last minute, I decided; it didn't keep very well, so it was best to wait.

When I'd finished washing the lettuce leaves and slicing up radishes and tomatoes, my mind turned away from the gruesome discovery of this morning to the more pleasant topic of the wedding. It was going to be small; Charlene was coming, as were Gwen and my sister, along with John's mother and a few folks from the island. We'd wanted to keep it simple, but part of me wished we were having it here on the island so that everyone in our lives could attend. John had wanted to go away to minimize the workload on me. When I'd talked about keeping it on the island, he'd hugged me and explained his reasoning. "You'll want to cater everything, you'll be cleaning the guest rooms, worried about making breakfast ... I want you to get away from everything and take a break!" I appreciated the thought, but felt a tug of wistfulness. I pulled out the computer and sent a quick e-mail to the resort, just to make sure they'd gotten the deposit check, then busied myself putting the rest of dinner together.

———

"It's hard to believe it was only this morning you were picking blueberries, isn't it?" John asked as he put the last dish into the dishwasher later that evening. Matilda had stayed for dinner, and the trout and the steamed pudding had been a big hit. Even Catherine had had a second helping of the pudding, despite her aversion to carbohydrates in any form other than a celery stick. The melding of the blueberries with the moist pudding, topped off with the butterscotch flavored sauce, was irresistible. The fish had been popular, too: flaky and flavorful.

"I know," I said. "Any word on Derek's death?"

"Nothing yet," he replied, "but I'm worried."

I glanced up from the cup of tea I was nursing at our big pine farm table. If I hadn't put the pudding in the fridge, I'd be on my fourth slice about now; the moist, berry-studded crumb covered in rich, buttery foamy sauce was absolutely addictive. "What are you worried about?"

"Adam."

I felt a frisson of worry. "Uh oh. Is Detective Johnson taking that threat he made seriously?"

"I get the impression he's the main person of interest." John tossed a dishwasher tab into the soap holder and closed the dishwasher, then grabbed a Thunder Hole Ale from the refrigerator and joined me at the table.

"Did he say anything about his interview with Derek's aunt and uncle?"

"Jeff and Elizabeth Abingdon?" He shook his head. "Johnson doesn't seem to think they're involved."

"But surely they know something!"

"He doesn't think so." John took a swig of his beer. "Apparently there was a falling out. Derek thought he was entitled to Jeff Abingdon's lobster license, and threatened to take him to court over it."

"Wouldn't that be a motive for murder?"

"You'd think so, but he dropped the suit six months ago. They haven't spoken since, and apparently Johnson doesn't think a lobster license is worth murdering someone for."

"Clearly he hasn't spent too much time on the coast of Maine," I snorted. "Didn't Derek live with the Abingdons for a few years?"

"He stayed with them for about a year," John said, "but that was a few years back, and they haven't been close."

"Did they find anything at his house?"

"Not that I've heard," he said.

"He said it was down by the pier, but it doesn't sound familiar."

"It's kind of hidden back in a clump of trees. There's no driveway; you have to walk through the brambles to get to it."

I pictured the raspberry patch not far from the pier; it was next to a meadow that in spring was covered with lupines, and in summer frequently hosted Claudette's goats, Muffin and Pudge, who traveled the island chained to an old tire so that, in theory, they wouldn't stray into people's gardens. There had always been what I took to be a shack hidden back in the woods. "You mean the small building with the peeling paint that's next to the meadow?"

John nodded and took another swallow of his beer. "That's the one," he confirmed.

"I'd like to take a look at the place myself," I mused.

My fiancé cocked a sandy eyebrow. "The police have already been through it," he said.

"I know, I know. I just feel like I have nothing to go on."

He grinned. "I didn't know the department hired you to take the case."

I rolled my eyes. "I'm worried about Adam, that's all."

"I'm just giving you a hard time." He reached over and squeezed my hand. "I realize you're probably going to ignore me, but I'd rather you hang back and let the detectives handle it." He gave me a crooked grin. "We're supposed to be getting married in a few months, after all. Hate to lose the deposit."

I kicked him under the table, and he laughed.

"Honeymoon's over already?" I asked.

"It hasn't begun yet," he said in a growly tone that made my insides do a little flip. Maybe Florida wasn't such a bad idea after all.

"On a more serious note," he continued, still holding my hand, "I have to say, Detective Johnson seems a bit surprised that things here aren't as quiet as he'd expected."

"Really? What else is going on?"

"The department is trying to crack a drug ring they think is working the coast," he said, "from here to Canada. They're working in tandem with the Coast Guard, but so far they're coming up empty."

"What kind of drugs?"

"Marijuana, mostly. Some heroin."

I took another sip of my tea. "Isn't there a bill in the legislature right now to legalize marijuana?"

"They're talking about it," John said, "but it's still illegal, unless you're growing it for medical purposes. There's still a booming business for recreational pot."

"I'm not a fan of the stuff myself, but I wish they'd just go ahead and legalize it," I said. "Tax the heck out of it and spend the money on education and Medicare, rather than spending oodles of money trying to tamp it down."

"Prohibition didn't work, either," John said, raising his beer and taking a sip.

"I just hope they don't spend so much time worrying about who's transporting pot that they don't look further than Adam when they're rounding up suspects."

"That makes two of us," John said. "Three, if you count Gwen."

"She'll be here in just a couple of days. I hope they get it ironed out by then."

"Me too," my fiancé said in a tone of voice that did not inspire confidence.

SIX

"How DID IT GO with Matilda last night?" I asked as I served plates of shirred eggs to Agnes and Beryl the next morning. I'd whipped up a batch of my Wicked Blueberry Coffee Cake and some bacon to go with it, and the two were eating as if last night's supper had been a week ago.

"Oh, wonderful," Agnes said. "She was telling me all about the island's history. We're going with her to see the lighthouse this morning," she said, "and we're going to see if we can get Murray Selfridge to let us take a look at where the old rectory used to be. I understand they're renovating it, but I'd love to take a look"

"Isn't that right near where they found the body?" I asked as I poured more coffee for Beryl.

"Right next to it, in fact. We were hoping your fiancé's mother could put in a good word for us." She smiled up at me hopefully.

I stifled a sigh. Did everyone on the island want a favor from Murray? And was Catherine's apparent hold on him already legendary? "I'll talk to her," I said, "but I can't make any promises."

"Well, if we can't get to the rectory, Matilda tells us there's a lot of history elsewhere on the island."

"She told us there's a ghost in the inn, too!" Beryl added between forkfuls of coffee cake.

"There may have been," I said, remembering the eerie apparition I'd encountered one day in the kitchen, "but I think we laid that one to rest."

Agnes's eyes were big. "Wasn't she murdered here?"

"That's the rumor," I said, not wanting to confirm it. "But something like that has happened in most old houses. It's not unusual when you have houses that have been standing for centuries."

"Matilda did tell us about another place, too. You can only get to it by boat, and legend is that bootleggers used to use it."

""Smuggler's Cove," I suggested.

"That's it!" Her eyes shone with excitement. "Is there any way to get there? It sounds like it would be a perfect setting for a murder mystery!"

"I can take you, if you'd like. We have to go at low tide, though. That's the only time you can get in and out of there." As soon as I'd offered, I regretted it; the cove was hard to get in and out of even with calm waters, and after a bad experience I'd had there not long after taking over the inn, I wasn't too keen on going back. Still, it was my job to keep the guests happy, and I didn't have plans for the afternoon anyway.

"Oh, that would be terrific. I've got the tide tables right here, on the back of the Visitors' Guide." She pulled a rolled-up brochure out of her bag and smoothed it out on the table. "Low tide is at two today," she said. "Would that work for you?"

"Sure," I said, trying to sound enthusiastic. "Why don't we meet at one-thirty, down by the dock?"

"Wonderful. How exciting! We'll get to see where all the action is." She held up a piece of coffee cake. "This is delicious, by the way. I'd love the recipe, if you're willing to share."

"I'll make a copy," I said, then refilled everyone's coffee and escaped to the kitchen.

———

"I'll take care of the breakfast dishes." John already had the dishwasher open and was filling it before I'd finished clearing the tables. He'd been up early, putting the finishing touches on his most recent sculpture while I got breakfast together, and was planning to carry it to one of the galleries on the mainland on the mail boat. I had made a small grocery list of things to pick up while he was over there; I knew he'd be stopping by the police station, too, to follow up on Derek.

He wiped his hands on a dishtowel and put his warm hands on my shoulders as I set down a plate. "Why don't you go berry-picking today?" he asked, kneading my tense muscles. "You seem stressed."

I shivered. "That's what I was coming back from when I found Derek."

"Go for a walk, then. Head down to the store and have a cup of coffee with Charlene. Mom will take care of the rooms, and you're free until dinner."

"I might do that," I said, thinking it would be a good opportunity to get a read on what was up with Adam. I wanted to talk with Zeke, too, to see if he knew anything that might help me figure out what had happened to the young man. Not to mention taking a walk around Derek's house.

John seemed to be reading my mind. "No investigating, though."

"I'm worried about Adam."

"They haven't even decided if it was a homicide yet, Natalie."

"But I'm betting they will. Why else would he be lying in blood—and why else would Detective Johnson be questioning everyone?"

"I know it looks bad, but Johnson knows what he's doing. He spent twenty years investigating homicides in New York."

"So you're saying it is a homicide?"

"There was a bullet hole in his chest, so it's likely, though it could be suicide. But I'm saying I want you to stay out of it. So if it was a homicide, and the person who did it is still hanging around, they have no reason to target you." His green eyes were solemn.

I wished I had John's confidence in the police. His concern was like a warm blanket, though; it was so nice to have someone wonderful to look after you.

"And if it is ruled a homicide?" I asked. "And if Adam is implicated? What then?"

"How about we cross that bridge when we get to it?"

———

I left the inn not long afterward, a container of my Texas Ranger Cookies in my hands. The chewy cookies were a toothsome combination of toffee bits, coconut, chocolate chips, and pecans that both froze and traveled well. I tried to keep a couple of bags of them in the freezer, but both John and I enjoyed them frozen, so it was a challenge. I'd managed to scrounge up a dozen for my purposes, though, and resolved to bake another triple batch soon.

As I walked toward Seal Point Road, my curiosity kept growing. I was looking forward to meeting Derek's relatives, but I also wanted to visit the little house where the victim had lived. The police had searched it yesterday—it wasn't that big—so I couldn't imagine there being any harm in at least walking around the place. When I reached the crossroads, instead of making a left toward the Abingdons' house, I turned right toward the pier, passing a low line of apple trees as the road dropped toward the harbor.

Derek's house was more of a shack than a house; in fact, it looked like its original purpose had been to store fishing supplies in the off-season. It was a squat, wooden structure with a flat roof that looked less than watertight. It had at one point been painted blue, but what little paint was left was peeling off in strips. The windows were cloudy, and even from the road, I could see that a spider web crack spread through one of them. I wouldn't want to spend the winter there, I thought. Or the summer, either.

The house was tucked in the trees just a short way from the town pier. A dirt path led to it from the main road, half-buried in a thicket of raspberry bushes and nettles that scratched at my legs as I passed, and I couldn't imagine having to push through this just to get to my own front door. I didn't know how much Derek had been paying to live here, but I hoped it wasn't much.

An old recliner with half the stuffing leaking out of it in yellow clots sat in a clearing not far from the front door, accompanied by two card-table chairs that had had better days. The dirty tips of hand-rolled cigarettes littered the ground; evidently this was where Derek had kicked back and enjoyed a smoke. Had Tania spent much time here? I couldn't imagine it being very appealing.

I clutched the container of cookies intended for the Abingdons as I stepped past the rotting recliner and reached up to knock on the peeling front door.

The door swung open when my knuckles hit it, and I jumped back, startled. Nobody was there, though; the door had just been slightly ajar. The smell of stale beer wafted out, and I wrinkled my nose.

"Hello?" I called—not that I expected anyone to answer, but it seemed like the right thing to do.

When nobody answered, I glanced over my shoulder and took a step inside.

I stepped on a piece of stale pizza with my toe and knocked over a beer can as I crossed through what I suppose could be called a living room. A formerly overstuffed and now half-stuffed couch of indeterminate color was in the middle of the room, festooned with dirty clothes. In front of it, an upturned crate doubled as a coffee table—or a beer table, if the number of cans lined up on it was any indication. An overflowing ashtray was tucked in between the cans, adding a stale smoke aroma to the spilled beer and spoiled food scent. Housekeeping had evidently not been a priority for Derek Morton.

By the time I got to the kitchen, I decided "messy" didn't really do it justice. "Filthy" was closer to the mark. Tania's description of the house as a "bachelor's pad" was an understatement. The sink overflowed with bowls and plates, and a pot with what might once have been ramen languished evilly on an electric burner. I swallowed back nausea and retreated down a short hall to the house's one bedroom.

I reached in and flipped on the light, then surveyed the room, which resembled the kitchen, only with more clothing. I could make out the general shape of a mattress on the floor among the piles of dirty clothes. A poster of Jimi Hendrix hung lopsidedly from the dark paneled walls. I knew the police had been here, but the jumble looked just like the rest of the house. Evidently Derek's mother hadn't gathered the courage to come and collect her son's things—either that, or she'd decided nothing was worth picking up.

I stepped into the dead man's bedroom with trepidation. There were flannel shirts and T-shirts, none of them clean, and a stack of dog-eared magazines. If he'd had a cell phone or computer, the police had taken them; there was no sign of electronics here. I rifled through the piles of clothes, but either the police had taken everything of interest, or there was nothing here. A suitcase lay in the corner; I searched its compartments carefully, but found nothing. I was about to give up when something gleamed in the corner. I bent down and picked up a light bulb. It was an odd color—blue instead of white—but didn't look suspicious. A moment later, I noticed a slip of paper poking from the back pocket of a pair of jeans on the floor. I retrieved a folded piece of notebook paper, on which were scrawled what appeared to be a series of dates and times. Three of them were in the past, but one was scheduled for the coming week, and one the following. Perplexed, I tucked the paper into my back pocket and looked through the rest of the jeans pockets. There was one other piece of paper, folded so many times I almost didn't recognize it as paper.

I sure recognized the intent of the note written on it, which was scrawled with a heavy hand in thick pencil on a creased piece of notebook paper.

Stay away from her or I'll kill you.

I had just tucked the note into my back pocket when I heard a sound. Someone was at the door. I hurried to the room's small closet and tucked myself inside. Whoever it was came through the house; I could hear footsteps in the bedroom. It sounded like a woman, and she was sniffling as if she'd been crying. I could hear as she moved through the room—it sounded as if she were searching for something—and wished I'd thought to leave the door open a crack. A moment later, I heard the footsteps retreat, and the front door creaking open, then thudding shut. I hurried to the window and peeked out in time to see a thin woman with brown hair disappear into the brambles.

———

I was still picking raspberry thorns out of my jeans when I arrived at Derek's aunt and uncle's house on Seal Point Road twenty minutes later, still wondering about the woman I'd seen. Had it been Tania? If so, what had she been looking for? I fingered the note in my pocket, thinking about Derek. Who might have written it? Someone jealous of Tania? I made a mental note to ask Charlene about other suitors as I climbed the porch to the Abingdons'.

The bright geraniums sparkled with dewdrops of water—someone had watered them this morning—and the front porch was well swept. A wind chime tinkled in the breeze as I knocked on the freshly painted door and waited.

I heard voices behind the door, and then it opened a few inches to reveal a gruff looking man in his thirties. He wore a Patriots T-shirt that looked as if it dated from the '70s and had seen pretty constant wear, and I caught a faint whiff of herring. "Can I help you?" he asked, sounding put out.

"I'm Natalie Barnes, the owner of the Gray Whale Inn," I said, the words tumbling out. "Sorry to bother you," I continued, proffering the container of cookies, "but I wanted to tell you how sorry I am for your loss."

He grunted in acknowledgment, then looked at the container in my hands. "What's in the box?" he asked.

"Texas Ranger cookies," I said. "I brought them for you and your wife."

He reached for the container and pulled it through the door. "Thanks," he said shortly. If I was hoping for an invitation, it didn't appear to be forthcoming.

"It must have been a terrible shock losing your nephew," I continued, trying to extend the contact. "I understand he stayed with you a few years back."

"He did," Abingdon said, "but once he left the island, we washed our hands of him."

"Someone told me he tried to contest your lobster license a year or two ago."

He snorted. "Some thanks for taking him in, wasn't it?"

"I'm curious. I know his mother is in Ellsworth; why did he live with you?"

"His mum asked us to take him in. Thought it would be better for him to be on the island, away from bad influences. Problem is, he took trouble with him."

"What kind of trouble?"

"The kind that lands you in jail if you're not careful. Or worse … like what did happen to him."

"You think he was killed?" I asked.

His eyes darted to the side. "They seemed mighty interested in that young lobersterman he was working for."

"Adam?" I asked, feeling a kernel of ice form in my stomach.

"Yeah," he said. "The cop seemed to think he had it in for Derek. Anyway, thanks for the cookies. Not sure I should take them, really; we had nothing to do with him, but I'll tell the wife you stopped by."

"So you have no idea who he was mixed up with?"

"Sorry, ma'am. Can't help you," he said. "Thanks again for the cookies," he added as he shut the door in my face, leaving me on the front doorstep.

I stood there for a moment, and as I turned to walk down the steps, I heard voices again from inside the house. Only this time there was a note of anxiety I hadn't heard before. I paused to see if I could make anything out, but the television drowned out the words.

It gave me something to think about as I headed down to the store, though.

———

"No goodies today?" Charlene looked up from the bag of mail she was sorting. Today she was dressed in a yellow sundress accessorized with large, sun-shaped gold earrings; she looked more ready for a Caribbean cruise than a day on Cranberry Island. Tania was nowhere to be seen, unfortunately. A few of the island's summer people were congregated on the couches at the front of the store, talking about a sailboat they were thinking of buying. I smiled and nodded as I passed them by and pulled up a stool at the empty bar.

"I gave them to Derek's aunt and uncle," I told her as I settled onto the stool.

"I'm dying to hear how that went. Want a cup of tea? I just brewed it a few minutes ago. I can deal with the mail later, and we can sit on the couches and be comfortable."

"Absolutely," I said. Charlene handed me a mug, and I filled it with the fragrant brew; Charlene had discovered Twinings Black Currant tea over the winter, and drank gallons of it. I added a splash of milk and some sugar and stirred.

I followed Charlene to the soft, worn couches in the front of the store and sank into one of them while Charlene arranged herself across from me. "I was hoping Tania would be here today," I said as I took a sip of the sweet, warm tea.

"She is," Charlene replied, straightening the skirt of her yellow dress, "in body, at least. I made her go for a walk about an hour ago, and she just got back, but I'm not sure she went anywhere."

So she had been out and about, I thought to myself. "Did she happen to stop by Derek's?"

"I don't know; she won't tell me anything." My friend sighed. "I'm worried about her, Nat. She barely eats, and she won't tell me what's going on." Despite the cheerful dress, I could see lines of worry in her face. "Do you think it's just grief?"

"I imagine so," I replied. "Where is she?"

"Hiding in the back, as always." She took a long sip of tea. "Anyway, how did it go?"

I told her about my visit to Derek's house and my brief stop at the Abingdons'.

"You went inside Derek's house?"

"The door was open," I told her. "I figured I'd go in, since the police had already been there."

I knew I could trust my friend not to chide me. Instead, she had a curious glint in her eye, and leaned forward. "Find anything?"

I reached into my pocket and pulled out the two pieces of paper I'd retrieved. "A weird note," I said, "and a piece of paper with some times on it. I don't know what the times mean, but the other one was clearly a threat."

"'Stay away from her or I'll kill you,'" Charlene read. She glanced up at me. "Detective Johnson seems to have forgotten how to conduct a search if they missed this. Where was it?"

"In a pocket of his jeans," I said. "Do you think 'her' means Tania?"

"Maybe. I don't know of anyone else Derek was seeing. In any case, it seems there's a suspect other than Adam," she said. "Gwen is out in California, so he couldn't be after her, and I know Adam's not seeing anyone else."

"Who would it be, then?"

Charlene arched a tweezed eyebrow. "I've heard Evan Sorenson's been carrying a torch for her."

"What do you know about him? Last I heard, he was in rehab."

"He was," she confirmed. "He was a nice boy growing up. Too bad he got into all the trouble with the drugs, the gambling..." I knew that he'd gotten himself into trouble over gambling debts, and also seemed to have drug problems his mother had tried hard to cover up. It always seemed to be something with Evan. "He used to love hot chocolate with marshmallows when he was a kid. Sat right there on that stool after school," she said, pointing to the stool at the end of the counter.

"I wonder why he's back," I mused, wishing I could go to Ingrid's house and just ask. But I really couldn't—not without an excuse.

"Me too." Charlene looked pensive.

"Did Tania spend much time at Derek's place?"

"She was over there a few times." Charlene wrinkled her nose. "She told me it's definitely a bachelor pad."

"More like a homeless camp." I told her about the cigarette butts and the de-stuffed chair, and the rotten food in the kitchen.

"Sounds like a picture," she said, wrinkling her nose. "And how did your visit with the Abingdons go? I barely ever see Turtle, it seems. Her husband does most of the shopping."

"Turtle?"

Charlene shrugged. "Her real name is Elizabeth, but she was shy, and always wore enormous turtlenecks as a kid. It kind of stuck."

"Poor thing," I said. "Anyway, I have no idea if she was wearing a turtleneck, because I didn't see her. Her husband answered the door," I told Charlene, "although only wide enough to get the box of cookies through it."

"He's never been the chatty type. Did you get anything out of him?"

"Not much," I admitted. "He said he'd had nothing to do with his nephew since he left the island a few years ago, and implied that he'd been into trouble when he stayed with them."

"That's not what I've heard." Charlene made a tsking sound and patted down a stray strand of highlighted hair.

"Oh, really?"

"Tania said they had a dust-up just a week or two ago."

"About what? The lobster license?"

"Maybe we should ask her." In a lower voice, she added, "I need your opinion about her, anyway. I'm really worried!" With a sigh, she got up and walked behind the counter, cracking open the door to the back room. "Tania, honey! Can you come out here for a moment?"

Charlene's niece emerged from the rear of the store looking deathly pale, with dark circles under her eyes. "I'm sorry to bother you, sweetheart," Charlene said as they walked toward the couches near the front door, "but Natalie had a couple of questions about Derek."

As she sank back into the cushions of the couch, Tania gave a half-shrug, her eyes bloodshot and puffy.

"I'm trying to figure out what happened," I told Tania as Charlene poured her a cup of tea. "I know it's really been a horrible week for you, but I'm worried the police are going to blame Adam for what happened to Derek." *Or you*, I added silently, remembering the note I'd found in the dead man's hand. "I was hoping you could help us figure out who else might have been involved."

"I don't know." Her head hung low, and her response was almost a whisper.

"Tania, honey." Charlene put an arm around her niece. "Natalie found a note warning Derek to stay away from a girl. Do you know who might have wanted to warn them off of you?"

She shook her head, and her voice was dull. "I think Evan liked me, but I wasn't seeing him."

"Did you visit Derek's house today?" I asked.

She stared at the floor. "No. I haven't been back since … you know." I looked at her, wishing I'd paid attention to what the woman I'd seen was wearing. Was Tania telling the truth?

"I know you said something about Derek having an argument with his aunt and uncle," I said. "What was it about?"

"I don't remember," she said dully.

"How about the contact he had?" I asked. "The one who was a 'cash cow'?"

"I don't know who it was. He wouldn't tell me anything about it. And now he's dead." Her face crumpled. "I'm sorry…" With that, she ran to the back room and shut the door, leaving Charlene and me staring after her.

"So," Charlene said after a long moment. "That's what we're dealing with."

"She's not herself at all." I felt a stab of worry. "This started with Derek's death?"

My friend nodded. "I've called a counselor, but she refuses to go see her. All she does is mope."

"Is she scared?" I said, my eyes drifting to the door.

"What would she be scared of, though?"

Maybe that the murderer would come after her next? I thought. Did she know something she wasn't telling us? She'd run off when I'd asked about Derek's contact. I didn't voice my fears to my friend. "I'd keep her close, if I were you, just in case," I told her. "And keep trying to get her to the counselor."

Charlene adjusted a fallen strap on her pale shoulder. Sundress or no sundress, it was hard to become bronzed on Cranberry Island. "To be honest, I'm glad she's not involved with him anymore—although this is not how I would have wanted it to end. I just didn't expect that she would be so … lost." Her shoulders sagged, and the strap fell again.

"Do you know what she talked to Detective Johnson about?" I asked. "Other than Adam?"

"He wanted to know where Derek was staying, how long he'd been here, who he hung out with … basic stuff." She took a sip of tea.

"Who did he hang out with?"

"I don't know, really. He and Evan appeared to be friends, and like I said, he had a contact he met sometimes—was paying him big bucks, according to Tania—but never said who it was."

"Did he say if the contact lived on the island?"

Charlene shrugged again. "I don't think she knew." She gave her tea a moody stir, then looked up. "I almost forgot. You haven't told me a thing about Murray Selfridge and John's mom."

I winced. "I've been trying to forget."

Charlene leaned forward, the prospect of new gossip temporarily lightening her burden of worry. "I hear he's pulling out all the stops trying to impress her. Someone told me he used to know her when John's family came to the island, and has had a crush on her for twenty years. Are they serious?"

Murray had had a crush on her for twenty years? Catherine hadn't mentioned that. Then again, we'd hardly talked since he started courting her. "He's pretty smitten," I told her. "Zeke Forester wants me to put in a good word for him—he wants to lease more land from Murray, and thinks he's putty in Catherine's hands."

"I never thought I'd see the day," Charlene said with a look of wonder. "Speaking of Zeke, how's he doing?" Charlene asked. "Every time I go over there there's a line at the farm stand. We're going to be carrying his eggs here, and I'm thinking about selling his produce, too; I've had to cut back on the vegetable orders from town."

"He's looking to lease more land, so it can't be that bad."

"I just hope he makes it through the winter," she said. "He's so sweet to his brother, and they both seem so happy here. I worry sometimes. Not a whole lot of farming to be done from October through May."

"He seems to think things are going to be all right."

"Let's hope he knows what he's talking about," Charlene said. "He may need to do more than farming if he's going to survive winter here." She bit her lip. "He's gotten a lot of correspondence from some regulatory division of the Department of Health and Human Services lately."

"Maybe it's about the cows he's planning to bring over," I said.

"Think cows will be enough to keep him in business," she asked.

"He'll figure it out," I said, hoping I was right. I took another sip of tea, and the bell above the door jangled.

Charlene and I turned to see who was walking in, then traded quick, wide-eyed glances. It was Ingrid Sorenson.

"Natalie," Ingrid said, looking as if she were about to go out for a hunt in the country in her tweed jacket and boots. Her eyes, pale blue above an aquiline nose, fixed on me as she strode to the counter. "I heard about the discovery you made out on the water." She shook her head; her carefully styled hair didn't move. "Terrible tragedy. Do they know if it was homicide yet?"

"If they do, they haven't told me," I said. "Did you know the young man?"

She shook her head. "Never met him," she said. "Derek something. I heard he was from Ellsworth."

"Really?" I said, glancing at Charlene and bucking up my courage. "I understand he and your son hung out together."

"You're not implying that my son had anything to do with that young man's death, are you?"

"We're not implying anything, Ingrid," Charlene said in a placating voice.

Ingrid's blue eyes were icy. "I'm glad to hear that."

Charlene smiled at her. "If you could just ask him if he knows who Derek was friendly with, that would be a big help. Apparently he had some kind of contact, but we can't figure out who it is."

"I'll ask if you want," she said, "but I'm sure he knows nothing about it." She straightened her tweed-clad shoulders. "Now, if you could just ring up a gallon of milk, I'll be on my way."

"I've got to run, too," I told Charlene as she extricated herself from the deep cushions of the couch. "I promised I'd take my guests over to Smuggler's Cove this afternoon."

She shivered. "Be careful."

"Keep me posted on Tania, okay? And let me know if she comes up with anything that might help."

"I will, Nat." She reached over and squeezed my hand before returning behind the register to ring up Ingrid's milk and continue sorting the mail. "Thanks for the support."

SEVEN

AGNES AND BERYL WERE waiting for me by the time I got back to the inn. Despite the fact that it was a beautiful, sunny day, both were dressed as if we were headed to Newfoundland in a Nor'easter. Agnes wore a rain slicker and matching plastic pants, while Beryl was decked out in knee-high rubber boots and a purple poncho.

"You guys sure are prepared," I said as I threw on a windbreaker, grabbed a flashlight from the drawer in the kitchen, and led them down the path to the dock.

"I know it seems like overkill, but everyone says the weather changes fast here," Agnes said. "Plus, I live in Southern California. How often do I get to wear rain gear?"

"Better safe than sorry." I grinned at the two women as we stepped onto the small dock.

In almost no time at all, Agnes and Beryl had clambered into the boat and I was casting off, ignoring the twist of worry in my stomach. I checked to make sure the oars were in the boat—and the life jackets—and revved the engine, heading toward Smuggler's Cove.

Although I'd visited Smuggler's Cove more than once, and both the tide and the smooth water were in our favor, visiting the small cove was a tricky proposition. It was really more of a sea cave—although the inside held a few spacious "rooms" that rumor had it had been used for nefarious purposes in the past, the entry was only accessible when the tide was low, and even then it was a tight squeeze. I'd been caught in there with a murderer once, and although he was long since behind bars, my stomach still clenched when I remembered being trapped in the cold, dark cavern.

"How did you figure out you were related to someone on Cranberry Island?" I asked, hoping to distract myself from the prospect of another visit to the little sea cave.

"We found a bunch of letters in my grandmother's attic," Beryl said. "I knew he was a priest on one of the islands when he disappeared, but we didn't know which one until we saw the postmark."

"Have you been into the cove before?" Agnes asked over the roar of the motor.

"A few times. It's hard to get in and out of, and there's not much there."

"Any sign of the rum runners?"

"There's an old iron loop driven into the rock where they used to tie up their boats," I told her, "but other than that it's pretty bare."

"That's a shame," Agnes said. "I was hoping for at least a few old bottles."

I glanced at her. "If there were any, they were taken long ago."

"Well, I suppose it will be interesting just to see what it looks like now. I can imagine the rest."

I could practically feel my blood pressure rise as we approached the rocky face of the cliff in which Smuggler's Cove was carved. The underwater rocks were more visible with the tide low, but no less dangerous, and I worked to maneuver the boat for a straight-in approach; the opening was fairly small, and it was less likely I'd scrape the sides of the skiff that way.

"Eerie." Agnes pulled the collar of her rain slicker together, as if it could protect her from whatever was in the cove. "It looks like something out of *Pirates of the Caribbean*."

"Shh." Beryl put a hand on her friend's sleeve. "Let her concentrate."

I was thankful for the request; getting into the little cove was easy for most of the locals, but tough for a landlubber like me. Last time I'd made this trip, I'd almost put a hole in the side of the *Little Marian*. This time, thankfully, I skirted the rocks without incident and shot straight through the small dark hole in the cliff.

The light faded almost immediately, and I reached for the flashlight and switched it on, using it to guide the skiff to where I knew an iron ring protruded from a rocky shelf.

"Cold in here." Agnes hugged herself as I handed Beryl the flashlight and tied up the skiff.

"You're used to Southern California," I teased her, trying to shake off a chill of my own. Absence had not made the heart grow fonder—at least as far as this little cove was concerned.

"Who put this here?" Beryl directed the flashlight at the rusty iron loop to which I'd tied the skiff.

"I don't know, but it's been here a long time." I climbed out of the skiff and offered a hand to the two women, who made their unsteady way out of the little boat.

"Was it used for anything other than rum running?" Beryl asked, her flashlight beam darting around the cove.

"I don't know. I'd love to find out how old these iron rings are, though," I told her as we clambered out of the *Little Marian* and stood on the rocky ledge next to the water.

Beryl's light did a quick sweep of the walls. "Not a whole lot of space. Is this it?"

"This is just where boats tie up. The main area is back here." I directed the light to an opening toward the back of the cave. "Follow me."

A feeling of foreboding descended on me as I ducked through the crevice that led to a dank, cavernous room. The last time I'd been here, a murderer had almost killed me. Time had not improved the place, although at least there weren't any killers in residence at the moment. The rocky room was empty.

"So, this is it," Agnes said, disappointment tingeing her voice. "Just looks like a cave."

"No writing on the walls or anything, is there?" Beryl asked, flashing her light into the crevices in the wall.

"Nope. And nobody ever comes here these days, either. Makes sense, really. It's not very nice in here, and it's hard to get to."

"It's not completely abandoned," Beryl said, shining her light on the floor of the cave. There was a big smudge of mud on the rock. She crouched down and touched it with one finger. "Still wet," she said. "Either of you have mud on your shoes?"

Agnes and I looked down at our boots; the soles were clean.

"Smells bad, too," Beryl said, wrinkling her nose and wiping her hand on the rocky wall. Now that she mentioned it, I did smell something unpleasant. "Ick. Horse poop."

She was right. It was faint, but distinctive.

"I guess we're not the only sightseers," I said lightly, but something about the fresh mud unnerved me. I flashed the light around the cave. "There's a lot of it, isn't there?"

"Yes," Beryl said. "Almost as if someone were pacing."

Beryl's light followed the track; it led to where the boat was tied up. "I know Matilda was talking about the cove the other day. Think she might have paid it a visit?" she asked.

"Maybe," I said, inspecting the walls of the dank room, looking for clues. The rocky walls were silent, though. Unyielding. If only they could talk, I thought, wondering what they'd seen over the centuries.

The sense of foreboding deepened. "Well," I said, trying to sound casual, "that's about all there is to it. Not much to see, is there?"

"It's fascinating," Beryl replied, still training her flashlight on the rocky floor.

"Yes, but we should probably head out while the tide's low. It gets tricky when it rises, and we don't want to spend the night in here." I shivered. "Trust me."

"Did you spend the night in here once?"

"Not by choice. My boat was damaged, and I got stuck." I didn't tell them the circumstances; no need to make them think the island was a dangerous place to be. "But I'd rather not risk it again. Ready?"

"Let's go," Agnes said, but Beryl seemed to want to linger.

"I feel like there's a secret here." She reached out to touch the cold, damp stone. "These walls have seen so much. I wish there were some way to know what all has happened here."

Her thoughts echoed my wish that the walls could somehow talk, but the sound of the water slapping against the rocks seemed louder, suddenly, and I just wanted to leave.

"Come on, Beryl. I think we've seen all there is to see." Agnes headed back to the boat, and after a lingering moment, to my relief, Beryl followed.

The tide was coming up more quickly than I expected; already we'd have to duck to make it through the cove's entry. When everyone was situated in the boat, I warned them to watch their heads and cast off, gunning the engine to make sure we made it through the cove's entrance without scraping the walls.

Agnes squealed a little and tumbled back as the little boat shot forward. Eyes on the water in front of me, I piloted the *Little Marian* out into the sunshine.

As I opened the throttle, there was a roar from somewhere over my right shoulder. And that's when another boat plowed into the starboard side of the skiff, knocking Agnes into the cold, dark water.

EIGHT

"Agnes!"

There was a hole gouged in the side, and water was pouring into the small craft. Agnes was flailing in the water a few yards away. Horrified, I reached for a life jacket and tossed it into the water toward her. The jacket flopped a few yards away from her.

"OhmyGod!" Beryl stood staring at her friend, eyes huge, both hands over her open mouth, then down at the water that was quickly engulfing our feet. She turned to me. "What do we do?"

"Agnes!" I called. She didn't answer, though. The flailing had stopped. Panic washed over me. I grabbed the two remaining life jackets and threw one at Beryl, then started stripping off my windbreaker. "What are you doing?" Beryl asked, her voice high and panicky.

"Going in after her," I said, strapping on the life jacket and kicking off my shoes. "Put yours on; you're going to need it soon." By the time I snapped the last buckle of the jacket, Agnes was already sinking. I leaped after her, praying I'd get there in time.

The cold water sucked the air right out of my lungs, and I came up gasping.

"She's over there!" Beryl called. I kicked my legs, which seemed abnormally heavy in their waterlogged jeans, propelling myself in the direction she had pointed. I couldn't see her anymore. "Is she still there?" I yelled back to Beryl.

"I see her jacket," Beryl said. "Hurry, Natalie. She's going down!"

I splashed through the inky water, tasting the salt in my throat—I'd swallowed some water when I gasped—and hoping I was going in the right direction. "You're almost there!" Beryl called, and a moment later, to my immense relief, my hand closed on the slippery fabric of Agnes's jacket.

"I've got her," I said as I grabbed her arm and hauled her up. She was heavy—a dead weight, I thought with a sick feeling. Had the boat hit her and hurt her, or was it just the shock of the cold water?

Her face was pale as it surfaced, and I struggled to keep her afloat. I glanced around for the other life jacket; it was a few yards away, on the open water side of the skiff. What was left of the skiff, anyway. Beryl was making panicked noises, and only an inch of the craft was visible above the waterline. Smuggler's Cove had not been kind to the *Little Marian*, I thought; twice now, it had sunk her.

And me.

But it wasn't only me. There was Beryl—and Agnes, whom I was struggling to keep from sinking again. My jacket wasn't enough to support the two of us.

Lying on my back with Agnes's head on my chest, I kicked toward the life jacket, reaching one arm back to grab it. I glanced toward Beryl, who had not yet abandoned the boat, but appeared to be up to her knees in water. "You okay?" I called.

"I'm scared." Her voice sounded young, childlike.

"Can you swim?"

She nodded.

"You'll be okay, then." My words sounded reassuring, but I glanced toward shore, estimating how far we'd have to swim. Most of this coastline consisted of sheer cliffs. There was a beach not far from Smuggler's Cove, but it was impossible to access from land. The other option was to go into Smuggler's Cove itself and wait for the next low tide to get out. But without the skiff, we'd end up in the same boat, so to speak: stranded with no transportation and unable to do anything but swim for land.

If I didn't get that third life jacket, though, none of that would matter. Agnes and I would never make it anywhere.

I kicked hard, but the tide and the current—not to mention the weight of an unconscious woman—were against me.

"Beryl!" I called. "Can you swim to get that other jacket?"

She was up to her waist now, and looking lost—until I asked for help. Something shifted in her. Her shoulders straightened, and I could hear it in her voice. "I'm on it," she yelled, and before I could respond, dove headfirst into the icy depths.

She hadn't been lying when she said she knew how to swim. Despite the jacket she'd neglected to remove, her arms sliced through the water, propelling her quickly toward the floating jacket. In less than a minute, she had reached it and was swimming toward Agnes and me. I felt for the unconscious woman's pulse as I waited, relieved to feel the flutter of a heartbeat under my fingertips. There was no blood—at least none that I could see—and no sign of obvious trauma. Good news. I hoped.

It wasn't long before Beryl had reached us. Together, she and I fitted the life jacket around Agnes's neck and belted it around her waist. My fingers were going numb from the cold. If we were going to head for land, we'd have to do it soon. It might be summer, but the water was still cold—somewhere in the vicinity of 50 degrees—and I was losing energy fast.

Beryl was obviously thinking the same thing. "Where do we go from here?" she asked, pushing wet hair out of her eyes. Mascara streaked down her cheeks, and although she'd only been in the water a few minutes, her teeth were chattering.

I looked behind her at the sheer cliffs, and then beyond at the impossibly distant gray-shingled inn, nestled into the green hillside. We'd never make it back without a boat. Our only chance was to swim for the little sliver of beach where the black-chinned terns nested and hail a boat—or attempt to climb the cliff.

"Let's head for the beach," I said, nodding to where several birds whirled in the breeze. "We'll figure it out from there."

"Got it. I'll take this side of the jacket and you take the other."

Together we swam toward the little strip of sand. My skin was stinging from the cold by now, and my fingers were so numb I had to look back to make sure I was still holding onto Agnes's jacket. Beryl's strength pulled me along, though, and together we inched toward the shore. Despite the effort, questions kept bubbling up in my mind. What would we do when we got there? Would anyone find us? Was Agnes just knocked unconscious, or had something worse happened?

For the first time since the skiff had been hit, I found myself wondering who had done it—and why. "Did you see the boat that hit us?" I asked Beryl as we kicked toward shore.

"Only briefly," she said. "It was a little one, about the size of yours."

"Did you see any other boat?"

"I think there was a lobster boat," she said. "But I wasn't really paying attention."

"Me neither," I said, but wished I had. A lobster boat. "Did you see a buoy on it?"

"No," she said.

I turned briefly and scanned the water, but there was no lobster boat in sight. Whoever it was had disappeared fast—and probably with the skiff that had hit us. Any local lobsterman would have stopped to help us, not disappeared. Which meant whoever had sideswiped the boat wasn't local—and I was guessing they were displaying a turquoise and orange buoy.

By the time we made it to the beach, there was no sign of the *Little Marian*, and the boat that had sideswiped us hadn't returned. Within a few minutes of laying her out on the beach, Agnes woke with a start and sat up.

"What happened?" she asked, teeth chattering. "Where are we?"

While Beryl explained what had happened and we helped her take off her waterlogged clothes, I scanned the water for a boat. I'd waved down the *Sea Queen* from here before; we'd be cold, but with any luck, George McLeod would spot us when he went on his next run.

As I hugged myself and shivered—it wasn't cold, but the breeze sucked the warmth out of my wet clothes, and the icy water had chilled me to the bone—I thought again of the boat that had run us down. What had they been doing near the cove, and why hadn't they stopped to render aid? Had they been about to enter the cove themselves?

Someone had been in Smuggler's Cove recently. And it was a good guess that whoever had left that mud on the floor wasn't there for sightseeing—and didn't want anyone else there, either.

But who? I wondered.

And more importantly—why?

———

We were lucky; the next mail boat run was only twenty minutes after we dragged ourselves ashore. I jumped up and down, waving my waterlogged jacket. Several passengers waved back, and when I saw George, the captain, hail me, I knew he'd send someone to retrieve us.

It was only another fifteen minutes before I heard the thrum of an engine, and John appeared in *Mooncatcher*.

"Is everyone okay?" His green eyes scanned us—both my guests had dark mascara streaks down their faces, and we all resembled drowned rats—but lingered on me. A deep furrow appeared between his eyebrows.

"We're fine," I said. "We probably want to get Agnes checked out, though—she took a nasty knock to the head." There were no signs of concussion that I could see, but I was hardly a trained medical professional.

"How did this happen? Where's your skiff?"

"We got blindsided on the way out of Smuggler's Cove, and the skiff went down," I said as I helped Agnes into John's skiff.

"And they didn't stop?"

I shook my head. "None of us got a good look at it, either. It was a skiff, and Beryl saw a lobster boat nearby, but that's all we've got." I was no Sherlock Holmes, I thought with a grimace. On the other hand, I'd been more worried about saving Agnes than about identifying boats.

"Well, let's get you home and warmed up," John said as I climbed into the boat after our guests. As he gunned the engine and we turned toward home, his face was grave, and his eyes were turned toward the now-disappearing cove in the side of the cliffs. "I'll ask around and see if anyone knows anything. We'll have to report this."

As I huddled down and tried to stay warm, I knew both of us were wondering the same thing. Was there any connection between the skiff that had rammed us and the death of young Derek?

I sighed and looked back at the dark cove. Sometimes I thought the island might be better off if it were somehow boarded up permanently.

We were back at the inn within minutes, and less than an hour later, the three of us were warming up in the kitchen with mugs of hot tea. Beryl had called the hospital and was planning to take Agnes over on the next mail boat. She seemed fine, but it was best to get her checked out. When Agnes tried to decline, Beryl insisted. "That was quite a knock you took," she said. "Better safe than sorry."

Although I offered to accompany them over to the mainland, Beryl declined. "There's no need for all of us to go. I'll keep her company."

"I'll drive you to the mail boat dock at least. Do you have a car on the mainland?"

"The rental's parked at the harbor," Beryl told me. "All I need is directions."

I drew her a map to the hospital and told her to tell me if they were back too late for the mail boat. "Call me and let me know which boat you're coming back on, and I'll drive down to the dock with the van. If you're too late for the mail boat, I'll head over and pick you up in the skiff," I offered.

"Not your skiff," Beryl reminded me.

I sighed. She was right; in all the excitement, I'd totally forgotten that the *Little Marian* was on the bottom of the ocean. I made a mental note to contact Eleazer ASAP.

"*Mooncatcher* will do just fine," John said.

Agnes grinned. "Thanks for the offer, but after today, I think I'd rather go on the mail boat."

NINE

JOHN WAS ON THE phone when I got back from dropping Agnes and Beryl off at the mail boat dock.

"She's right here," he said when I walked in the door. "I'll see if she's up to it."

I gave him an inquisitive look.

"Detective Johnson," he whispered, hand over the mouthpiece, handing me the receiver when I nodded. I spent the next twenty minutes giving the details of what had happened to the *Little Marian*.

"You didn't get a look at the boat or the person driving the skiff?" he asked.

"No," I said. "I was too focused on getting out of the cove in one piece, and then, once we were hit…" I sat down at the kitchen table as John opened the fridge and took out a bag of lunch meat and a jar of mayonnaise.

"Going to be hard to find out who it was," Johnson told me, stating the obvious.

"Do you think this might be connected with Derek's death?" I asked.

"I don't see how."

My fiancé cut a few slices of French bread and slathered them with mayonnaise, then reached for a few tomatoes. "The accident happened right near where I found Derek," I told the detective, thinking of the woman I'd seen crying just before I ran across the skiff with its awful load. Was it possible she was crying because she knew Derek was dead? It was highly unlikely, I decided; and besides, I had no idea who she was. I turned my mind back to the business at hand. "By the way, it looked like someone's been using the cove for something; there was fresh mud all over the floor."

"I thought you said the cove was empty."

"It was," I confirmed, watching as John laid thick tomato slices on our sandwiches. "But that boat could have been coming to drop something off."

The detective sighed. "Did you see anything in the boat?"

"I told you, it happened too fast, and I was mainly worried about my passenger." John, who was carrying two plates to the table, raised an eyebrow at the irritation in my voice. "I think it should at least be considered as a possibility."

"It sure would help if we could ID the boat," he said.

"I'll ask around and see if anyone saw anything. But I was wondering if it might not be the boat with the turquoise and orange buoy. Any luck tracking that one down?"

There was a brief pause. "I'll check, but I don't think so," he admitted, and something told me it had not been a top priority, to say the least. John had asked around; although the local lobstermen had noticed the buoys, they didn't know whose they were.

"Maybe someone could take a closer look at that cove, too," I said. "Or at least keep a watch on that, somehow."

Again, the pause. "I'll let the Coast Guard know," he said. I could tell it wouldn't go far. Maybe John would have better luck getting that through. I made a mental note to keep an eye on the entrance to the cove, which I could see from the back windows of the inn—and keep a camera handy, too.

"Is there anything else?" I asked. "Any progress on the murder case?"

"We'll be sure to keep you informed if there are any developments," he said, telling me exactly nothing, and I hung up a moment later, feeling grumpy.

"Didn't go well?" John surveyed me from across the table, a turkey sandwich in his hands.

"Not particularly." I reached for the plate with the sandwich, suddenly ravenous. "Thanks for this, by the way."

"My pleasure. Now, eat. We'll talk more when you've got food in your stomach."

I scarfed down the sandwich in no time, then followed it with the remains of my tea. "You make a mean turkey sandwich, sweetheart."

"So I've been told," he said. "I'm planning on making a mean fettuccine Alfredo with shrimp for dinner tonight, too, unless you've got other plans."

A perfect dish: easy to put together, warm and comforting, and it would hold well if the ladies were late getting back. Agnes had brought her cell phone with her, and as it worked on the mainland, they'd be able to be in touch. I smiled fondly at my fiancé, who had saved me in more than one way today. "You're my knight in shining armor, you know that?"

He grinned. "If you would just stay out of trouble, I could leave the armor at home some days."

"How was I supposed to know we'd get run down by a rogue boat?"

"That cove is jinxed for you, Nat."

"I think someone's using it."

"The mud does sound suspicious," he admitted, stretching out his long limbs while I watched with admiration. "But even if it is being used, there's no evidence of wrongdoing."

"What about the boat that ran me over?"

"That was a pretty aggressive act, and dangerous," he agreed, "but the only thing you found in the cove was some mud. No sign of any other crime."

He finished stretching and leaned forward, elbows on the table, fixing me with his green eyes. "I'm not saying we shouldn't keep an eye on it. It's possible you got rammed because someone didn't want you in there."

"You think?" I said dryly.

"There could be other reasons, too, of course. Someone having too much to drink, not paying attention…"

"In the middle of the afternoon? And it was awfully close to where I found Derek," I reminded him.

"True." John ran a hand through his sandy hair. "I'm not saying you're wrong, Natalie; there's a good chance it is connected. I'm just saying we shouldn't jump to conclusions just yet."

"Part of me thinks we should take another look at the cove, in case I missed something, but I'm in no hurry to go back in there."

"I'm glad to hear it; I don't want you anywhere near that cove, and in fact, I'm wishing I could get you a chaperone. You seem somehow to be a natural target."

"I don't think it was me in particular," I said. "I think anyone who was in the cove would have been a target."

"Be careful, Nat," he said. "You didn't see them, but they probably got a good look at you."

"I thought you said it was probably an accident."

"It might be, but I'll admit it does seem suspicious. Sometimes," he said, "I think the island would be better off if we filled that cove with concrete."

"I've had the same thought," I said. "It seems to attract trouble."

"Just like you." John gave me a pointed glance. "I'll ask around, see if anyone's seen anyone going in and out of there. On an island this small, someone's bound to know something." He stood up and walked around the table, putting his arms around me from behind. "Warmed up yet?"

"Not completely," I confessed.

"I hear body heat works really well." The seductive tone of his voice made me shiver in a way that had nothing to do with cold.

"Well…" I began. But before I could finish, the door opened, and Catherine walked in.

She eyed John and me. "I'm not interrupting anything, am I?"

"Of course not," I replied, feeling my cheeks redden. Despite the fact that I was almost forty, she could still make me feel like a schoolgirl.

"Good." She sat down at the table across from me, pushed John's plate out of the way, and adjusted the pearls around her neck.

I glanced up at the clock and realized I had another secret to decipher: the contents of tomorrow's breakfast menu, along with meal plans for the next couple of days. I stood up and stretched. "I'd better get the rest of the meals figured out," I said. "Thanks for taking care of the rooms. You've been a huge help."

"My pleasure," she said. "I hardly need to do anything; they even make the beds themselves!"

My favorite kind of guests. "By the way," I said, as a thought occurred to me. "Is Murray still trying to get the school closed?"

"He thinks the tax burden is unfair," Catherine said. "I have to say I agree with him."

"Does he realize that having no school on the island will decimate the year-round population?" I asked.

She smiled. "That would suit his plans, actually. He'd really like to make the island a resort."

So he hadn't given up his long-term plans. "But who's going to be here to take care of things?" I asked. "Once it's closed, you know, it's almost impossible to undo. And many of the lobstering families will have to move off-island. Without a school, the Lockharts couldn't stay."

Catherine frowned. "I hadn't considered that. Still, it's not my business, is it? We're only dating. It's not like we're planning to be married. Speaking of which, how are your wedding plans going?"

John and I exchanged glances, but neither of us wanted to respond. We had a good bit of work to do in that department. "Please, just put in a good word for the school if you can, Mom," John said. "Murray listens to you."

"I'll think about it. I don't know enough about it to have an opinion, really." She sighed. "In the meantime, I need to go and get freshened up."

John raised an eyebrow. "Freshened up? For what?"

"We're going to Spurrell's Lobster Pond for dinner," she said as she brushed off her skirt and trotted toward the kitchen door. "Don't wait up!"

John stared at the door as it swung back and forth in her wake. "I wish she'd picked anyone other than Murray Selfridge," he said.

"I know." I walked up behind him and wrapped my arms around his waist. "But I don't think there's anything either of us can do about it."

TEN

I spent the next hour putting together menus and calling in a food order, then gave Eleazer a ring to let him know about the *Little Marian*. John had headed down to Island Artists with another batch of the toy boats, and planned to spend the rest of the afternoon in his workshop putting the finishing touches on another sculpture.

When I told Eleazer about the collision, he tsked into the phone. "That little skiff hasn't had much luck," he said. "It may be time to retire her."

"You think? I'm kind of attached to her."

"It's going to be hard to retrieve her, and the motor is probably shot after being underwater. Besides, I've got a new skiff I've been working on—a beauty. Why don't you come down and take a look?"

"How much?" With the wedding coming, I didn't want any extraneous expenses.

"I'll cut you a deal. Claudette was just saying she wanted to have you over for tea, anyway."

"How about tomorrow afternoon?" I asked.

"I'll let Claudie know."

I hung up and grabbed my favorite cookbook off the shelf, then leafed through it until I found a recipe for Chocolate Express Muffins. The boat incident had made me jittery, and I needed something to do to calm me down. Despite the coffee in the batter, the moist chocolate cakes would be just the ticket for breakfast tomorrow. And maybe for tea this afternoon.

As I gathered the flour, sugar, and coffee crystals from the pantry, my mind turned back to the events of the last few days. A dead young man in a boat—not from here, but connected to people here—who bragged about "big things" on the horizon before he died. A threatening note found in his house. A mysterious lobster boat with foreign colors lingering not far from Smuggler's Cove. And the attack on the *Little Marian* today.

Why would someone run down the skiff? I wondered. It hadn't seemed accidental; there had been no attempt to evade our skiff. It didn't make sense—unless whoever did it was trying to warn me away from the cove, I thought as I measured flour and baking soda into a bowl. Derek's body had been displayed as a warning, too. Did we interrupt somebody else's plans?

I mixed milk and the coffee crystals into a bowl, stirring them until the coffee had dissolved, then added a cup of melted butter, two eggs, and a splash of vanilla before fitting the beaters into their sockets and whirling the aromatic mixture. The mud on the cove floor was fresh, and there was a lot of it. Was someone doing something in the cove they didn't want other people to know about?

And if so, how was that connected with Derek's death? Or was it just a coincidence?

I glanced out the back window toward the little cove as I stirred in the dry ingredients, making a rich, chocolatey batter. Although I couldn't see it, I knew by now the cove entrance must be covered by the tide. Was the cove the reason I'd seen that lobster boat idling just off the coast recently? I wished I'd gotten a closer look at the boat that had rammed us, but I had been too concerned with my waterlogged guests. As I folded the chocolate chips into the batter, my mouth already watering at the thought of the chocolatey little cakes, I realized I hadn't heard about Agnes yet. I reached for the phone and dialed the cell phone number she'd given me. When she didn't answer, I left a message, asking her to call as soon as she knew something.

As I returned to my muffins, placing muffin cups into the pans, I thought again of Charlene's niece, Tania. She was the closest islander to Derek—along with Ingrid's son. What was he doing back on the island, anyway? I knew Evan had been addicted to drugs of some kind a while back. Was he dabbling in it again? I'd have to check in with Charlene and see if she could gently grill Tania for more information.

Still, recreational drug use didn't usually get you killed. And it didn't explain the boat that had just about split my skiff in two that morning.

There was something else going on, I thought as I poured the batter into the muffin cups. And I had a hunch Derek knew something about it—something someone didn't want him to know.

I put the pans into the oven, washed the bowls, and made myself a cup of tea as I waited for them to finish. Before long, the kitchen was filled with a warm, comforting chocolatey smell that made my mouth water. The muffins would be terrific tomorrow morning alongside a fruit salad and shirred eggs with toast, I decided, with bacon or sausage on the side. With the menus I'd made, I was in pretty good shape … except that I'd forgotten to pick up carrots. Which would be a great excuse to drop by the farm; after all, Derek had worked there for a while, and things hadn't ended well. I'd been looking for a reason to stop off at Zeke's farm for a chat. With any luck, I'd be able to come home with more than a few bunches of root vegetables.

When the timer buzzed, I took the muffins out of the oven, admiring their plump, chocolatey tops. I tried a bite of one that hadn't risen quite as well as the others; the rich, chocolate-coffee crumb studded with melted chocolate was heavenly, and for a blissful moment, I forgot that anything else existed.

Unfortunately, the feeling was short-lived.

———

Agnes was no worse for wear, it turned out, and if anything, the near-disaster had added a fillip of interest to her trip. She and Beryl wolfed down John's fettuccine when they got back, and were still chatting about it over coffee, muffins, and eggs the next morning.

I walked through the sunlit dining room with a coffee pot as Agnes speculated on who might have driven the boat that rammed us. "It was bizarre—and I can't think why anyone would do something like that. I mean, we're just tourists."

"I've never known of anything like that happening before," I told her. I was relieved that she was just a little bit cold and banged up—nothing serious. "I'm really glad you're okay."

"Me too," Agnes said. My eyes were drawn to the stretch of buoy-dotted water just outside the cove. No lobster boat now, although it wasn't anywhere near low tide. Had it been low tide when I'd spotted the boat in the past? I wished I'd paid more attention. "What are you two up to today?"

"We're going to see if we can talk our way into the old rectory," Beryl said.

"I forgot to ask Catherine about it," I remembered suddenly. "Sorry about that. She's not made it up to the inn yet, but I will."

"No worries. Matilda's going over there this morning. She told us that since she put together the exhibit on his family, Murray Selfridge been very amenable."

"Well, good luck," I said, thinking I had a visit of my own to make today. I'd decided to see if I could talk with Fred Penney, the other lobsterman Derek had sterned for. Even if he didn't have any new information on Derek, maybe he'd have a lead on the boat that I'd seen outside Smuggler's Cove.

"We'll let you know what we find!" she said, peeling the wrapper from her third muffin. "These are absolutely irresistible. If I lived here, I'd weigh 400 pounds by now."

"Sometimes I feel like I'm on my way," I grimaced, tugging at my snug waistband. Weight gain certainly was an occupational hazard. I wondered if, by the time September came around, I'd still fit into my gown.

Speaking of weddings, I realized I hadn't heard back from the resort. After checking on everyone, I excused myself back to the kitchen and sat down at the computer.

No response.

I pulled up the bookmarked web site. Instead of an image of the gorgeous, palm-tree-studded resort, all I got was a page that said the web address was unavailable. I switched to Google and typed in the hotel's name. The second entry was an article in the *St. Petersburg Times*. As I read it, my heart lurched.

There would be no wedding in September for John and me—at least not at the Sandpiper Resort.

It had gone out of business.

———

I'd hurried through the rest of breakfast in a daze. John, unfortunately, was out of reach, as he'd headed to the mainland for the day, so I hadn't had a chance to share my bad news. I was still thinking about the wedding—the now nonexistent wedding, that was—as I rode my bike down to Zeke's farm an hour later. What were we going to do? Was it possible to get our money back? Would we ever get married?

Taking a deep breath, I forced myself to look around and take in the view. The ferns and moss lining the road were brilliant green, and the pines and firs soared above them, perfuming the sea air with their piney scent. Every once in a while, I spotted a patch of lime green leaves I knew belonged to low-bush blueberries, along with swathes of bright red bunchberries—beautiful, but not edible, at least not by humans. John and I would figure it out, I told myself. Right now, I had more important things to worry about. Like keeping Adam out of jail.

It was a perfect day, with temperatures edging up toward the seventies and a gentle breeze off the brilliant blue water. The trees parted, and I found myself scanning the buoy-dotted harbor. Surely someone on the island other than me had seen that orange-and-turquoise buoyed lobster boat, I thought; the local lobstermen were known to guard their territory closely. I'd have to ask down at the co-op.

By the time I parked the bike in front of Zeke's farm, I had decided to tell John that evening and not to worry about it until then. I took off my helmet, ran my fingers through my hair, and retrieved my bags from the basket on the front of the bike.

"Hey, Zeke!" I called as I rounded the farm stand. The fit young farmer, who was pulling up weeds from a long line of lush tomato plants, waved and started toward me. His brother, Brad, who was at the far end of the field, waved too, his face splitting into a toothy smile. I waved back, grinning. He never seemed to have a care in the world.

A few chickens pecked among the tidy rows of vegetables: natural pest control, Zeke had told me last time I was here. He let them out in the morning and closed them back up in the evening. There'd been a few problems with loose dogs, but overall they lived a happy life.

As the farmer headed my direction, I let my eyes drift across the fields. There were three long rows of tomatoes, a patch of what appeared to be lettuce, and several rows of pole beans. Behind them, like a benevolent parent, stood an old red barn that Zeke had told me housed horses and cows in the old days. There was rumored to be a blacksmith's anvil inside it somewhere; apparently the farmer who built it also knew enough to shoe his horses and do basic smith work for the locals. All of it—the horses, the blacksmith, even the stables in the island's many carriage houses—had gone away with the automobile, though. It was amazing how quickly things changed.

"What can I do you for?" Zeke asked, tossing his handfuls of weeds onto a pile at the end of the row and smiling.

"I need carrots, and could use a bit more lettuce," I said. "I thought I'd stop by and pick some up; and eggs, too, if you've got some. I used up most of mine at breakfast this morning."

"Just picked lettuce this morning," he said, "and the hens are laying faster than I can pick up the eggs. Follow me!"

He turned and headed toward the shed next to his farmhouse—a white clapboard building with a leaning front porch. A line of gloves was strung from a line hung between two posts, and a variety of spades and hoes leaned up against the side of the house. The shed beside it was filled with crates of produce, and outside it was a reclaimed laundry sink fed by a hose—Zeke's produce-washing station, with a little trench that led back to the fields. The chicken coop was located about fifty yards beyond the house, where the sea breeze would carry the aroma away from the house.

Zeke unlatched the shed and opened it, releasing the scent of earth and vegetables. A few bins of compost stood in the corner, along with a variety of organic pesticides.

"No fertilizer?" I asked. I was surprised; I used copious amounts of organic fertilizer on the roses and window boxes at the inn.

"Too expensive. I have an arrangement with a dairy farmer on the mainland," he said as he lifted a crate of fresh lettuces from the back corner of the shed.

"How do you get it over here?" I asked, trying to envision George McLeod heaving bags of cow manure over to the dock. "I can't imagine it being popular with the mail boat crowd."

Zeke laughed, exposing a line of bright white teeth. "Fortunately, the pasture is right on the water, so I use an old skiff I got from Eleazer. It's an aromatic trip, but not a long one."

"Ugh." I wrinkled my nose.

"I'm not saying it's pleasant, but it's cheap—and 100 percent organic. Like I said, if I can square things away with Murray and the USDA, I'm hoping to get a few cows into the pasture soon; that should solve the transportation problem, and get me into the dairy business, besides." He glanced at me, and said in a nonchalant tone, "Any luck persuading John's mother to talk to Murray?"

"Not yet." Saving the school, leasing land: the list of things I wanted Catherine to talk to Murray about was growing. A brown hen with bright, beady eyes wandered into the shed, picking at the dirt, and Zeke shooed it away. It half-hopped out the door, clucking imperiously. "The chickens seem happy."

"They are." He grinned as he selected a few lettuces and put them into a bag for me. "And as long as they keep laying like this, I'll be happy, too."

"It seems like a lot to keep up with. Do you have any helpers?"

"I do," he acknowledged. "A couple of young guys come out and give me a hand when they're not out on the water. The pay isn't terrific, but it helps them make ends meet."

I leaned up against the rough wood wall and tried to look casual. "I heard Derek Morton worked for you for a while."

"He did." The smile dimmed. "Not for long, though; he didn't work out."

"Not very reliable?" I guessed.

"We had a difference of opinion," he said shortly, glancing up at me from eyes that reminded me somehow of the hen's for a moment. Sharp. "And no. Not very reliable at all. I understand he found different work."

"Evidently he was working for Fred Penney," I confirmed. "Who do you have working for you now?"

"Evan Sorenson."

"Ingrid's son?"

Zeke nodded. "He's not a bad worker, but he's a late riser."

"How long has he been working for you?"

"Since the beginning of May." He opened the ancient refrigerator that was humming in the corner of the shed and pulled out a dented carton of farm eggs.

"Do you know if he and Derek hung out together?"

Zeke closed the refrigerator and smiled at me, but it didn't make it to his eyes. "I see living on the island has rubbed off on you."

My face heated up. "I'm sorry—I know I sound nosy." I forced a laugh. "I guess I am turning into an islander. Actually, though … I was more worried about Derek. He worked for Adam Thrackton, too."

"I heard." He handed me the eggs.

"Did you also hear the police are thinking it's a homicide?"

A shadow of some emotion crossed over his face, but was gone before I could identify it. Surprise? Or fear? "I wondered why the police asked so many questions," he admitted. "I'm sorry to hear that."

"Any idea who might have wanted to kill him?"

He let out a deep breath and shook his head from side to side. "He was only here for a couple of weeks. When he didn't show two days in a row, I had to let him go."

"I heard it wasn't a very warm parting."

Zeke shrugged. "It's business. Now, then, lettuce and eggs. And carrots, too? They're beauties." He lifted a bunch and tucked it into the bag, taking care not to bruise the tender lettuce leaves. "I'll toss these in for free."

"Thanks." I reached for the bag, feeling mildly guilty for my questions, and felt in my back pocket for my checkbook. "Shoot. I left my checkbook home. Is it okay if I come back later today?"

"I'll put it on your tab. You can pay me next time."

"Are you sure?"

"Absolutely." I followed him out of the shed, standing next to it as he closed the doors and latched them. I squinted at the barn on the far end of the fields. "Are you going to keep the cows in there?" I asked, pointing to it.

"What? Oh, in the barn?" He waved a dismissive hand toward it. "It's in pretty bad shape; needs a lot of work. Besides, it's pretty far from what I hope will be my pasture." He glanced at the land I knew he was hoping Murray would rent to him.

"Matilda Jenkins told me there's an anvil in it, from when the local smith lived here. He used to shoe all the island's horses."

"Really?" He seemed uninterested.

"I'd love to take a look inside sometime. I'll bet there are all kinds of fascinating old farm implements. It's hard to imagine that there were two farms on the island, isn't it?"

"I've only been in there a couple of times. Didn't see much but piles of moldy hay," he said quickly. "A fire hazard, really. One day I'll fix it up, make sure it's structurally sound. I put a *No Trespassing* sign up just to make sure none of the neighborhood kids get into it and get hurt. Or Brad," he said, glancing over his shoulder at his brother, who was peering at something on the ground near the barn.

"Good thinking."

"I'll get to it someday, I suppose. I've got plenty of things to do in the meantime, though. Speaking of which ..." He adjusted his gloves and gave the fields a meaningful look.

I took the hint. "Thanks for the lettuce and eggs. And the carrots, of course; what a treat!"

"Anytime." He nodded, then turned back to his row of tomatoes while I fitted the carton of eggs and the bag of vegetables into the bike's basket and hopped onto the bike, mulling over our conversation. I was burning with questions about Derek. Why had he quit— or been fired? Would Tania be able to tell me? As I rode toward the top of the hill, the cool breeze behind me, my mind turned again to that fleeting emotion I'd glimpsed when I told Zeke that Derek had been murdered. Had it merely been surprise?

Or something else?

ELEVEN

JOHN WAS IN THE kitchen when I rolled up to the inn a half hour later. He smiled and waved at me from the kitchen window, where he appeared to be washing dishes. Handsome *and* thoughtful, I thought as I waved back.

The kitchen was filled with the mouthwatering aroma of cranberry bread when I opened the door, the bag of veggies looped over one arm and the eggs in my hand.

"Hello, gorgeous," John said, putting down the dish and giving me a bear hug.

"Thanks for doing the dishes," I murmured into his chest.

"My pleasure."

"Smells wonderful in here. What's in the oven?"

"I was mentioning your cranberry bread to Agnes, and she said it sounded so good she wanted me to make it."

"So half of breakfast is taken care of?"

"And dinner. I intercepted the grocery delivery and took the liberty of marinating the salmon."

I hugged him again, loving the smell of him. "Will you marry me?"

"In a heartbeat." He kissed my head gently.

"Speaking of weddings," I said, "I have some bad news."

"What is it?" he asked, suddenly alert.

I took a deep breath. "It looks like the resort we booked went out of business."

He blinked. "What? What about our deposit money?"

"I don't know," I said, "but the web site's gone, and nobody's responded to my e-mail. There was an article in the *St. Petersburg Times* saying it had gone out of business. "

"Damn," he said, tossing the dishrag into the sink. "Are you sure?"

"I don't think the newspaper would have picked it up if it wasn't true," I said, feeling my spirits sink.

"So much for planning."

"Why don't I make a cup of tea and we'll see if we can figure something out?" I suggested.

"I think I'd rather have a beer, but you're probably right," he said as I filled the kettle with water and fished a box of Irish Breakfast tea from the pantry. "Cookies?" I asked.

"I wouldn't say no to a few of your Texas Ranger cookies."

I grabbed the last bag of cookies from the freezer and arranged a few of them on a plate, then gathered cups, sugar, and a pitcher of milk from the fridge. "Where's your mom this afternoon?"

"She took care of the rooms and then headed over to Murray's."

"Ah, Murray Selfridge." I snorted. "At least she's going there instead of having him coming here."

"That's looking on the bright side of things," John said with a wry grin.

"How are things going with the current investigation?" I asked.

John reached for a cookie and took a bite of it, then said, "I've got some news, actually."

"What?" I leaned forward, cookie momentarily forgotten.

"Homicide." He grimaced. "Gunshot wound killed him. It was from several feet away; there wasn't much powder residue near the wound."

I shivered. "Guess that's a pretty clear call." Not much chance of a suicide or accidental death if you've been shot from a distance, with no gun in sight. "Any new leads?"

"They talked with his mother in Ellsworth. She said that he'd been mixing with bad company and staying out late. She gave him an ultimatum six months ago, and he chose to leave rather than abide by her rules."

"Poor woman," I breathed.

"She's racked with guilt. Tough love usually works for the best, but sometimes …" John shook his head. "It's a sad situation."

"I stopped by his aunt and uncle's house this morning. They didn't seem too broken up about their nephew's death."

"Why did you do that?"

"I brought them some cookies," I said, feeling my face color. "That's all."

"Hmm," John replied, narrowing his eyes. "And what did you learn in exchange for the cookies? Although they are pretty darned delicious," he admitted.

"Not a whole heck of a lot," I admitted. "I did drop by Derek's house, though."

"Oh?"

"The door was open."

He winced. "Tell me you didn't go in."

"Well, like I said, the door was open…"

He groaned. "Did you find anything?"

"Actually, I did," I said, pulling the two pieces of paper out of my pocket—and suddenly realized that with all the excitement over the skiff, I'd forgotten to tell Detective Johnson about what I'd found.

He leaned forward, intent. "Where did you find these?"

"In his pants pocket," I said. "And I forgot to tell the police."

"I'll tell them." He shook his head. "I can't believe the investigators missed these. This letter could be important, but now that it's not in the house, we've got chain of custody issues."

"I could always put it back," I said.

"Still. What are we supposed to do, call the detective and tell him you found a note while you were breaking and entering?"

"He'd suggest I planted it," I realized.

"Exactly."

"Here's the other thing I found," I said, handing him the note with dates and times on it.

"What's this?"

"I don't know," I said. "I just thought it might be relevant."

"Some of these times haven't happened yet," he said.

"What do they mean?"

"Maybe we should keep an eye on things at the times listed," he said.

"But keep an eye on what?" I asked.

"Wait a moment," he said, his green eyes lighting with an idea. "Where's the newspaper?"

"Right here," I said, handing him the folded copy of the *Daily Mail*. He flipped through until he got to the tide tables.

"When's the next one?" John asked.

"Tomorrow at ten," I said.

He ran his finger down the page and stopped halfway down. "That's it," he said. "Low tide. Give me another one."

I read off another time and date. Sure enough, it was another low tide.

"I'll bet Derek was going to and from Smuggler's Cove," he told me.

"But why?"

"That's what we'll have to find out," he said. "Although now that you've been in the cove, whoever's using it might change tactics."

"Are you going to tell Detective Johnson about what I found?"

"Unfortunately, I can't figure out a way that doesn't involve me mentioning your breaking and entering."

"If they'd done a better job searching the place, it wouldn't have been a problem," I pointed out.

"We'll just keep an eye on the cove the next time the tide is low," he said.

"Good idea," I said. "We can watch it from here."

"How's Charlene doing, by the way?" he asked.

"Worried about Tania. She seems ... scared."

John's brow furrowed. "Scared?"

"I don't know why. I asked Tania if she knew who Derek's contact was—apparently he had a new source of money—and she got up and hurried into the back room."

"Well, at least Tania knows he had a contact. His mother had absolutely no clue who might have killed her son."

"So Tania has no idea what was going on with him?"

"Detective Johnson told me she hasn't talked with him since he left."

"And now she never will again." My heart felt heavy in my chest. "What kind of trouble was he into before he left?"

"Drinking, for sure."

"Drugs?" I asked, thinking of Evan's history.

"His mother didn't know, but she didn't rule it out."

I sighed. "Depressing subject. Let's talk about something else."

John poured us two cups of tea, then grinned at me. "Like our star-crossed nuptials?"

My heart sank further, thinking of our disappearing wedding plans. "Think we'll ever get married?"

"Absolutely" he said. "We need to see if we can chase down that money, but in the meantime, I've got an idea I'd like to run by you."

I felt something inside of me relax. I leaned forward, elbows on the table, and stared into John's green eyes. "Tell me all about it."

———

By the time we'd drained the teapot, I was in much better spirits than I had been. As I cleaned up the table, John stopped and gave me a kiss, then headed out the back door. He was gone barely a moment before bursting back in. "Natalie, come here."

"What?" I asked, putting down a plate and hurrying to the back door.

"Is that it?" he asked, pointing to a white lobster boat that was motoring away from the vicinity of Smuggler's Cove.

"I can't tell," I said, squinting and trying to see the buoy. "There's no name on it, is there?"

"No," he said. "No dinghy, either, which would make it hard to get into the cove."

"Let me get the binoculars." I hurried inside and dug through the drawers until I found our bird-watching field glasses, but by the time I got back outside, the boat had passed around the point and was lost from sight.

"Just because there isn't a dinghy doesn't mean that isn't the boat," I suggested. "Maybe the dinghy was damaged when it hit us, and it's somewhere being repaired."

John gave me a meaningful look. "Or maybe it's in the cove." The tide was low, I realized. It was entirely possible that the dinghy was hidden inside. "When does the tide turn again?"

I headed back into the kitchen and grabbed the tide tables, then returned to the deck with the paper in hand. "According to this, low tide is at three-fifteen today."

"Ten minutes ago," John said, consulting his watch. "They've got another thirty minutes or so before the water rises too high to get a dinghy out of the cove."

"It's a beautiful day to sit outside."

"It sure is, isn't it?"

We turned the two rocking chairs I kept on the porch so that they faced the cove. Time ticked away, and although the breeze was lovely and the company delightful, we were both disappointed. If the dinghy had gone into the cove, it wasn't coming back out; and the lobster boat didn't seem interested in returning, either.

"Were they scouting to see if anyone was around?" I asked.

"Why use a boat to do that, when you can see from land?"

"That only works if you're on the island," I pointed out. "If you're not from here, it's hard to get here without being noticed."

"True," he admitted.

"We could always head to the cove during the next low tide and see if anyone's there," I suggested.

"That would be at three in the morning," he pointed out. "Besides, it's dangerous. And if what's going on in the cove has anything to do with Derek's death, there's a good chance the people involved are armed."

"Why would anyone shoot him?"

"He was mixed up in something he shouldn't have been, is my guess."

"But what? Here on Cranberry Island?"

"There's more goes on here than you know."

I glanced over at the little island, and noticed a plume of dark smoke rising. "Somebody must be burning leaves," I said.

"Odd time of year to be doing that," John said. "Maybe it's garbage."

"Awful lot of garbage."

As I spoke, the phone rang.

"Back in a minute." I hurried into the kitchen to pick up the phone. "Gray Whale Inn," I answered.

"Natalie?"

"Charlene."

Her voice was breathless. "Tell John to get over to the farm as fast he can."

My heart clenched. "Why?"

"One of the buildings is on fire."

———

Half the island was gathered around the farm by the time we got there, and what was left of the shed was a smoldering ruin. Tom

Lockhart was still spraying water from the pumper truck, but there were no open flames.

The black smoldering ruin seemed out of place next to the verdant rows of vegetables, the venerable barn, and the small farmhouse. Zeke was pacing back and forth beside it, wearing mud-stained jeans and a worn T-shirt and looking agitated. Brad was curled up in a fetal position on the ground near the house, with Emmeline patting his back.

"What happened?" I asked as we climbed out of the van and hurried over.

"The shed caught fire while I was behind the house," Zeke said. "I can't believe it. How could this happen?" A gust of breeze set the wind chimes on the front porch tinkling. It was incongruous next to the smoking black shed.

"Thank God for the pumper truck," said Emmeline, who looked up from where she was comforting Brad. Today she wore a pink flowered housedress, and her bright brown eyes were soft with compassion.

"Did you have anything flammable in the shed?" John asked.

"Not that I know of," Zeke said, running a hand through his hair. "I'm glad it was only the shed, but it's still an inconvenience. I just don't know how it could have caught fire."

"How much did you lose?" John asked.

"A lot of tools," he said, "and the washing sinks. It might not seem much, but that's going to put me back a good bit. Cash flow isn't terrific right now."

"Shouldn't have been much of a fire risk; we've had a lot of rain up till this week," I said, peering in at the blackened ruins.

"You're insured, right?" I asked.

"Yeah. I hope they cover it."

"Don't worry about it, Zeke," Tom said. "We'll have a shed-raising sometime soon. Everyone will pitch in and help out, right?"

"Of course," John said.

"I can hammer," I said. "And bake cookies."

He smiled at us all. "Thanks, guys. What I can't figure out is how it caught fire in the first place."

As I scanned the smoldering ruins, something caught my eye. "I think I see what might have caused it," I said, pointing to a blackened can lying askew in the middle of what used to be the shed. "Did you store a gas can in here?"

"No," he said, shaking his head.

"Well, somebody put one in here," I said.

"Do you know of anyone who might have a grudge against you?" John asked him. He picked up a fallen branch and flipped the metal can over. It was definitely a gas can.

"That's not mine," the young farmer said. "Mine are plastic. I keep them in the barn."

I glanced at John. "I think this may be a crime scene," he said.

"Wait," Zeke said, holding up his calloused hands. "I did have one of those metal cans. I forgot; I found it in the cellar, and was going to fill the lawnmower with it."

John gave him a searching look. "Are you sure?"

"Yeah," he said. "Sorry about that; I just forgot about it."

"I still think we need to check it out," John said. "Having a gas can is one thing; they don't usually burst into flames. Besides, the insurance company will probably require an investigation."

"It's fine," Zeke said, looking at John with a level eye. "It's not a big deal. I'll handle it." There was a warning in his voice I'd never heard before.

"Just trying to help, Zeke," John said, taking a step back. "Are you sure nobody would have wanted to vandalize your place?"

"Positive," he said firmly. "Now, if you'll excuse me, I need to thank the folks who came out to help. Thanks for the offer to help me rebuild." Then he walked away, leaving John and me to exchange puzzled glances.

"That was strange" Emmeline said quietly. She'd heard the whole exchange.

"I thought so too," I told her.

Emmeline stepped away from Brad, then spoke in a low voice. "He's an odd fellow," she said. "Spends a lot of time in that barn of his, but he doesn't have any livestock."

"He told me he's working on fixing it up," I said.

She tsked and smoothed her pink dress. "I haven't seen any building supplies."

I looked at the barn, which he'd said was too dangerous to show me, and thought about his reluctance to call in an investigator. Was there more to Zeke Forester than he let on?

After a few minutes saying hello to our neighbors, we got back into the van and headed for the inn.

"That was weird," I told John as he made a U-turn and headed back to the inn.

"He was lying about that gas can." John's face was grim. "And he sure didn't want the police at his place."

"That's what I thought," I said as we passed the little house of the lobsterman who had tried to give Charlene tourmaline earrings.

Most of the rest of the island's lobstermen were out on the water, but Fred's traps were stacked up beside his small house. I still meant to talk to him about Derek; with everything that had been going on the last few days, I hadn't made it over there.

As we passed the pier, I noticed the police launch moored at the dock. I pointed it out to John. "Looks like they're back on the island."

"I wonder why they didn't give me a call," he said. "Maybe they're taking a second look at Derek's house."

"I've been thinking about Derek, and wondering if Ingrid's son had anything to do with him," I said.

"I found out why Evan came back to the island, by the way," John said.

"Really?"

"I ran into Adam down on the dock, and we had a beer at the co-op. A few of the guys told me that Evan's had a crush on Tania since high school; he just can't stay away from her."

I looked at John. "I hate to even suggest it, but that sure sounds like a motive for getting rid of Derek. Particularly with that note I found warning him to 'stay away from her.' Do the police know about this?"

He shook his head. "I haven't told them yet. Besides, we can't give them the note, so the connection is tenuous."

"Still. It might be worth mentioning. Are they still focusing on Adam?" I asked.

"I haven't heard about any other suspects," John said, and my stomach knotted.

No sooner had we returned to the inn than the phone rang again. I picked it up, expecting it to be Charlene asking for details about the fire. As it turned out, I was half right.

"Natalie?"

"Charlene. I've been meaning to call you…"

"I've got terrible news," she said.

My heart clenched. "What?"

"The police arrested Tania."

———

The world seemed to swirl around me. "What are you talking about?" The words seemed to tumble out of my mouth. "John didn't know anything about it."

"The officer said he didn't want to alert John because he knew you and I were friends. He was afraid she'd run."

I gripped the phone and sank down onto a chair. "What evidence do they have?"

"I don't know, but they're searching my house right now," she said. I heard a muffled sob. "They say she's into drugs."

"No," I breathed. I stared out at the mountains of the Mount Desert Island, but the serene view of the green slopes did nothing to soothe me.

"Derek was, too."

No surprise there, from what I was learning about him. "Do you have an attorney?" I asked.

"No, but Murray recommended one," she said.

"Let me talk to John, and I'll be right over."

I hung up and turned to John, who had a deep furrow in his tanned brow. His voice was urgent. "What's going on?"

"They arrested Tania." Just saying the words had a ring of finality.

His jaw tightened. "Johnson didn't have the courtesy to tell me?"

"They're searching her house right now," I said.

John grabbed the keys from the hook by the door. "I'm going down to Charlene's."

"Take me with you, okay? I need to be with Charlene."

"I hope she's getting an attorney."

"She's calling one now." I gave him a quick hug. "Call me at the store if you get back before I do."

His face looked dark with anger. "Don't worry, I will."

TWELVE

CHARLENE'S EYES WERE RED and swollen, her mascara smeared across her cheeks. "Oh, Natalie," she moaned as I put down the plate of cookies I'd brought and took her into my arms. "I just can't believe it." There were a few other islanders at the bar; at a look from me, they retreated to the couches near the front. Eli was among them; so was Fred, who lingered at the bar for a moment.

"If there's anything I can do to help, Charlene, I'm a phone call away," he said, looking at her with longing in his eyes.

"Thanks, Fred." She wiped her eyes. "Right now, I need to talk to Natalie, if you don't mind."

"I'm here if you need me," he said, and followed the others to the front of the store.

"Let's get you sitting down," I said, guiding her to one of the bar stools. "Is Tania doing okay?" I asked in a low voice.

"They came with a search warrant," she said in a low, trembling voice. "They found a bag of pot in her room."

"I thought you said they were still searching the house," I said.

"They are. I'm just praying they don't find anything else."

"Did Tania answer any questions?"

She shook her head. "I told her not to say anything until I got her an attorney. I called Murray for a recommendation—I didn't know who else to turn to."

"He found you someone?" As little as I liked Murray personally, I was glad he was willing to use connections to help Tania.

Charlene nodded. "She's on her way down to the jail now. They're holding her on the launch at the moment. I wish I could be with her..." Tears began flowing again, and I hugged her.

"Poor thing," I said, thinking both of Tania and Charlene. I glanced over my shoulder at Eli and Fred, who were talking quietly and stealing glances back at us.

"Her mom is a wreck. So am I. What do we do if they sentence her to jail?" Charlene swallowed. "Or me?"

"We'll find a way through this," I told her, wishing I felt half as confident as I sounded. "Now. Sit down and let me get you some tea, and then I want you to tell me everything you can think of that might help her."

"Okay," she said, taking a deep, shuddery breath. "Okay."

As I filled a mug with hot water from the pot next to the coffee maker, Charlene dabbed at her eyes with a napkin. I handed her a cookie and tossed a tea bag into the mug. When she had managed to pull herself together, I pulled up the stool next to her.

"Tell me everything," I said. "What has she told you about Derek?"

She glanced up at me. "She was in love with him."

"Do you think he's the source of the marijuana?"

"I don't know, Nat, but once she started dating him, she seemed so … different. Making bad judgments, moody. Just not herself at all."

"She seemed almost scared the other day," I said. "Do you think someone was trying to make her life difficult?"

Charlene's mascara-smeared eyes widened. "Like setting her up?"

"I don't know, but it's possible."

"Oh, Natalie." She buried her face in my sleeve. "I've done such a terrible job of being an aunt. She was under my care, and now she's going to jail."

"She hasn't been convicted of anything," I said in a soothing voice. "Talk to the attorney," I advised her. "And I'll talk with John. You can stay at the inn tonight if you need company; I've got your favorite room open. You can join us for dinner, too."

"Thanks, Nat. I can't do dinner, because with Tania in jail …" She broke into tears again, and I stroked her back. When they subsided, she looked up at me with raccoon-ringed eyes. "I don't know what I'd do without you. You always make everything better somehow."

"I'll try," I said, trying to sound comforting, but praying I wasn't giving her false hope.

———

"How's Charlene holding up?" John asked. I'd walked back to the inn to make dinner, and John had arrived a few minutes later.

"As well as can be expected." I took a break from rummaging through the fridge and sat down at the kitchen table, feeling as if all the air had been sucked out of me. "They're still searching her place. Any word on how they got a search warrant?"

"Someone called in a tip," he said.

"Who?"

"Johnson didn't know much, or wasn't telling me. I'm going to head down to the station in person tomorrow." He sighed. "I hope there wasn't much of whatever they found."

"Why?"

"It could be the difference between a misdemeanor and a felony."

A felony. I felt like I'd been sucker-punched. "I wish she'd never gotten involved with Derek Morton," I said bitterly.

"You think it was because of Derek?"

"That's what my gut says. He was a shady type, and it seems to me the drugs had to come from outside."

"Makes sense. Cranberry Island isn't exactly drug central."

"Exactly," John said, nodding.

I looked up at him. "Most of the people here think getting high means climbing the stairs to the top of the lighthouse."

Despite the dire situation, John cracked a smile.

"Maybe she was keeping it for him," I suggested. "Did they find any at his house?"

He shook his head. "They didn't find anything, but you were right about Derek and drugs."

"What do you mean?"

"Detective Johnson told me there were track marks on his arms, and the autopsy results showed several drugs, including marijuana, in his system. And since she and Derek were close…"

I groaned. "I hope it wasn't anything other than marijuana. I know it's illegal, but it's so much more benign than the others. Even if there's not enough for a felony, if she's addicted…"

"It's a scary situation," John concurred. "Even so, at least she's still alive."

"I suppose that is a silver lining, of a sort." I got up from the table and headed for the cookie jar; times like this called for sweets. I took the lid off the cookie jar and reached inside, but the jar was empty. "Shoot," I said, putting the lid back on. "No more Texas Ranger Cookies in the freezer, either."

"We've got pecans and butter," John said with a hopeful look in his eyes.

"Are you thinking about Turtle Bars?"

"They're Charlene's favorite," he said in a cajoling tone of voice.

"And yours," I pointed out.

"True."

"I need to make dinner," I said.

"Don't worry about dinner; I'll take care of it. You need some chocolate therapy."

"All right," I said, retrieving my recipe book and flipping through it until I got to the recipe. The page was dog-eared from frequent use. "Baking helps me think, anyway." As I reached for the brown sugar and butter, I wondered aloud who might have called in a tip on Tania.

"A friend?" John suggested. "Someone who was worried about her?"

"Now she's at risk of a police record, though; it doesn't make sense." I measured brown sugar and flour into the mixing bowl, combining them with a fork. "Why not confront her directly? Or talk to Charlene, or Tania's parents?"

"Maybe whoever it was did talk to Tania, and thought it wasn't working."

"Or else they wanted to get her in trouble," I suggested. "Someone connected with Derek's death?"

"If she knew something about what happened to Derek, why would you want her in police custody, though?"

I unwrapped a stick of butter and sighed. "You're right. It doesn't make sense."

"Did anyone have a grudge against her?"

"I'd have to ask Charlene about that." I added the butter to the bowl and started the mixer, creaming the butter together with the dry ingredients. "Can you call and find out what they found?"

"They weren't done with the search, and I couldn't get specifics out of them. I'll try again in a few hours," John said. "Hopefully they'll post bail soon—and it won't be too high."

"Bail?" I hadn't thought about bail. Feeling slightly sick, I turned the mixer on low, scraping the sides of the bowl as the butter and dry ingredients combined into a crumbly mixture.

Before John could answer, Catherine breezed into the kitchen, looking like Jackie O. in dark glasses and a scarf. For the first few months when she came to the island, her wardrobe had moved from cashmere twin sets toward jeans and wool sweaters, but with the advent of Murray Selfridge, her sartorial selections were swinging away from the practical and more toward the decorative. At least it was tasteful decorative—and although she was in her seventh decade, she still had the figure to pull it off. I found myself tugging unconsciously at my waistband, which was a bit more snug than usual, and glancing ruefully at the bowl of butter and sugar. Weight gain is an occupational hazard of innkeeping, unfortunately. At least it was for me.

"I was hoping I'd find you two here."

"Hi, Catherine." I turned off the mixer and waved a wooden spoon in her direction.

"Terrible news today!" She perched the glasses atop her coiffed silver-blonde hair and took a can of sparkling water from the fridge. "Murray and I were just talking about your friend's niece."

"Tania?" I asked as I poured the crumbs into a baking pan.

"That's the one." Catherine tossed a few ice cubes into a highball glass and filled it the rest of the way with sparkling water. She used to be a Perrier girl, but since she'd had to cut her budget, she had started drinking the grocery store brand. I had still never seen her drink from the can, though. She took a sip and sat down at the table. "Poor dear was arrested, I hear."

"We were just discussing that," John told her. "Has Murray heard anything?"

She set down her glass and crossed her stockinged legs. "He knows the judge—they play golf at Kebo Valley on Mount Desert Island every Wednesday—and put in a good word for her character. It should help with bail."

"That was awfully kind of him," I said, impressed with Murray's willingness to help—and hoping it would be enough. I patted the dough into the pan and began pressing pecans into it. How much are we talking?" I directed the question to John, who was the most likely of the three of us to know.

"I have no idea. Not a lot of drug busts in this part of the world, thankfully, but I think it depends on what—and how much—they found."

"I hate not knowing."

"I'm sure she'll be taken care of," Catherine reassured me. "And although the situation is unfortunate, maybe it will scare her straight."

"As long as she doesn't end up with a felony conviction, that would be great," I muttered as I plopped the remaining butter into a saucepan with half a cup of brown sugar. "Please tell Murray thank you for interceding on Tania's behalf, Catherine. And for finding her an attorney."

"He's a prince, isn't he?" she beamed, then took another dainty sip of seltzer.

I glanced at John, who looked as if he were in pain. Like him, I was having a hard time believing Murray had somehow gotten in touch with his softer side; I suspected he was trying to impress Catherine. Still, there was no denying John's mother was an excellent influence.

As I stirred the gooey mixture in the pot, Catherine stretched daintily. "Well, I'm off to go and change; do you need any help this evening?"

"No hot date?" John raised an eyebrow at her.

"A lady needs to have other engagements from time to time," she replied with a glint in her eye. "Otherwise, her suitors won't have an opportunity to miss her."

"Suitors?" John teased. "Don't tell me you're dating Fred Penney, too."

"Fred?" She raised a thin hand to her chest. There was a necklace there I didn't recognize, I realized: a tasteful sapphire pendant. "The surly lobsterman who spends all of his time down at the store and hasn't shaved since the Reagan administration?"

"That's the one," John confirmed. "Not your type?"

"Oh, John." She gave him a withering look, but there was still a sparkle of amusement in her expression.

"You're welcome to join us for dinner if you'd like," I told her as I poured the caramel mixture over the pecans and dough in the pan, then put it in the oven. In twenty minutes, I knew, the caramel would be bubbling, and I could swirl milk chocolate chips over the top.

"Thank you for the invitation, dear, but I had a rather large luncheon today, so I think I'll stay in and have something light. I'll be happy to set up the dining room before I retire, though."

"That would be great." I was grateful for the help. Catherine might look as if she felt housework was something best handled by aproned maids, but she was always quick to pitch in. Although we still had our differences, and I often felt her mild disapproval at the high-fat, high-sugar fare I made at the inn (and tended to consume, as well), I had grown to like her a lot since she moved to Maine. For her part, she seemed more than happy to have me as a future daughter-in-law. Or at least she hadn't expressed any opinions to the contrary.

"What delicious treat are you making now, anyway?" she asked, watching as I disposed of the butter wrappers. "My. Two sticks of butter?"

I sighed audibly. I was just going to have to get used to this.

"Natalie is just whipping up another batch of cookies for the guests," John said, tactfully not mentioning the empty cookie jar in the kitchen. Gosh, did I love that man.

"Good idea; the plate in the dining room is almost empty," Catherine said. "Those guests certainly do cut a swath through them, don't they? I thought about whipping up some of my Oatmeal Delites this morning after breakfast, but I ran out of time."

"It's fine," I said, perhaps a little too quickly. I had sampled her Oatmeal Delites once when John and I visited her in Boston, and they resembled nothing more than crispy sawdust patties. "I'll just get these whipped up and then make a pan of blondies, and that should keep us for a few days."

"Fabulous. I'll go and put the dining room to rights and then head down to the house. Give me a jingle if you need me!"

"Will do," I said, as she disappeared through the swinging door in a faint cloud of Chanel No. 5.

———

The caramel pecan turtles came out looking as good as they smelled, and I couldn't help but snag a few as I finished whipping up a batch of brownies. John had offered to be in charge of dinner, and after refilling the plate in the dining room, I put a few turtles in the kitchen cookie jar and loaded the rest in a storage container, along with some brownies. I bundled everything into a cloth bag with a tub filled with frozen Beef Stroganoff; Charlene might not be able to join us for dinner, but that didn't mean I couldn't bring dinner to her.

"See if you can find out who might have called in a tip," John said, kissing me on the forehead. "And be careful."

"I'm not going in the skiff, remember?" I asked. "Oh, yeah—I almost forgot to go see Eli!"

"You can drop by on the way back home. Are you walking, or do you need the van?"

Glancing out the kitchen window at the sunlit trees, I said, "I thought I'd walk."

"Good; I could use the van today."

"For what?"

"I have some things to take down to Island Artists," he said. "Plus, I've got other errands." He gave me a wink, and I felt my insides quiver a little bit.

"I love you, you know."

"I love you too," he replied. "Enough to leave you a cookie."

"Just one?"

"If you're nice, I might leave two."

I laughed and headed toward the kitchen door. As I pulled on my sneakers and a windbreaker, I had a thought. "While you're down at the dock, can you stop by the co-op?"

"Good idea," he said. "We need to find out who owns that orange and turquoise buoy."

"Could be a Miami Dolphins fan," I joked. John raised an eyebrow; we were deep in Patriots territory. "Shouldn't be too hard to find. A snowbird, maybe?" I suggested.

"Wouldn't last ten minutes here," he said with a grin. "Let me know what you find out, okay?"

"Of course," I told him as I headed out the door.

It was a lovely walk to the store—being outdoors in the fresh air always soothed me—and I even resisted the temptation to break into the container of turtles and brownies, instead limiting myself to plucking a few roadside blueberries.

The sun was still fairly high in the sky when I stepped onto the wooden porch of the store. News of Tania's arrest had obviously traveled across the island; even from outside the mullioned windows I could see a gaggle of islanders tucked into the couches and chairs at the front of the store. The bell above the door jingled as I entered. Charlene sat behind the counter, her face startlingly devoid of her customary Mary Kay products.

I smiled and nodded to inquisitive islanders and headed to the counter, where Charlene looked up at me with a bleak expression. "I brought you dinner." I dangled the cloth bag enticingly. "And Turtle Bars."

She barely batted an eye, which is when I knew it was time to be worried.

I glanced behind me and spotted Eli in the crowd. "Can you man the front counter for a few minutes?" I asked. He hurried to the counter, allowing me to escort my limp friend to the back room. "Sit here," I ordered her, leading her to a battered, stuffed armchair. "I'm getting you tea and cookies."

She sat listlessly as I bustled to the front of the shop, returning to the back room a few minutes later with a cup of tea—two sugars, heavy on the milk—and a plate of warm cookies.

"Drink this," I ordered, and she mechanically lifted the cup to her lips.

"It's all my fault, Natalie." Her voice was a monotone. "I should have seen the signs. I should have taken better care of her. And now her life is ruined."

"It's not ruined," I corrected her. "We don't even know what the evidence is yet. Plus, I hear Murray got you in touch with a great attorney."

Charlene shook her head. "I don't know how we're going to get her out of this."

"For starters," I replied, "we can start thinking about who might have called in that tip."

My friend looked up at me. "What tip?"

"That's what made them get the warrant. Someone called in a tip."

"Why does that matter?"

"I don't know. Because whoever did it wanted to hurt Tania. Or because it could be that whoever called in the tip planted something for the cops to find," I suggested.

Her eyes widened. "You think she was framed?"

"I don't know if she was framed, but if we don't do some digging, we'll never know. I need your help, though."

"What do you want me to do?" The voice was still monotone, but her posture had straightened a bit.

"Tell me who she hung out with. Who her friends were—and her enemies. Does her mom know?"

"Her mom lives over on MDI," Charlene said. "She isn't that involved."

"So it's up to you, then."

Charlene hesitated, then reached for a turtle. My heart lifted a bit as she took a bite. "She and Kaitlyn Bennett have been friends since third grade," she said. "But they haven't been as close lately. I don't know what happened."

"Worth looking at. Any reason she might hold a grudge?"

"Not that I know of. But Tania didn't tell me much."

"All right," I said, grabbing a pad and a pen from a shelf. "We've got one potential person. Anyone else you can think of? Ex-boyfriends, maybe?"

"There is Evan," she mused.

My mind began working. Evan would almost certainly have access to drugs. If he held a grudge against Tania, he could simply plant them in her place and call the cops. He knew she was dating Derek; maybe jealousy played a factor. The spurned lover thing. But Derek was dead; would he still need to get revenge?

"They weren't an item," she told me. "But he's always liked her."

"Definitely an option, then," I said, writing down the name. "Anyone else? Anyone at all?"

"Not that I can think of right now." She finished her cookie and reached for another.

"Well, we've got two people to go on, and that's a start." I ripped off the page and folded it in half. "I know where Evan lives, but what about Kaitlyn?"

"She's up on Harbor Lane. Third house from the end, on the left. It's blue with green shutters."

"I'd like to go ask her some questions," I said. "Do you want to come with me?"

"But the store ..."

"Don't you have anyone else who can fill in?"

She looked at me bleary-eyed. "To be honest, Nat, I don't think I'd be much help. Plus, I want to wait here in case the attorney calls."

"You sure?"

She stood up and pushed her hair out of her eyes. "Yes, I'm sure. But I have a favor to ask."

"You name it," I told her.

"Can you fill in for me tomorrow morning? So I can go and visit Tania?"

"Of course," I said. "When do you want me?"

"Will ten o'clock work?"

I squeezed my friend's shoulder. "I'll be here with bells on."

THIRTEEN

CHARLENE HAD BEEN LOOKING, if not happy, at least more like herself when I left the store a few minutes later. I wasn't sure how much we could do to help Tania, but we had to try.

Despite the events of the day, the weather was fresh and gorgeous, with a cool breeze off the water and the trees glowing emerald green. I leaned down to pick a few blueberries from time to time; the raspberries were turning red, but not quite ready, and I found myself making a mental note of where the best bushes were. There was nothing better than fresh raspberries and cream, and if Zeke did manage to get a few cows on the island, it would be even better. My thoughts turned to his strange behavior after the fire. Why hadn't he wanted the police to come? Or had he just not wanted to make a fuss?

I felt for the list of names in my back pocket as I turned up Harbor Lane a few minutes later. Although I hardly needed it: there were only two names on it. I had decided to visit Kaitlyn's house first.

It was a short walk from the store to Kaitlyn's, and the house was hard to miss; the paint was royal blue, and the trim was the color of pistachio ice cream. Two salmon-colored rocking chairs stood on the porch, surrounded by pots and pots of flowers—a riot of colorful pansies, marigolds, and nasturtiums that had somehow escaped Claudette's voracious sheep.

Wind chimes tinkled behind me as I knocked on the door; a moment later, I could hear footsteps approaching from inside.

A young woman answered the door, looking puzzled. I'd seen her from time to time, but never met her. "Can I help you?" she asked.

"I'm sorry to bother you, but I'm Natalie Barnes, Charlene's friend. Are you Kaitlyn Bennett?"

"I am. You're the lady who runs the inn, right?"

"That's me."

"I love your brownies; I can't ever resist them when they're at the store."

"Thanks," I said, taking an instant liking to the girl. "Anyway, Charlene said you might be able to help out. You've heard about Tania?"

"Tania?" Her brow furrowed. "What about her?"

"She was arrested today," I told her.

Her eyes widened, and she took a step back. "No. For what?"

"Drug possession."

"That's horrible," the young woman said. She was a fresh-faced, athletic-looking young woman. Unlike Tania, she wore no make-up, and was dressed in loose faded jeans and a University of Maine T-shirt.

"I know," I said. "I was hoping you could help us find a way to help her out."

"Come in, please." She opened the door wider and invited me into the small house. The inside was as colorful as the outside, but it all worked. "Poor Tania. I'm so worried about her. Ever since I got back from school this summer, she just hasn't seemed the same." She led me into the kitchen, and gestured to one of the chairs around the small table. "Can I get you a cup of tea?"

"No thanks," I said.

"Please, sit down," she said, gesturing to a chair at the small, round kitchen table. The cabinets were a gorgeous periwinkle blue, and matched the hand-painted blue-and-white tiles of the back-splash. A variety of copper molds hung on the wall, and the table was covered with a Provençal-style tablecloth. "I love the decor in here."

"My mom did it," she said. "She's always wanted to be an interior designer. I keep telling her to go for it, but she doesn't want to leave her job. She raised me herself, you know."

"Maybe she can start part-time," I suggested. "She really has a knack."

Kaitlyn smiled, exposing a line of white but slightly crooked teeth. "I'll tell her you said that."

I nodded at her shirt. "Are you a student at the university?"

"Just finished my first year," she said. "I wanted Tania to go, but she was kind of tired of school, and wanted to take a year or two off before going to college." She sighed. "Now I wish she hadn't. I knew she seemed different this summer, but I had no idea she was into drugs."

"Do you know anything about her relationship with Derek?"

"I don't like to speak ill of the dead, but that dude was bad news." She twisted her hair around one finger as she spoke. "He actually tried to get me to go out with him one night when I ran into him waiting for the mail boat." She shuddered. "I told him he could take a flying leap."

"Charlene said Tania had a major crush on him."

Kaitlyn rolled her eyes. "She did. She was totally into him. I have no idea why; I thought he was sleazy."

"She seemed to be dressing differently this summer, too."

"I saw that, too. I think she was trying to keep him interested," Kaitlyn suggested. "He wasn't that into her; like I said, I think he was always hitting on other girls."

"Did she ever get together with Evan Sorenson, do you know?"

"They hung out, but they were never a couple; although he wanted to be. He came back to the island for her, you know. He's had a thing for her since the eighth grade."

"I'd heard that," I said. "How much time did they spend together?"

"A good bit." She sighed. "I think he was her only friend on the island, honestly, other than me and Derek—if you can call Derek a friend. She wasn't really returning my calls lately. I feel kind of bad about it now, but I was always trying to get her to break up with him." She frowned slightly. "I think she felt judged, but I was just trying to help."

Had she "helped" her friend by calling in an anonymous tip, I wondered? "I'm sure you were trying to help her. She'd probably appreciate a visit, if you've got the time."

"I don't know how to do it, but maybe Charlene can go with me," she suggested, looking uneasy at the thought.

"Do you know anyone who might have wanted to get Tania into trouble?"

She shook her head. "Evan would have walked on water for her. She didn't have a lot of other friends here—a lot of them went off-island after graduation. I can't think who would have wanted to mess with her, though. I'm sorry I'm not more help."

"I appreciate you taking the time to talk with me," I told her as she let me out the colorful front door a few minutes later. The sun was dropping in the sky, and there was a chill in the breeze; I hugged myself, wishing I'd taken a jacket with me.

My next stop was Ingrid's house. I was hoping to touch base with Evan; if, as Kaitlyn said, he had a crush on Tania, he should be willing to do anything he could to help her.

I walked past Eli and Claudette's on the way, smiling at the bits of boat sprawled out across the yard, along with Claudette's goats Muffin and Pudge, who were working in concert to pull their tire toward a pot of geraniums, and realized I'd never made it over to check out the skiff Eli had offered. There was no time today, but maybe tomorrow, after I finished keeping an eye on the store, I'd give them a call and see if Eli could spare a few minutes.

Ingrid's house was immaculately kept, as always, with two urns of geraniums showing only a little bit of goat damage flanking the stairs to the porch. As I was about to mount the first step, I heard voices through the open window, and paused.

"You never should have come back. I knew she would be a bad influence on you." I recognized the voice as Ingrid's.

"Mom. You're jumping to conclusions." Evan, I thought.

"First her boyfriend gets himself killed, and now this."

"He wasn't her boyfriend. They weren't serious."

"Serious enough to get her into drugs. And you, too."

"I'm not into drugs. That's all behind me now."

"Really?" Ingrid spat. "Why won't you do a drug test, then?"

"You never have faith in me," he said. He was yelling now. "You won't be happy unless I'm locked up in some rehab facility, will you?"

"I'll do whatever it takes to keep you safe," she answered. "I know you care for that girl, but I'm glad she's not around to tempt you anymore. And that drug dealer, too. I heard he was dealing at the school. Innocent children! And now that girl Tania is involved, too."

"She was clean, Mom. I know Derek tried to get her to smoke, but she wouldn't do it."

"Oh?" The voice was near hysteria now. "Then how come she got arrested for having marijuana today?"

"I hate you." The voice was so savage it made me shiver. A door slammed so hard the entire house seemed to shake, and then I heard a woman sobbing.

Quietly, I crept away from the house into the cooling evening, wondering to what lengths Ingrid might go to protect her son—and if those lengths might extend to murder.

———

"I hear we're going to visit the old rectory!" Beryl was grinning from ear to ear the next morning as I poured coffee and checked to be sure everyone had enough food. I'd made Kat's Stuffed French Toast for breakfast that morning—I'd gotten the recipe from a friend of mine in Texas—and had finished two of the sweet, apricot- and cream cheese-infused French toast "sandwiches" myself that morning. I wasn't the only one enjoying it; Agnes was on her third slice, and my hopes of leftovers had been dashed.

"Catherine pulled it off," I told her with a smile. John's mother had set things up with Murray, and we were scheduled to meet Matilda at Murray's construction site the next day.

My fiancé had, as promised, fixed salmon for everyone the night before, sending me upstairs for a bubble bath as he handled the guests. He'd been frustrated and angry at the detective, who hadn't shared any new information about the case against Tania with him, but he had managed to put it aside and charm Beryl and Agnes, who had both told me they wished they'd gotten to him first. I thought of our wedding discussion earlier that week; I loved his plan, but with Tania in jail, it might change everything. I pushed the thought from my mind and focused on my guests.

"We've got the day free, and Agnes wanted to research locations. Any suggestions?"

"I'd definitely head to Mount Desert Island and visit Jordan Pond House," I said. "Tea and popovers on the lawn are an unforgettable experience."

"I've heard about that place," Beryl said. "How do we get there?"

"It's easy; if you take the mail boat over, you can catch a bus to the restaurant. There's a lovely hike around Jordan Pond, too. A family of beavers has built a dam at the far end—and you might even see some loons!"

"That sounds fabulous," Agnes said as she forked up another bite of French toast. "I just hope I'll have room."

"I'll call and make reservations for one o'clock," I said. "That'll give you plenty of time to digest."

Agnes smiled. "Thanks, Natalie."

"Any word on the DNA test yet?" I asked.

"No," she said, "but I'm going to call again this afternoon. There's a possibility we might find some other evidence, too, once we get to the rectory. Matilda's been looking at the letters my grandmother found after he disappeared."

"Old letters are often useful," I said. "Let me know if you find anything out!"

"Of course," she said with a smile. Satisfied, she took another bite of stuffed French toast while I retreated to the kitchen to make the phone call to Jordan Pond House.

Everyone finished breakfast early that morning; the guests were eager to start their adventure, and raced to catch the mail boat. I finished the dishes and was on my bike by 9:45, arriving at the store a few minutes before ten.

"Ready?" I asked Charlene, who was dressed in jeans and a linen jacket, accented by a scarf with bright red poppies.

"I suppose so." Although her makeup was expertly applied, it couldn't completely cover the dark rings under her eyes. "I barely slept last night."

"Take this with you," I said, offering her two plastic bags filled with leftover muffins and cookies. "I would have brought French toast, but my guests ate it all. These are for you and Tania."

"Thanks, Nat." My friend hugged me. "I'll be back by three at the latest. She's got a bail hearing at eleven." She patted her stylish leather purse. "I brought my checkbook. I hope I have enough."

"I'm sure it'll be fine, but if you need help, let us know."

She gave me a grim smile. "Thanks."

"I'm glad they're moving it along," I said. "Do you know the specifics of what they found yet? They wouldn't say much to John when he went and talked with them."

Charlene shook her carefully coiffed head. Normally she liked to style her hair in sexy caramel waves, but today she'd pulled it up into a neat French twist in the back. It was a good look for her, but not one I was used to seeing. "I'm still not sure she wasn't set up," my friend said. "Did you have any luck talking to Kaitlyn and Evan yesterday?"

"I only talked with Kaitlyn, briefly—but I saw both of them." I explained what I had seen yesterday afternoon. "Did you know Evan came back to the island for Tania?"

"No, but I'm not as in touch with the teen scene as I am the affairs of the older crowd. So to speak." She gave me a saucy wink that made me smile; despite the situation, Charlene's spirit was still intact.

"We'll have to ask Tania about it."

"We'll have to ask Tania a lot of things." Charlene's voice was stern.

"Let's get her home first," I said, and glanced at my watch. "You'd better run—give me the quick lowdown on what you need me to do."

"Just keep the coffee on and ring people up," she said. "You remember how to use the register?" She pointed to the 1970s-era behemoth at the end of the counter.

"I think so."

"You'll be fine," she said breezily. "The mail comes at noon, and you have to go down to the pier to meet the mail boat. Someone usually is here to mind the store while you run. The outgoing is in that bag there"—she waved a manicured hand toward a gray bag in the corner—"and you can just sort what comes in and stuff it into the boxes." She inclined her head toward the wall of post office boxes everyone on the island used. "I'll have my phone with me, if you get in trouble. It's spotty, but it's better on Mount Desert Island than it is here." She sucked in her breath through her pink-painted lips. "The *Daily Mail* will be here at noon, too. Let me know if you see anything in it."

"You know it'll show up in there sometime," I said. All the arrests were listed in the crime watch section—a part of the paper read with intense interest by everyone on the island.

"I know," she said, with a sigh that seemed to deflate her.

"Go," I said. "Your niece needs you. And your sister." I knew Charlene was meeting Tania's mother at the jail.

"Wish me luck," she said, lingering at the door.

"Always."

―――――

The first half hour was peaceful; a couple of locals came in for milk or eggs, and I managed to wield the cash register without accidentally charging anybody $100 for a gallon of milk. At noon, I wandered down to the pier to exchange outgoing mail for ingoing mail, leaving Eli at the register, and spent the next half hour tucking envelopes into boxes. My mind kept returning to Tania, though. When there weren't customers at the bar, I found myself fretting. To distract myself, I grabbed a week-old copy of the Portland paper, poured myself a cup of coffee, and settled onto one of the squishy couches in the front of the store.

It was easy sometimes to forget that there was a world outside of Cranberry Island, and after a few pages reading about congressional tussles, global warming, and gun violence, I was ready to close it up and rearrange cans of pear slices instead. On the other hand, maybe the outside world wasn't so far away after all. Gun violence wasn't exactly absent on Cranberry Island. Derek Morton had been shot to death just days ago.

I turned a page of the paper to an interesting article on the drug trade. Evidently Portland had had a recent resurgence of the problem, with major influxes of marijuana they suspected was coming from Canada. It was Prohibition all over again, complete with gangs and murders. Although I wasn't interested in drugs myself, sometimes I wished they'd just legalize marijuana and tax the heck out of it instead of flushing millions of dollars down the drain trying to stamp it out. And turning young, foolish women like Tania into felons.

Was she going to be a felon? The thought made my stomach churn, and I put down the paper and walked to the phone behind the counter. John's voiced answered on the third ring.

"Hey," I said.

"How's it going down there?"

"Quiet. Charlene told me that Tania's bail hearing is at eleven, so I'm here for a while."

"I just got off the phone with Johnson."

My stomach clenched. "And?"

"The good news is, there wasn't enough for a felony conviction."

All the air seemed to rush out of me. "The bad news?"

He hesitated. "They found a gun."

FOURTEEN

"Oh, no." Silence hung between us for a moment. "What kind of gun?" I had to ask, even though I dreaded the answer.

He let out a long, deep breath that answered the question before he spoke. "The same kind that killed Derek Morton."

I sat down on a stool, feeling as if I had just been shot myself. "How could she have a gun? She's not even old enough to have a gun! Don't you have to be 21 or something?"

"They're researching the registration papers and doing ballistics tests on the weapon."

"How about fingerprints?"

"That, too. Even if they don't find any, though, they're going to be wondering what it was doing in the trash behind her house."

"So it wasn't in the house—it was in the garbage can?"

"The one by the back door," he confirmed.

"Anyone could have put it there," I pointed out. "What does she say?"

"I haven't talked to her, but Tania claims she didn't know anything about it."

"Well, that's something. If her fingerprints don't turn up on it…"

"It was still at Charlene and Tania's house. And she might have used gloves. I'm worried they're going to come after Charlene, too, Natalie."

I gripped the phone. "John. You really don't think either of them had anything to do with Derek's death, do you?"

He sighed. "No, I don't. Just because I don't, though, doesn't mean the detectives will agree with me. In any case, I'm afraid it's going to make bail a challenge."

The bell over the door rang, and my eyes swiveled to the front of the store. Ingrid Sorenson was walking in. "Can I call you back?" I asked.

"Love you."

"Love you too," I said, hanging up and smiling at Ingrid.

"Hi, Ingrid."

"Natalie." She lifted her sunglasses and blinked in surprise. "What are you doing here?"

"Filling in for Charlene. She went to visit her niece."

"Oh, yes. I heard she'd gotten into some trouble. I hope everything gets worked out," she said, not sounding entirely convincing as she disappeared into one of the aisles.

"Me, too," I said, playing with the phone cord.

Fred, who had come in a few minutes earlier, slouched toward the register with a six-pack of Pabst Blue Ribbon and a giant bag of Doritos, I turned to him with a smile. "Surprised to see you here, instead of out on the water."

"Where's my mermaid?"

"Off on the mainland this morning," I said. "You're stuck with me, I'm afraid." As I rang up his purchases, I asked, "What's your buoy color, anyway?"

He gave me a wary look from under heavy brows. "Why do you want to know?"

"I always like to look for them," I said. "It's fun knowing who's who."

"Black and white," he said grudgingly.

"Original," I quipped as I tucked the beer and chips into a bag. "Do you need to get your mail?"

"Why not?"

I reached under the counter for the keys and turned back toward the bank of mailboxes. "What number?" I asked.

"316."

I unlocked the brass box and withdrew two envelopes: one from the electric company, the other, hand-addressed, from an address in Portland.

"Here you go," I said, turning back to the counter. He just about snatched them from my hand. "It'll be $11.37 for the purchases."

As he pulled out a battered wallet and laid a ten and two ones on the counter, I noticed a smudge of orange paint on the cuff of his canvas jacket. I counted out his change and dropped the coins in his hand. "Have a good day," I said as he turned and stumped toward the door.

"Tell Charlene I'll be looking for her," he said.

"Of course."

I rang up Ingrid, who wasn't too inclined to talk, despite my many questions about her son. She scuttled out the door, clutching her bag of orange juice and milk tightly.

As I sat back on my stool, I thought about my conversation with Fred. I hadn't seen a whole lot of black and white buoys around the island, I realized. But I had seen an orange one.

Hmm.

———

Charlene was a wreck when she got back to the store around half past two. Black mascara streaked down her cheeks, and her eyes were red.

"How's Tania?" I asked, rounding the counter in a hurry. I was thankful the afternoon mug-up group had exited the store a few minutes earlier. The news would be across the island before dinner—that is, if it wasn't already spreading. Charlene had, after all, come and gone on the mail boat.

"They set bail at $500,000," she said. "On account of the gun."

"I was afraid of that. John called after you left."

"They can't charge her with murder." Charlene jutted out her chin. "She barely knew him!"

"Did she hire the lawyer?"

"Yes, and I'm covering the cost," she said.

"What about her parents?"

She shook her head. "They're down on their luck right now."

"But Charlene …" Although Charlene wasn't poor, I knew she wasn't making money hand over fist, either. Few of us who lived on the island were.

"I was saving for a college fund for her." She lifted her chin. "Now it's her defense fund." Her lower lip trembled. "It's still not nearly enough to get her out of jail."

"Poor thing," I said, wrapping my arms around Charlene.

"We have to get her out of there," she said. "I'm sure someone framed her."

"Me too."

"We've solved other crimes, haven't we?"

I nodded. "We have. And we'll do everything we can to solve this one. Did she tell you who might have wanted to get her into trouble?"

"I didn't get a chance to ask. We only had about ten minutes together."

"Maybe next time, then."

"I'm going back to see her the day after tomorrow," Charlene told me.

"Be sure to ask her then." I glanced at my watch. "Actually, I hate to run, but I'd better get going."

"What do you mean?"

"I promised to stop by Eli's and take a look at a skiff he finished. I'll check in with you later, okay? We'll make sure Tania's okay."

"I just hope they don't arrest me too," she said gloomily.

———

"Natalie!" Eli greeted me with a gap-toothed smile as I walked up the lane to the house he shared with his wife, Claudette.

When I arrived, Claudette's goats, Muffin and Pudge, were straining at the tire they were chained to, attempting to get to a particularly tasty geranium on the Whites' porch. I knew Claudette prized both her goats and the wool she gleaned from them, which she knitted into mittens and hats for the long Maine winters. I also knew the neighbors were less than enamored of her ravenous ovine duo. Many a rosebush had fallen victim to their insatiable appetites.

"Sorry I missed tea," I said. "Between the murder and Tania's arrest, it's been a bit chaotic."

"No worries," he said. "Poor little Tania. Wouldn't hurt a fly. I've known her since she was a babe in arms."

"I know," I said. "I'm doing everything I can to clear her name."

"Rum business, it is. Now, then. Are you here to see Claudie, or your new skiff?"

I sighed. "You really think the *Little Marian* is toast?"

He eyed me from under his cap. "You've been lucky twice. Do you want to try for a third time?"

"Well, when you put it like that ..." I shivered. "On the other hand, maybe I just need to stay out of Smuggler's Cove."

He grinned. "That would be a good plan, too, lass."

I followed him into his workshop, which like the yard outside, was cluttered with bits of boat: oars, curved boards, rudders, and seats he had salvaged from other boats.

As he closed the workshop door behind him, I glimpsed an old buoy in the grass, which made me think of the mysterious lobster boat that had been hanging around lately. "I've been meaning to ask you; has anyone seen a lobster boat with a turquoise and orange buoy hanging around the island?"

"I know that boat, and I've seen her a few times. She's called the *Green Zephyr.*"

"I haven't seen any turquoise and orange buoys around, though," I said.

"That's because she belongs to a friend of mine in Southwest Harbor. Couldn't say why he's hanging around Cranberry Island. I wonder if someone's been taking out the *Zephyr* on the sly."

"Where was she when you've spotted her?"

"Not too far off the point," he said. "Near the lighthouse."

And Smuggler's Cove, I thought. "Did she have a dinghy on her?"

"That she did." He eyed me. "You think she's up to funny business in the cove?"

"I don't know," I said, "but I've seen her there at low tide. And I think there was a lobster boat hanging around when we got rammed."

Eli shook his head. "Shady business."

"Yeah," I said.

His eyes glinted. "You know, we need to take this skiff of yours out for a ride. Want to go visit the *Zephyr*?

I hesitated, thinking of all the things I should be doing—after all, I'd been at the store most of the day—and then decided to go ahead. "Why not? I need a skiff, and I want to see the boat."

"Well then, we'll be off," he said. "I put her in the water yesterday for a trial run, and she's tied up down at the cove; let's head down and see how she goes!"

"Terrific," I said, and followed him down the wide path to the water.

It was a beautiful day for a boat ride. There had been rain overnight, and now everything seemed washed clean.

"Here she is," he said, pointing to a pretty white skiff painted with gray-blue accents. She was about the same size as the *Little Marian*, but practically sparkled with the new paint. "Brand new motor," he said. "Plenty of horsepower, and I designed her to be extra-steady."

I laughed; he knew I would always be a landlubber. I couldn't count the number of times I'd almost pitched over getting in and out of the *Little Marian*.

"She's beautiful," I said, admiring the smooth paint job. "How much?"

"Why don't you try her out for a few weeks, and we'll talk?"

"But Eli…"

"No buts. I know you don't have a skiff right now, and with this one just finished, it was meant to be. You ready to test her out?"

"Absolutely. She's so cute!" I said as I stepped in and sat down in the front.

"No, no. You're the captain," Eli said, pointing me to the back of the boat.

"Are you sure?" I always felt like a rank amateur with Eli in the skiff with me. Largely because I was.

"I'll navigate," he said, hopping into the front with the agility of a mountain goat and untying the little skiff.

We pulled away from the island quickly, the little boat cutting through the sapphire waves. It was cooler on the water, but also freer, somehow. I watched as a little group of ducks bobbed past us, unconcerned by our passing. "Where am I going?" I asked.

"Make for Southwest Harbor," he called back to me, and I steered the boat away from the island and across the water that separated us from Mount Desert Island.

FIFTEEN

THE LITTLE SKIFF RAN like a dream, and it seemed no time at all before we were pulling into the picturesque harbor, which was dotted with pleasure yachts and working boats and lined with mansions the locals called "cottages." I had spotted a few turquoise and orange buoys on the way across the water; evidently we were in the *Zephyr's* territory.

"Do you see her, Eli?" I asked as we entered the crowded harbor.

"Over there," he said, pointing to a lobster boat nestled among the yachts, close to the dock.

I squinted at the name on the back of the boat. Sure enough, the words *Green Zephyr* were painted in peeling script letters, and it sported the familiar turquoise and orange buoy. A dinghy was tied just off the stern; either the captain had replaced it, or this wasn't the same lobster boat I'd seen outside the cove the other day.

I slowed the engine as we approached the boat. A short, burly man was coiling ropes on the deck, and Eli hailed him.

"How's the fishing, Mike?"

"Eli! Haven't seen you in ages, my friend!" The man adjusted his cap, and his weathered face split into a smile. "Lobstering's good this month. Want a couple?"

"Only if you can spare 'em," Eli said.

"I'll get two for you in a moment," he said, and his eyes turned to me. "Who's your lady friend?"

"This is Natalie Barnes," Eli said. "She owns the inn over on Cranberry. Natalie, this is Mike Donavan."

"Nice to meet you, Mike." I smiled up at him, squinting into the sun.

"Care to come aboard, or are you heading into town?"

"We came to talk to you, actually."

"I can guess why," he said darkly. "Come around the stern, and I'll help you tie up." I guided the skiff to the back of the lobster boat. Eli put out the bumpers, and Mike and I tied it to the bigger craft and stepped up onto the *Green Zephyr*.

"I'd shake your hand, but I've been filling traps all day," the short lobsterman said. It was a small deck, and smelled powerfully of salted herring, the bait used to catch lobsters.

I smiled at him. "I understand; my niece's boyfriend is a lobsterman, too. Nice to meet you."

He grinned back and adjusted his cap. "You here about the craft that's been borrowing the *Zephyr's* name, I suppose."

"Is that what's been going on?" Eli asked. "We wondered if someone had been taking the *Zephyr* out on the sly."

"No, no one's been on her but me," Mike said. "But I've heard reports that I'm in lots of places I never go."

"Like where?" I asked.

"Cranberry Island, for starters. And farther out to sea, too."

"How long has this been going on?" I asked.

"Since the spring," he said. "She's been in Northeast Harbor, too, from what I hear. She usually runs at night."

"We've seen her during the day on the island," I said. "Right near Smuggler's Cove."

"Somebody's up to something," Mike said darkly. "And I don't like them pretending to be me, either. I may not keep my boat clean, but I always keep my nose clean." Despite his assertion to the contrary, the boat looked pretty darned spotless to me.

"I think you're right; somebody's up to something," I told him. "I don't know what, though. I went into the cove the other day, and there was nothing there. Someone's been using it, though."

"How do you know that?" Eli asked.

"Fresh mud on the floor. And someone rammed my skiff on my way out."

Eli nodded. "Bad business, whatever it is."

"I'm convinced it may be connected with Derek's death," I said.

"Young Derek Morton?" Mike said.

"You know him?"

"Knew him, more like. That young man was trouble. He sterned for a friend of mine here in Southwest a few months back. Always showing up late, and hung over. He took the boat out once without permission, and that was the end of him."

"He did the same thing on Cranberry Island," I said.

"Got himself killed, I hear," Mike said. "Did they figure out who did it?"

I swallowed and glanced at Eli. "They've arrested a young woman, but I don't think she's the one who did it."

"Terrible shame. Two young lives." The stout lobsterman shook his head angrily. "And now that damned boat is going around pretending to be the *Zephyr*."

"Have you talked to any of the harbormasters?" Eli asked.

"I'm about to," he growled.

"If anyone knows where she's docking," I said, "we'd be interested to know."

"If I hear anything, I'll give Eli a jingle. Now, before I forget..." He opened a hatch and reached in. "How many do you need?"

Eli turned to me. "Want any?"

"No, thanks. You've been help enough, Mike," I said.

"You sure?" Mike asked.

I smiled. "Positive."

"We'll take two then," Eli said. "One for me and one for Claudette. We owe you one, Mike."

"No problem, Eleazer. Thanks for stopping by. How's the missus, anyway?"

"Enjoying the grandkids," Eli beamed. "We'll have to have you and Pat over sometime."

"I'll have the wife ring Claudette up," Mike said, then handed Eli the two lobsters—good two-pounders, it looked like.

Eli thanked him and clambered down to the skiff with his dinner. "Let me know if you find out anything."

"I'm on it," Mike said, and a moment later we were motoring back toward Cranberry Island with two lobsters crawling around on the floor of the skiff. Thankfully, their claws were rubber-banded shut.

"Why would someone pretend to be the *Zephyr*, do you think?" I asked as we motored home. A few rain clouds were forming far over the water, and a loon bobbed to the right of the boat, taking flight as the little skiff neared it.

"Trying to keep something secret."

I thought about that for a moment. "Where's the tide right now?" I called over the thrum of the motor.

"About a half hour away from low tide," he replied.

"Do you mind stopping by Smuggler's Cove?" I asked.

He glanced back at me, a bushy gray eyebrow cocked. "You think this fake *Zephyr's* using it?"

"Maybe," I said. "It's been hanging out nearby lately."

"That's a bad luck place for you, Miss Natalie," he warned. "You sure you're up for it?"

I nodded. "I think so." My voice sounded more confident than I felt. "As long as you'll take us in."

"Ayuh," he said. "Can't hurt to have a look-see."

The storm clouds had come closer by the time we reached the little black cavern on Cranberry Island. Although the water was studded with multicolored lobster buoys, there was no sign of a lobster boat.

"I'll hand her over to you now," I said, idling the motor as Eli and I switched places. He slowly approached the cove, deftly guiding the little skiff around the submerged rocks we both knew littered the water around it.

"Ready?" he asked.

"Let's do it."

I gripped the sides tightly as he urged the little skiff forward, using just enough power to keep her moving past the rocks, but not so much that we'd approach the rocky, dark mouth of the cove too fast.

The sound of the little skiff seemed to be magnified a hundred times as we entered Smuggler's Cove, the thrum of the motor ricocheting off the rock walls. I realized as soon as we passed into the cove that I had forgotten an important thing: a flashlight. As I opened my mouth to tell Eli we had to go back, a narrow beam of light came from behind me, darting across the rocky shelf.

"Where did that come from?" I asked, relieved. It was hard enough to maneuver in the cove with light; turning the skiff around in the small space without it would be treacherous.

"Always carry one on my keychain," he answered as I scrambled to put out the bumpers and tie the little skiff up to the rusted iron loops that had been there for decades. Maybe longer. "Never know when it'll come in handy." He hopped up onto the rock shelf first, nimble despite his years, and reached out a hand to help me up.

"Let's take a look." His calm voice helped soothe my jangled nerves, and I followed him through the little opening into the larger cave.

"Muddy," he pointed out, scanning the rough floor with his penlight. It was impossible to tell if the cove had been used since the last time I'd been here, or if the mud was old. "Not much else here, though."

"Think they stopped using it after they saw me going in here?" I asked.

"Was there anything in here then?"

"Just mud. Same as now." He swept the floor with the light again, and I spotted something. "Wait. Point it back over here." I moved toward a crevice near the back, where I'd spotted something shiny.

He moved the light over the area until it caught on something that looked like crumpled plastic. I reached for it; it was a sandwich bag. It looked empty at first, but then I took a closer look. Little bits of green clung to the inside, and when I opened it, my suspicions were confirmed.

"Marijuana."

———

Eli made a "tsking" noise. "Probably some high school kids," he said. "Up to no good. Used to be liquor they filched from their parents' houses, but nowadays …"

"Let's look and see if there's anything else." While I listened nervously for the sound of an approaching boat, Eli carefully ran the light over every nook and cranny of the cave, but came up with nothing.

"Looks like they're using the cove for a smoke," he said, resignation in his voice.

"That doesn't make sense, though," I replied. "The window of time for getting in and out of here is too small. Surely there are enough hidden-away places on the island that would be better." I pushed my hair back behind my ear. "Besides, why go to the trouble of disguising a lobster boat just to have a smoke in Smuggler's Cove?"

"People do odd things. But in the meantime, unless you'd like to spend the next twelve hours in here, we should think about heading back out."

I shivered. I didn't relish the thought of doing that again. Particularly if that lobster boat decided to make a return visit. I tucked the bag into my shorts pocket and followed Eli back to the skiff, untying the ropes as he revved the engine. At my request, he paused in the mouth of the cove. Wherever the fake *Zephyr* was, she wasn't here today, though, so as the water crept up the sides of Smuggler's Cove, he zipped through the opening and turned the boat toward home.

———

"So," Eli asked when we pulled back into the dock behind his house a half hour later. "What do you think of her?"

I looked down at the beautiful white skiff and grinned. "I love her. How much?"

He grinned at me. "Consider her an early wedding present."

"Eli, it's too much …"

"You're one of us now, Natalie," he said. "And if you're going to be an islander, you need a boat."

I reached over and hugged him. "Thank you, Eli. Thank you so much."

"When is that wedding going to be, anyway?"

"There may be some news on that front very soon," I said. "We thought we were getting married in Florida, but there may be a change in plans."

"Oh, really? What do you have in mind?"

"It's still a secret," I said, grinning at him. "I'll let you know as soon as I can."

"Well, let us know," he said. "If we can make it, we will. Got time for a cuppa? The missus is dying to see you."

My heart expanded until it filled my chest. "Absolutely, Eli. Absolutely."

SIXTEEN

AFTER A LONG CHAT with Claudette, who also gave me a few skeins of handspun yarn for the knitting I never quite got around to, I stopped by the Sorensons' house again, but this time it was quiet. I knocked on the door, but there was no answer, so after a few minutes I gave up and headed back to the inn. John was hard at work in his workshop when I got there, looking grim.

The smell of fresh sawdust soothed me, as always, probably because I associated the scent with John. He was handsome as usual today in a green T-shirt that stretched over his muscular chest and blue jeans that looked like they had been cut just for him. He looked up at me with those green eyes of his, and my heart did a little skip. "Hey, beautiful," he said, putting down the sandpaper and walking over to hug me. I let him fold me into his arms, relaxing into his chest and inhaling the scent of him. "What have you been up to today?"

"We got a new skiff," I said. "A wedding present."

"From Eli?"

"He took me out on it," I said. "We found the mysterious lobster boat."

"What?" John stepped back, hands on my shoulders, and looked at me. "Where?"

I told him about our visit with Mike, and his theory that there was another boat posing as his.

"I wonder why?" he asked.

"Somebody doesn't want to be recognized," I suggested. "We also went back to Smuggler's Cove."

"Natalie." I could hear the concern in his voice.

"Eli was with me," I told him. "We found an empty baggie with some pot in it." I reached into my pocket and withdrew the crumpled plastic. He opened it and took a sniff, then closed it, looking grim.

"Was there anything else?"

I shook my head.

He sighed. "Teenagers. It appears we have a drug problem on the island; I'll have to let Detective Johnson know."

"It doesn't make sense, though. Why go to Smuggler's Cove to smoke? It's hard to get into, and once you did, you'd only have about a half hour before you had to clear out."

"It also doesn't explain the *Green Zephyr* double," he agreed.

"Another puzzle," I said. "Just what we needed." I looked up at John. "Any word on Tania?"

"No news," he said. "I've got three messages in to the detective, and I'm still waiting for a call back. I've been keeping myself busy while waiting." He pointed to his latest creation. "What do you think?" he asked, giving his work a critical look.

"It looks like it's going to fly right out that window," I said, admiring his sculpture of an eider duck in flight. While the tail still held the unmistakable look of driftwood, it seemed to magically morph into a graceful, streamlined waterfowl taking flight. John had long scoured the beaches of the island for chunks of driftwood he could transform into beautiful sculptures, and his work had earned the attention of a few major galleries, providing a nice change from the small toy boats he carved and painted every winter to sell at Island Artists. He always said the animal was in the wood, and he was just helping it out, but it looked like magic to me.

"They won't tell me what other evidence they have," he said, reaching for a piece of sandpaper and running it across the underside of the duck's wing. "And her alibi is challenging; she said she was asleep in her room all night. Charlene says she would have heard if she'd left, but there's a window without a screen in her room—it wouldn't have been any difficulty getting out without being heard. And she was supposed to meet Derek the night he died, which complicates things."

"What motive?"

"Jealousy," he said. "Adam told me he'd been with another woman; he talked about it down at the co-op."

"That's the first I've heard of that," I said. "Still. They'd only been going out a few weeks. Is that really a valid motive?"

John shrugged. "With the gun found in the trash can …"

"Are they looking for other possibilities?" I asked. "Have they found anything out about his big business plans?"

"I wish I knew. They're being awfully close-mouthed about the whole thing."

"I need to talk to Evan," I mused, sitting down on a stool a few feet from his workbench. "I tried to stop by today, but he and Ingrid were arguing."

"About what?" John asked.

"She thinks he's back into drugs," I said. "She told him she was glad Derek was gone ... and that she'd do whatever it took to keep Evan safe."

John's green eyes darted to mine. "Do you think that might extend to eliminating bad influences?"

"You think it's possible she shot Derek?"

"She's taken measures to protect her son before," he said. A few years ago she had gone to great lengths—not all of them ethical—to keep his drug addiction from going public. "It's certainly worth considering."

"What about Evan himself?" I asked. "I heard he came back to the island for Tania, but she was infatuated with Derek. Is it possible he was getting rid of the competition?"

"It is," he said, "but we don't have any evidence. It doesn't explain the 'T' on the note in his hand. And with the gun at Tania and Charlene's ... "

"We can at least tell Detective Johnson what we've found out," I said.

"Don't forget that Adam's also a potential suspect," John pointed out, looking worried as he sanded the tip of a wing. I found myself understanding a little of what John said about the animal waiting to come out of the wood as I noticed a knot placed perfectly for an eye. It almost looked like the bird had grown out of a tree. Why couldn't this murder investigation evolve as smoothly? My heart told me it had taken a sharp wrong turn—and the police were doing nothing to correct its course.

"Derek *was* found in his skiff, but I can't believe Adam would do something like that. Can you?"

"Of course not. But Johnson doesn't know him as well as we do." John put down the sandpaper and ran a hand over the wing. Satisfied, he retrieved the paper and set to work on the tail feathers.

"He sure seemed friendly—and was happy to eat my scones—but he hasn't been very helpful, has he?" I asked. "And we still have the drug bust to deal with." I groaned and closed my eyes. "Do you know how much marijuana they found?"

"Well, there's some good news there," John said. "If they hadn't found the gun, we'd be celebrating. It was only a couple of ounces, enough for a misdemeanor. She could get some jail time, but it could be worse—and at least she wouldn't have a felony conviction."

"Unless she's convicted for murder," I said dully.

"Well, there is that." John ran a hand down the smooth back of the duck. "But I'll pass on what you found to Detective Johnson. I need to find out if there are fingerprints on the gun, anyway."

"And we still have no idea who Derek's mysterious 'contact' was."

"Or why he was taking Adam's boat out late at night," John added.

"There's something going on here," I said, glancing out the window toward the blue water where I'd found Derek a few days earlier. "I just wish I could figure out what."

———

Agnes and Beryl were back already, talking excitedly in the parlor, when I walked back up to the inn.

"Must have been some terrific popovers," I said as I brought in a bottle of wine along with some Brie and a baguette, and set it down on the coffee table.

"Oh, Jordan Pond House was divine," Agnes said, stretching out in the overstuffed sofa, "but that's not what we're excited about."

"Did you hear back from the test?" I guessed.

"We did," Beryl nodded. "The bones belonged to my grandfather."

"How exciting! And yet sad, too," I told her. "It must be hard knowing someone murdered your grandfather."

"I know; I never got to meet him, and I always wanted to." Her eyes were a bit misty, and she took a deep breath before she spoke again. "I wish my grandmother were still alive; she pined for him for years. She never remarried, even though he was missing for more than forty years. She was always waiting for him to come home."

"Did your grandmother live here on the island with him?"

"She lived here for about a year, when he first was called here, but island life wasn't for her. She spent most of the time in Bangor, with my great-grandmother," Beryl said. "She had three kids, and her mother was a big help with them. He spent weekends up here at the Episcopal church and went back to Bangor during the week." She shook her head. "And then one week, he never came back."

"How tragic," I said.

"My great-grandmother didn't make it any easier on her daughter. She always claimed he'd run off to Canada with another woman, but my grandmother never believed her. She was loyal to him till the end."

"You mentioned you had letters," I said.

"I do," she said. "She kept all of them, and there's something in them I can't figure out. Maybe you can help?"

"I'd love to see them," I told her. The distraction would be welcome about now.

"I'll go get them," she said.

"Right now, I've got to get dinner going. Will you show me afterwards?"

"Of course," she told me, reaching for the cheese knife and slicing herself a thick wedge of Brie, which she sandwiched between two slices of bread and popped into her mouth.

As the two women talked excitedly, I excused myself to the kitchen. The buttery yellow walls and golden floors were warm and soothing, as was the sight of Biscuit curled up in her customary spot above the heater. I gave her head a rub, and she meowed at me, wondering where her wet cat food was. I opened a can of grilled chicken cat food—the only kind she didn't turn her nose up at—then washed my hands and set to work.

Comfort food was the order of the day, and although I'd been planning on roasting chicken later in the week, I decided that this evening would be a good time for it. I arranged the two chickens I'd ordered from the mainland on a roasting pan—I'd split them after cooking them, and serve each person half a bird—and rubbed olive oil and seasoned salt onto them. John had told me Catherine was eating at Murray's house this evening, so there were only four of us. I smiled at the thought of Gwen arriving for the weekend; as much as I liked Catherine, I missed Gwen's company. She was almost like a daughter to me, I thought as I emptied a bag of new potatoes into a colander and rinsed them under the faucet. I knew she'd spend most of her time with Adam, but I hoped she'd carve out at least a bit of time to catch up with John and me at the inn. The only cloud on the upcoming weekend was Tania's arrest.

Unfortunately, it was a pretty big cloud.

As I sliced the new potatoes in half, my thoughts turned again to who else might have wanted to kill Derek. I couldn't imagine Tania shooting him and setting him adrift in a dinghy. And speaking of dinghies, why had it been Adam's? Had someone been trying to set him up? And what had the gun been doing in Charlene's trashcan? Had that been what the tipster had in mind when he or she called the police?

I had answers to none of those questions. But if I wanted to help Tania, I needed to.

My information on Derek was sketchy, at best, I realized. And although I'd done a lot of prying, I hadn't really talked with his employer, Fred Penney, about him. I'd have to fix that tomorrow, I decided as I tucked onion slices and celery into the chickens and slid both the chickens and the potatoes into the oven. I'd make a salad with the greens from the farm, I decided, and for dessert I'd serve parfaits made with vanilla ice cream, lemon pound cake I'd put in the freezer last week, and a lemony blueberry sauce. I rinsed a pint of berries and put them into a pot with some sugar and a splash of limoncello, then turned the heat to low and returned to the parlor, where Agnes and Beryl were leafing through a stack of letters.

"Wow. That's a lot of letters."

"It is, isn't it?" Beryl grinned.

"He wrote all of those to your grandmother?"

"Actually, no." Beryl riffled through the stack and pulled out a yellowed sheet with florid script on it. "A lot of them are correspondence with a priest in Nova Scotia. A Father Probst. Here," she said, handing me a letter. "Tell me what you think."

I took the letter and read:

It pleases me to learn that your flock is doing well and that the weather has not been too adverse, allowing you to make your weekly trips to visit your parishioners. I am sending the liniment you requested, and it should arrive next week. I hope your congregation is generous in its tithing as always. I will be praying for you, and putting in a good word with the Bishop. Thank you, as always, for your dedicated service.

Yours in Christ, Fr. Probst

"Here's another one," she said, handing it to me.

Thank you for your donation to the mission; the bishop was very pleased to receive your support. I wonder, though, are you having difficulties tending to your flock? You seem to have fewer sheep. Is there another local church that is drawing off your congregation? I will be sending the supplies you requested; they should arrive next Tuesday.

Yours in Christ, Fr. Probst

"That's odd," I said as I folded up the letters and handed them back. "He seems to almost be reporting to this priest. Did he hail from Nova Scotia?"

"Not that I know of," Beryl said. "He grew up in Bangor."

"Why would he be concerned about what a Nova Scotian bishop thought of him?" Agnes asked.

"A mystery for your book," I told her with a smile. "Have you shown these to Matilda?"

"Not all of them. But what I can't figure out is, what's up with the liniment and supplies?"

"Maybe they're cheaper coming from Canada?" I speculated.

"Maybe," Beryl said. "It still doesn't explain why he ended up dead with a bullet in his head. Here's the last one, from about a month before he disappeared." She handed me another brief missive.

The Bishop is deeply concerned with the dwindling of your flock. The church's strength is in numbers, as you know, and as a shepherd, it is your duty to keep them from going astray. Perhaps a more personal form of guidance is in order? The Bishop has informed me that he will be sending an emissary to counsel you, and help you back to the path of righteousness.

In Christ's Name, Fr. Probst

A chill crept up my spine as I set the letter down. "This is the last letter?"

"The last one we found," Beryl said.

"It sounds like the Bishop sent a hit man, not a counselor," Agnes said in an ominous tone.

"But why?" Beryl asked. "None of this makes sense."

"No, it doesn't," I said. "But something tells me it has to do with why his body was buried next to the rectory."

Beryl shivered. "The problem is, how do we figure out what he was talking about?"

"I don't know. If Matilda can't help, your only hope is to find something at the old rectory, even though it's probably a slim chance. I think he may have been the last person to live there, and I don't know how much they cleaned out when he died. Maybe he left something there that can explain what happened." Personally, I thought it was a fruitless endeavor, but I didn't want to disappoint her.

Beryl sighed. "It's worth a try, I suppose. I just wish there were someone we could talk to."

"And if not, maybe I can come up with my own explanation, and put it in a mystery." Agnes's eyes lit up. "Maybe it was a slavery ring, or something!"

Beryl fixed her with a stern glance. "This is my grandfather we're talking about. He was a man of the cloth; he wouldn't have been involved in any wrongdoing."

I said nothing, but privately thought that the evidence—opaque as it was—tended to indicate the contrary. Strange missives to and from a priest in Canada, a bullet in the back of the head; something was going on, I was sure of it.

And something had been going on with Derek, too. I just hadn't yet figured out what it was.

———

John and I were just cleaning up from dinner—the chicken and potatoes had been roasted to perfection, and the parfaits had been summertime bliss—when Catherine came breezing in the kitchen door on a cloud of Chanel No. 5.

"Did you hear what happened today?" she asked.

John set down the bowl he'd been drying. "What? More bones?"

"No," she said, walking over to the table and sitting down primly on a chair. "Another drug arrest."

"Who?" I asked.

"Brian Knight," she said.

I was shocked. Brian was a great kid. I'd often seen him sterning with his father, a cheerful smile on his freckled face. "Brian? But he's only in high school!"

"They start younger and younger these days," she said, shaking her head.

"I can't believe it. How did it happen?"

Catherine took off her jacket and folded it neatly over one arm. "Another tip called in, apparently."

"Not to me," John said drily.

She breezed past his comment. "There seems to be quite a drug problem on the island lately. First Charlene's niece, and now this young man."

"Murray's going to use this to justify closing the school, isn't he?"

"Well, it is a problem."

"Closing the school won't help," I said.

She pursed her lips and said, "But that's evidently where the young man got the drugs."

"What?"

"Derek Morton sold them at the school, and would you believe the teacher didn't know anything about it?"

"Derek sold drugs at the Cranberry Island School?" John shook his head. "If I'd known that, I might have killed him myself!" He got up and headed for the back door, anger in the set of his jaw. "I'm calling Detective Johnson right now," he said. "If anyone from the police calls the house, I'll be in my workshop."

SEVENTEEN

I DECIDED TO HEAD out to Fred Penney's as soon as breakfast was over the next morning, leaving the dishes and cleanup to John and Catherine. Catherine, as usual, had made comments over the cheesy soufflé I'd served for breakfast, and again I found myself longing for Gwen's return. At least Adam wouldn't be in jail when she returned, I thought. On the other hand, it hurt my heart to think Tania still might. Adam had stopped by the night before to check up on us—and to make sure Gwen's travel plans were still intact.

"I can't wait for her to get back," the tall, dark-haired lobsterman had said, grinning. As sad as I was that Tania was implicated in Derek's death, I was relieved the shadow of suspicion hadn't fallen on him. At least not yet. "I've got something to ask her," he added.

John clapped him on the back. "It's about time."

"I know we've got plans for Saturday, so I'm thinking Friday night."

"Want me to cook something special?" I asked.

He shook his head. "I'm taking her to a restaurant on Mount Desert Island," he said. "I'm going to totally surprise her."

I felt a thrill of happiness at the thought of Gwen marrying this young man and planning to stay on the island for good. Although that would likely mean Gwen wouldn't be returning to her room over the kitchen—and that Catherine would be my long-term assistant. It would work, I told myself as I traipsed up the hill from the inn. It would work.

Instead of taking the van, I'd decided to get out and walk, since the weather was glorious and I didn't need to be back at the inn until two, which was when Agnes and Beryl and I were scheduled to head over to the old rectory. The walk went quickly, and it seemed like no time at all before I was standing in front of Fred Penney's small house. Although most of the islanders had all their traps in the water at this time of year, there was an enormous stack of them in his front yard. Charlene had told me he wasn't fishing as much as the other lobstermen, but from the looks of it, unless these were back-up traps, he wasn't fishing at all. I walked up to the little house, which didn't look to have room for much more than a kitchen, a bedroom, and a small living area. A juniper planted by some previous owner had grown to massive proportions, coming up to the roofline, but the rest of the front yard was overgrown grass. And lobster traps.

Behind the house was a weather-beaten shed, and beyond that, the land sloped down to the water. I caught the scent of the beach roses that lined the shore; it did little to cover the smell of old, rotted herring that emanated from the stack of lobster traps.

As I walked up to the metal front door, I heard the sound of a television. I knocked, and a moment later, the door opened, adding the smells of beer and frozen pizza to the bouquet.

"Something wrong?" Fred eyed me suspiciously, then took a swig of the Pabst Blue Ribbon he held in his right hand. Behind him, a basketball game played on a flat-screen TV.

"I just wanted to ask you a few questions about Derek," I said.

"Why?"

I put on a smile. "Because he worked for you, from what I understand. And because Charlene's niece is in jail for his murder, and unless we figure out who did it, she stands to spend a lot of her life behind bars."

His eyes darted to the shed for a moment. Then he leaned against the doorjamb. "Shame about Tania," he said. "I was thinking maybe it might be that fella who had a thing for her," he said. "What's his name? The Sorenson boy."

"Evan Sorenson is a possibility," I said. I didn't tell him that based on the conversation I had overheard in Zeke Forester's barn, I thought he sounded too scared to be the murderer. "Anyone else you can think of?"

"Well, he did have a lady friend," Fred said.

"Tania?"

"Well, her of course," he told me. "But he had another one on the side. He'd meet her on the sly, like. Apparently her husband was away from home a lot, and she got lonely sometimes." He gave me a lewd wink that made me want to head straight back to the inn and take a shower.

"He told you about her?"

"Men get to talking when they work," Fred said, taking another pull from his can. "Don't know who she was, but apparently she was happy for the attention, if you know what I mean."

"When did they meet?"

"Whenever her husband was out on the water," he said.

Well, that narrowed it down, I thought. "Speaking of out on the water, you don't seem to have many traps out."

He stretched. "I'm gettin' old. Can't do those long hours anymore." Behind him, the audience cheered as someone made a basket. He eyed me. "How's Charlene doin'?"

"Holding up," I said. "It's been hard on her, with Tania in jail." I gave him a meaningful look. "I'm sure she'd be very appreciative of anyone who was able to help her niece."

He stood up a little straighter. "Is that so? Well," he told me, finishing off his beer and crumpling the can in his hand, "I wouldn't mind Charlene being grateful to me. She's a looker, your friend."

"She is," I agreed.

"If I were you, I'd talk to that Sorenson boy. And ask around, see if you can find out who Derek's lady friend was. All I know is, she lives on Seal Point Road." His eyes twinkled malevolently. "Husbands can get mighty upset when they find out their wives've been playin' around while they're out haulin' traps."

"Seal Point Road? Anything else you know about her?"

He shook his head. "He just told me that's where he was headin' after we were done hauling traps. Although things had changed recently, I got the impression. She was bankrollin' him, somehow. Or someone was."

I thought of the drugs he had evidently been dealing at the school and guessed that was the source of Derek's newfound wealth. "Was he a good worker?" I asked.

Fred shrugged. "He was a typical young man. Too many hormones, and not enough sense."

"Tania mentioned he talked about some new opportunity that was coming up," I said.

"He was probably just trying to impress his girlfriend. Typical young buck." He gave me a knowing look. "Although the money was coming from somewhere."

"I'll look into it," I told him. "In the meantime, if there's anything else that you think of, please let me know."

"Will do," he said. He closed the door a moment later, and there was another burst of televised cheering from inside the small house.

As I walked down the porch, I caught another whiff of the beach roses. I'd been meaning to cut some for the tables in the dining room; maybe I could snip a few here before heading back to the inn. As I walked down the pine needle–strewn path toward the beach, I remembered how Fred's eyes had darted to the shed. The door was slightly ajar.

Glancing back at the house, I veered toward the shed, hoping Fred wasn't watching me. The house's shades were all shut tight, thankfully, so I decided to risk it, and slipped into the run-down building.

The shed appeared to be where tools and appliances went to die. The two high windows were grimy with years of dirt and cobwebs, but let enough light in to be able to make out headless brooms, a tube-style television, and a rusted bike buried among the piles of debris. My heart sank; there was nothing here to help me solve the mystery of what had happened to Derek Morton.

I took my time and examined everything anyway; since I was here, I might as well be thorough. As I listened for the sound of footsteps on the branches and pine needles outside, I ran my eyes over the piles, looking for anything that looked like it might have been discarded recently. The only thing that looked recently disturbed was an old brown tarp that had been spread over a pile in the near front corner. Unlike the rest of the objects in the shed, it wasn't felted with dust.

I stepped over a broken lawnmower and grabbed a corner. I drew in a breath at what was under it.

It was a gray dinghy—or what was left of one. The front had been smashed in, and from the pale wood exposed, it had happened recently. I bent down and took a close look at the smashed area, and wasn't surprised to find flakes of white paint. I was about to pull the tarp back over it when I spotted two cans of paint tucked up under what was left of the boat. One was turquoise, and the other was orange.

———

On the way home from Fred Penney's, on a whim, I decided to swing by and see how Zeke and Brad Forester were doing since the fire.

The farm appeared deserted when I arrived. The blackened remains of the shed reminded me of an empty socket in a mouthful of teeth; it looked strange in juxtaposition with the rows of verdant tomato, bean, and cucumber plants. Zeke had erected a tent-like shade structure next to where the shed had been; trays of washed carrots and beets were in bins on the tables.

I walked over to the farmhouse, figuring Zeke and Brad might be grabbing a snack inside—or maybe a nap—but no one came when I rang. I waited a few moments, then decided to walk around; it was a beautiful day, and I always loved seeing other people's vegetable gardens.

I walked down the nearest row toward the back of the property. Strawberry plants were lined up to my right, their red berries and white cup-like flowers like jewels against the green of the foliage, and to my left were the young plants of some member of the squash family. Watermelon, perhaps? My mouth watered at the thought of the crisp, crimson flesh—a real summer treat.

As I neared the end of the row, I heard voices. I paused, looking around, and realized they were coming from the barn. I opened my mouth to speak, but before I could say anything, I heard Zeke's angry voice.

"They're not going to intimidate me," he said. "As soon as my license comes through, I'm quitting."

"What about what happened to Derek?" It was another voice. Young, male. Not Brad's. "And your shed. They mean business."

Zeke gave a bitter laugh. "That's why I have a shotgun by my bed. They won't mess with me."

"I think you're making a mistake," the young man warned. "What if they come after Brad?"

"I'll look after Brad," the farmer said.

"It's your funeral." I heard footsteps, and hurried away from the barn, kneeling to inspect a strawberry. When the door opened, I pretended I hadn't heard it, instead busying myself by admiring the red fruit.

"What are you doing here?"

I looked up to see Zeke Forester looking at me in a less-than-welcoming manner. The barn door was already closed tight behind him, and a few yards away, Evan Sorenson stared at me, looking spooked.

"These berries look terrific," I said. "I was thinking of making strawberry shortcake tonight. Do you have any ready to go?"

The farmer's face relaxed. He threaded a short chain through the handles of the barn door and padlocked them shut, then walked down the row toward me. "I picked a few this morning, but haven't had a chance to wash them yet."

"I can take care of that," I said. "Are these watermelon plants?" I asked, trying to keep my voice relaxed as I stabbed a finger at the row of sprawling young plants.

"Sure are. Moon and Stars," he said. "They're huge, and speckled. Forty pounds, some of them. Brad loves how they look—that's why I planted them."

"Can't wait. I love watermelon, too." I smiled and decided to take a risk. "How's the barn renovation going?"

"Fine," he said shortly, the ease instantly evaporated from his voice.

"It's too bad about the shed," I continued. "Any plans to build a new one, or are you using the barn?"

"We'll see," he said. "I'm too busy weeding these days to think of building. Maybe this fall." We reached the end of the row. "How many pints of strawberries do you want?"

"Three should do," I said. "Drat; I forgot my checkbook again. I hate to ask, but ..."

He glanced up at me. "I'll put it on your tab."

"I pay interest in brownies," I joked as he eased three plastic baskets into a paper bag and handed them to me. "How's the dairy plan going?" I asked, wondering about the exchange in the barn.

"It all depends on Murray," he said. "Any luck talking to Catherine about it?"

"I asked her to bring it up, but I don't know if she's spoken to him yet."

"I'd love to have things in place by the end of summer," Zeke said. "So I can get them going on the pasture."

"I'll be sure to follow up," I told him.

"Will that be all?" He adjusted his cap, looking impatient to get away.

"That's it for now." I smiled. "Thanks, and please say hi to Brad for me. We'll enjoy these!"

As I walked back toward the inn, I tried to puzzle out what I'd overheard. At first I'd thought Zeke had been talking about his dairy license, but if the limiting factor was Murray's willingness to rent him land, that clearly wasn't it.

Who was trying to intimidate the farmer? I had suspected the shed fire wasn't an accident, and apparently Evan shared my opinion. But he also seemed to think he knew who was responsible for killing Derek Morton, and Zeke hadn't contradicted him.

Something was going on at Zeke's farm—something that might shed light on who had murdered Derek Morton. And the best way to find out what it was, I thought, was to take a peek into that carefully guarded barn.

EIGHTEEN

My mind was elsewhere as I ushered Beryl and Agnes into the van early that afternoon, with Catherine sitting next to me in the front. She had dressed in a silk blouse and slacks for the occasion, along with kitten heel pumps. Her hair was in a little French twist that looked like something Grace Kelly would wear. I had dressed more practically, in jeans, a polo shirt, and my old sneakers. Beryl and Agnes were slumming it, too; after all, we were going to be poking around an abandoned building.

Beryl handed me a photograph before we got into the van. "Is that your grandfather?" I asked. The image showed a tall, lean man in a clerical collar. An ornate gold crucifix around his neck.

"It sure is," she said.

"Good-looking guy." I handed it back to Agnes. "Where did the fancy cross come from?"

"It came from Italy," she said. "According to family history, my grandfather's great-uncle was a Catholic priest, and gave it to my grandfather when he decided to take the cloth. He wasn't Catholic, but it was a family heirloom. Apparently it originated in Italy."

"I didn't know you were Italian," I said.

"On my mother's side," she said as we bumped up the road from the inn. "It's where my dark hair comes from. Or what used to be dark hair." She grimaced as she touched her salt-and-pepper braid.

"It's still beautiful," I told her. "Did Matilda come up with any new information?"

"She found the church records from the time," Agnes told me. "Apparently he was a talented priest; his congregation swelled from the time he came to the time he left. People even came from the mainland to hear him preach."

"Must have been charismatic," I told her.

"Yes … but it doesn't make sense," Beryl pointed out. "The letters with the bishop in Canada indicated that his congregation was shrinking."

"And we looked it up," Agnes said. "His bishop was in Bangor, not Canada."

That was strange. "Did she find anything about the bishop in Nova Scotia?"

"No record yet. She's still looking, though."

"You're right," I said to Beryl. "It doesn't make sense. Was he doing some other kind of ministry? Going to different islands and preaching?"

"Not that we can find," Agnes said. "We even contacted the diocese headquarters in Bangor, but there's no record of him preaching anywhere but here during the time he was installed on the island."

I glanced up at the rearview mirror. "Do you know if he traveled to Canada?"

Beryl shook her head. "Not that I know of. I don't know what to make of it."

"If it's solvable, I'm sure Matilda will figure it out."

"Matilda is going to meet us at the rectory," Agnes said.

"Are you going to explore with us?" I asked Catherine, who had been sitting quietly in the front seat beside me.

"I'll probably go and visit Murray while you gals poke around," she said.

"Probably a wise choice. You look really nice today; I'd hate to see your blouse get dirty." As I spoke, we rounded a bend and found Murray's sprawling house in front of us. While the rest of the island was populated by quaint shingle-style and clapboard houses, Murray's was built of pink brick, with a circular drive on which his Jaguar was parked. It hadn't always been this way, of course; before Murray made his money in development, Charlene told me, the Selfridge home had been a typical clapboard house, complete with a tower from which wives could presumably search for their husbands.

Now, though, there was a house that looked like it had been picked up from Dallas and plunked down on Cranberry Island. If this is what Murray had in mind for his island developments, I was very thankful nothing had come to fruition. I was also thankful the driveway to his home was long and heavily treed.

The original rectory—or what was left of it—was off to the right, its simple white clapboard looking very incongruous next to its enormous brick neighbor.

"Does he have plans for it?" I asked.

"He's thinking of replacing it with a cabana," Catherine said.

"A cabana?"

She pointed to the pit in the ground beside it. "To go with the pool."

I looked at the dark hole from which the bones had been excavated and suppressed a shiver. How long had they lain there? And who had put them there? Although work had stopped for a bit, it seemed to be moving ahead now; a young man with a spade was deep in the pit.

"My grandfather's resting place," Beryl said.

"Just think," Agnes said. "If Murray hadn't decided to put in a pool, you never would have known what happened to my grandfather."

"We still don't," Beryl pointed out.

"I can't imagine putting in a pool on Cranberry Island," I mused, looking at the muddy pit. "It'll be heated, I hope."

"Of course," Catherine volunteered. "We're not polar bears. Now, if you'll drop me off at the house, that would be terrific; I'd hate to get muddy. I'm excited to hear what you find, though!"

"We'll let you know," I said, pulling up into the circular drive in front of the house. I waited until Murray answered the door. He gave us a quick wave, and headed to the car with a stack of papers.

"What's this?" I asked.

"Waivers," he said as a drift of Polo cologne wafted through the car window. He'd dressed for Catherine's arrival, in khakis and a pressed checked shirt. "Just in case something happens."

Only Murray would ask for legal papers, I thought.

As I handed them back to my guests, Murray said, "Catherine talked me into renting some more land to that young farmer."

"Really?" I said, not quite sure how to react. Yesterday, I would have thought that was a great idea. After what I had seen that morning, I wasn't so sure. "How about the school?"

"What about it?" he asked.

"I heard you're voting to shut it down."

"Natalie." Catherine gave me a warning look, which I ignored.

"It's a tax burden," he said.

"We'll have to pay taxes whether there's a school on the island or not," I pointed out. "This way, we have a year-round community here."

"It's not necessary." Murray's already ruddy face turned a darker shade of red.

"Who's going to take care of your resort people?" I asked. "Who's going to run the store, or build boats? Claudette's grandkids will have to move off-island."

"I thought you were here to go through the old rectory," he said, his ears reddening.

"Oh, yes. Thank you for that," Beryl piped up from the back seat. "Here are my forms, and Agnes's."

"Mine too," I said, reading through the pages quickly and signing at the bottom. I didn't speak legalese, but at least I didn't see any verbiage about giving him ownership of the inn.

"Is Matilda here?" Beryl asked.

"She's already at the rectory," he said.

"I appreciate you giving us the opportunity to check it out," I told him as I signed my form and handed it over. "And I'm sorry if I sounded sharp, but the school is important to the island. Please think about it."

He glanced at Catherine, who smiled at him. "She does have a point."

I could have hugged her.

"I'll let you get on with your day," I told him. "Thanks again."

"Let us know if you find anything," Catherine called. "And be careful!"

I turned around in the circular drive and parked near the pool site.

"You're pretty hot about that school, aren't you?" Beryl asked.

"I thought you were going to nix the whole rectory thing," said Agnes.

"Sorry about that. I'm just frustrated, that all."

"Well, we're here," Beryl said as I pulled in next to Matilda's ancient Dodge Omni. Like many vehicles on the island, the passenger door was held on with duct tape. "Come on," she said, and I got out of the van and followed my guests down a short, pine needle–strewn path to the old rectory.

"Halloo!" Matilda called as we got close to the run-down structure, her close-cropped hair gleaming bright white in the afternoon sun. "I've waited for you!"

"Did Murray make you sign a waiver, too?"

She peered at me over her glasses. "Are you kidding me? Of course. But we're in, so who cares?"

I surveyed the old building. "It's not in great shape, is it?"

The warped door was wide open, but the windows had long ago been boarded up. It was a small structure; probably only enough room for a bedroom, a kitchen, and a small living area. "I'm surprised he didn't tear the whole thing down."

"He's oddly frugal in some ways," Matilda said.

"But not others." I stared pointedly at the enormous hole in the ground that was slated for a pool. A pool that could probably be used for six weeks out of the year.

When we got to the front door, we all hesitated. I peered into the dark building; the wood floorboards were coated with dust and debris. "Do you think it's safe?" I asked.

"I imagine so," Matilda said. "Here goes."

The boards creaked as she walked in, but nothing seemed to give way. She snapped on a flashlight—I was impressed she'd thought to bring it—and ran the beam around the dim room. Beryl followed, eyes wide, and then Agnes.

"So this is where my grandfather lived," Beryl said. "Not very big, was it?"

"His family was in Bangor," Agnes reminded her. "He didn't need much space."

"It's a shame there isn't any furniture here," Matilda said. There was a cracked mirror hanging on one wall, and a pile of old newspapers in the corner, but the front room, which must once have been a living room, was empty.

"Not much of a kitchen, either," Beryl observed from a low-hanging doorway. I peered over her shoulder; the space couldn't have been more than six feet long. There were a sink and some falling-down shelves; if there had once been an oven or a refrigerator, they were long gone. "I can see why they changed the location of the rectory," I said.

"I just wish there were more here," Agnes said, walking into the small bedroom, which was also empty.

"It has been vacant for more than fifty years," Matilda pointed out. "It's not common to walk in and find things just as they were."

"I'm kind of disappointed," Beryl said. As she spoke, she took a step forward. There was a loud crack, and her right leg shot through the floor.

She caught herself with her hands as I hurried over to her. "Are you okay?"

"I think so," she said, her voice tight with pain. "Help me up, would you?"

Together we hauled her out, and inspected her leg. "Is it broken?" I asked.

"I don't think so," she said, bending it experimentally. "Just bruised and a little scraped up. Thank goodness I wore jeans today!"

"And thank goodness you didn't go all the way through," I added, staring at the hole in the floor where her leg had gone through and then inspecting the floorboards under my own feet. They seemed solid, but after what had just happened, I suspected all of us were nervous. As much as I hated to admit it, Murray had been smart to have us sign waivers. "You've had a heck of a week," I told both women. "First the accident in the skiff, and now this."

Agnes grinned. "At least it hasn't been dull."

I looked down at the floorboards. They seemed solid, but who knew? "We should probably get out of here," I said.

"First I want to find out if there's a cellar access," Matilda said.

"Other than that one, you mean," I said, pointing to the jagged hole in the floor. She approached it gingerly, aiming the light through the hole.

"See anything?" Beryl asked.

"Actually, yes," she said. "It looks like a bunch of bottles." She stood up and looked around. "Surely there's an access point."

"I didn't see any doors," I told her.

"Is there one outside, maybe?" Matilda asked. We were all relieved to file out the front door and circle the small house from the exterior.

Unfortunately, though, there was no sign of any access from the outside.

After inspecting the house multiple times, we stood outside the front door, reluctant to go back inside.

"There's got to be an access somewhere," Matilda said.

"I'm not sure it's safe to look for it, though. Beryl could have fallen all the way through."

"I'm going back in." The historian's jaw was set and her voice full of resolve.

"Matilda . . ."

"If I fall, just haul me out," she said firmly.

I groaned as she headed back in, training the flashlight on the floor. "All right, I'll join you," I said a moment later. I couldn't let her go in alone. As I followed her cautiously, I found myself regretting the second helping of coffee cake I'd had that morning, and tried to think light thoughts.

Keeping a safe distance from the wiry historian and skirting the hole in the floor, I watched as she studied the floors and walls, feeling them with knotted hands. She made the rounds of each room, including the kitchen, but came up empty.

"There's got to be an access somewhere," she said. "I've checked everywhere."

"What about those papers?" I asked, pointing to the unruly stack in the corner. "There might be something under there."

"It's worth a try, I suppose," she said. Together, we relocated the stack—"From the late '20s," she noted—and sneezed at the clouds of dust that rose in a cloud. When we got the last of them shifted, she shone the light over the area, but the floor looked just like the wood in the rest of the room. "So much for that," Matilda said, frustration in her voice.

"Wait. What's that?" I directed her light toward a slender seam in the wood.

"You're right, Natalie. There's something there!"

I brushed the dust away; there was definitely a seam there. "A trap door," I suggested.

"Looks like it. A big one, too. But how do we open it?"

I looked around the room for something to use to pry it open, but there was nothing available. "Maybe there's something in the kitchen, or outside," I suggested.

"I'll check the kitchen," she said. "You go look for a branch or something."

"We'll see if we can find something," Beryl said from the door. I sat near the door while Matilda tiptoed to the kitchen. "There's a bent butter knife in here," she called to me. "Think that will work?"

"It's worth a try."

She tiptoed back, glancing at the hole in the floor, and slid the thin blade of the knife into the seam and lifted. A section of the floor came up about an inch, and I grabbed the edge and pushed it up farther.

"Bingo," she said in a low voice as we both peered down into the murky depths of the cellar, which smelled of must and earth. A rickety staircase led into the darkness, and my thoughts turned to the bones buried just yards away.

"Ready?" she asked.

"Are you sure it's safe?" I asked.

"Not at all," she said drily, with a glance at the hole in the floor. "But I'm dying to know what's down there."

Before I could protest, she was already on the first step. It creaked ominously, but didn't give. "So far, so good," she said.

"What did you find?" Beryl called from the doorway.

"It's a staircase to the cellar," I told her. "Matilda's going down."

"Is it safe?"

"I doubt it," I told her honestly, then returned my attention to Matilda. "What do you see?" I asked the historian.

"It's amazing down here," she said from near the bottom of the ladder. "Like a time capsule. You should come see. The ladder seems perfectly safe."

Despite her assertions, I waited until she was all the way down before braving the first step. I didn't know if it could hold one person, much less two—and I had been hitting the pastries a bit hard lately.

"You coming?"

"Be right there." Saying a brief prayer, I lowered myself onto the first step. It bowed under my weight, but didn't break. Carefully, I made my way down the rest of the ancient staircase—which was more like a graduated ladder than a staircase—to where Matilda was flashing her light on a stack of dusty bottles.

"Isn't this incredible?" she breathed. "I'll bet nobody's been down here in ninety years."

"Are these all full?" There were hundreds of them, I realized, coated with dust. Some were stacked in wooden pallets, and others were crammed into makeshift shelves lining the wall.

"They seem to be." Matilda picked up a bottle, pried out the cork, and held it out to me. "Take a sniff."

I lowered my nose cautiously and took a light whiff that just about seared my nose hairs. "Good God. What is it?"

"Whiskey." She shone the light on the bottle; the liquid inside glowed amber beneath the dust, and a label proclaimed it as Toronto Club Whiskey. She ran the light around the basement; there were crates and crates of bottles. The basement was significantly bigger than the house above it. "This place is enormous," she said.

"What's that?" I asked, pointing to a contraption in the corner. There were two large metal containers linked by a narrow tube; the whole thing was felted with dust.

She walked closer. "I think it's a still."

"As in for making moonshine?"

"I think the reverend was spreading more than the good word, Natalie," she said slowly, running her light over a line of barrels that were tucked behind the still.

NINETEEN

"I've often heard that rum runners used Smuggler's Cove," Matilda said, still staring at the bottle. "Now I know who it was."

"You really think a priest was responsible for this?" I asked.

"What better cover?" She glanced at me. "Nobody's going to go after the local priest."

"Apparently someone did," I pointed out.

She replaced the cork on the bottle. "True."

"Natalie?" It was Beryl, from somewhere up above us. "What did you find?"

"Lots of bottles," I called up. "I'll be right up." As I headed for the bottom of the ladder, Matilda's light found a crate of empty bottles stacked in front of a line of barrels. "Aha."

"What?"

"I think I know why someone may have done him in."

I paused. "Why?"

"Ever heard of the Real McCoy?" she asked.

"You mentioned him the other day," I said. "But what does that have to do with this basement?"

"McCoy was a rum runner who was known for importing genuine liquor. He used to go up and down the Atlantic seaboard, smuggling Canadian whiskey, among other things."

"And?"

"Well, we've got a basement full of liquor bottles marked Canadian whiskey here. And some of them are empty." She flashed her light on the crate nearest the still.

"And there's a still ..." All of a sudden the letters Beryl had showed me popped into my mind. "He was corresponding with a Canadian bishop who was complaining about his congregation thinning." I looked up at Matilda. "Do you think the 'bishop' was a rum runner?"

"That would be my guess," she said. "I'm guessing Beryl's grandfather started smuggling Canadian whiskey, but then started manufacturing his own whiskey and passing it off as Canadian stuff."

"We're coming down," Beryl called from the top of the ladder. One by one, the two climbed down the ladder to join us in the dusty cellar.

"Oh, my word," Beryl breathed when she took in what was around us.

"It's a surprise, isn't it?" Matilda asked.

"I think we've figured out who killed your grandfather," I told her.

"You're kidding me," she said.

"We're guessing his Canadian bishop was a rum runner, and your grandfather was making moonshine."

She gulped. "My grandfather? The priest?"

"And rum runner," I added.

Matilda piped up, "Don't forget distiller."

———

By the time we emerged into the sunlight, Matilda and Beryl had located a stack of labels and a ledger that showed a rather active business venture, but no sign of any cash. We all surmised that whoever had done in Beryl's grandfather had taken any cash on hand with him (or her), and abandoned the whiskey as second-rate. "What a find," Matilda said, as she headed up to the house. "I'll let you know what Murray says; I'm hoping he'll let me make an exhibit out of it!"

Beryl was thoughtful on the way back to the inn. We all had dust and cobwebs in our hair, and I, for one, was looking forward to a shower. "I wish I knew who that 'bishop' was. I'm pretty sure he was responsible for my grandfather's death."

"I'll bet Matilda can help you with that," she said. "She's got contacts all over the place."

"It's just so sad." Her voice sounded hollow. "If he hadn't been involved in rum running, I might have gotten a chance to know him."

"People do all kinds of strange things," I said.

"What do you think happened to all the money he earned?" Agnes asked.

"I bet I know," Beryl said.

We all looked at her in surprise.

"I didn't say anything before, but my grandmother had mental problems," she said. "The reason the kids were in Bangor was so that my great-grandparents could take care of them. She spent a lot of time in institutions. I always figured my great-grandparents paid for it, but now I think it may have been my grandfather."

"So he might have gotten into rum running for a good cause?"

"The end justifying the means, so to speak," Catherine suggested. "Too bad it didn't work out for him."

———

When Agnes and Beryl were settled, I picked up the phone and dialed the Whites. "Hey, Eli," I said into the phone when my friend answered. One mystery might have been solved—or at least the motive figured out—but I still needed to make progress on the more recent one.

"Natalie! How's the new skiff doing?"

"Just fine," I said.

"You name her yet?"

"Not yet. Hey … can I ask you a favor?"

"Anything for a woman who makes the best brownies in Maine."

I chuckled. "I promise I'll bring you a batch soon. In the meantime, do you know where Fred Penney moors his lobster boat?"

"Absolutely," he said, "since it almost never leaves these days. Why?"

"I have a hunch she may be our false *Zephyr*," I told him. "Has he asked for a new skiff lately?"

"Now that you mention it, yes. I just sold a new one to him a few days back. Why didn't I think of that?"

"Can we take a look this afternoon?"

"I'll be right over," he said.

It was less than fifteen minutes before Eli showed up at my back door. I handed him a bag of brownies from my freezer, and his eyes lit up.

"Don't tell Claudie," he said. "She'd kill me."

"My lips are sealed," I said, knowing his wife's insistence on sugar-free everything. He took one out and popped it into his mouth, even though it was frozen, as I followed him down to the dock. "You make a mean brownie, Miss Barnes," he told me once he'd swallowed.

"Thanks." I grinned at him.

"Which skiff you want to take?" he asked.

"Why don't we take yours?" I suggested. "I'm still breaking mine in."

"With your track record, I'm a bit worried about the breaking," he joked as I hopped into the little boat and helped him untie it.

It was only a few minutes before we were in Cranberry Island's small harbor. Fred's lobster boat was moored on the far end, away from the pier. "Could be her," Eli mused as we drew closer. The buoy on the front was navy and red, not turquoise and blue, and the name emblazoned on the back of the boat in peeling paint was, appropriately, *Lazy Susan*.

"How could you change the name of the boat?" I asked.

"Paint a sign on a board and hang it on the back," he suggested. "Replace the buoy, and you're a new boat."

"Can you get a little closer?" I asked. He slowed the motor and drew up behind the lobster boat. I wasn't surprised to see two shiny nails driven into the stern of the boat. "I wish we could go aboard and see if we could find that buoy. I found paint cans in Fred's shed."

Eli glanced back at the island. "I won't tell if you won't."

I stared at him. "But we'll be seen!"

"Not if you board from the starboard side," he said. "Be quick about it, and crouch down low. I'll go a short ways off and cast a line." He picked up his fishing rod. "When you're ready, give me a shout and I'll come back and get you."

He drew close enough to the lobster boat for me to clamber onto it. "Are you sure?"

"I'll be back in five," he said. "Gonna catch me a mackerel."

"More like a red herring," I muttered and clambered aboard.

Speaking of herring, there was less of a smell of it than I expected, compared to my experiences on Adam's lobster boat. I hunched down, trying to stay out of sight, and half-crawled into the wheelhouse.

The first cabinet held old, water-stained charts, and the second held life jackets. The third had all kinds of tools, along with extra gas and oil, and the fourth was stuffed with dirty old towels. I was about to close it when I caught a glimpse of orange.

Eagerly, I pushed the towels aside. I'd found the orange and turquoise buoy. And behind it was a rolled-up piece of canvas. When I opened it, I wasn't surprised to find the words *Green Zephyr*.

I shoved the two things back into the compartment and rearranged the towels, then squatted down to think. Fred Penney was the driver of the faux *Green Zephyr*. But why? And if he wasn't out lobstering, what was he doing?

I headed toward the stern of the boat, to the bins where the lobsters are kept. I opened the lid to one to find it filled with water. But the other was dry. I leaned in, wondering why there were granules of what looked like dirt spread along the bottom of the compartment. When I took a whiff, I realized it was pepper.

For a few more minutes, I poked around the boat, but found nothing. I gave Eli a wave, and he came looping back; I hopped back into the skiff and we were off.

"Find anything?" he asked.

"She's the other *Zephyr*," I said. "The buoy and a canvas sign are tucked into a compartment in the front."

"Anything else of interest?" His intelligent eyes were bright.

"One of the lobster compartments was empty, except for a bit of black pepper."

"Pepper?"

"I know," I said. "Weird."

"He's up to something," Eli said.

"How do we find out what?"

"Only way I can figure is to follow him," Eli suggested.

"Actually, I think I know when it'll be at Smuggler's Cove next," I told him.

"What, are you psychic?"

"No." I told him about the list of dates and times I'd found at Derek's house—including the closest date on the list.

"That's tomorrow night, isn't it?" he asked.

I nodded.

"Need some help?"

"I'd love it," I said.

"Count me in."

TWENTY

I WAS STILL RESTLESS when Eli dropped me off back at the inn. Nobody was around, so I set to work assembling a cake for the next morning as I ran through everything I knew, ignoring Biscuit's plaintive meow from her customary perch on the radiator. I couldn't stake out Smuggler's Cove tonight—but there were other things I could do. I grabbed a turtle bar from the cookie jar and picked up the phone, chewing as I dialed.

Charlene answered on the third ring. "Cranberry Island Post Office and Store."

"It's Natalie."

"Any news?"

"Lots of it," I said, and told her all I'd discovered as I measured flour into a bowl for streusel.

"But you can't find out about the *Zephyr* until tomorrow night," she said. "You're stuck."

"Not completely. Something's going on in that barn," I told her.

"Why do you say that?" she asked.

I told her about the conversation I'd overheard between Zeke and Evan.

"Evan thinks Derek's death is linked to something involved with the farm?"

"Exactly" I replied. "I've been trying to figure it out. I think something's going on in there—that's why Zeke didn't want the cops to investigate the fire, and that's why he scares everyone away from the barn."

"Well then. When are we going to check it out?"

"It's not that easy," I told her as Biscuit wove between my legs. I cut the butter into the streusel and added walnuts, my mouth already watering. The creamy batter was finished and waiting. "It's padlocked shut."

"It's an old barn, isn't it?" Charlene asked. "Surely there's another way in."

"He guards it pretty carefully. I'd be surprised if he was that careless."

"We'll never know until we try, will we? How about tonight?"

"John will kill me."

"Just tell him you're coming to visit me," she said. "Bring some cookies. It'll make it more convincing."

"I'm out of Caramel Turtles," I warned her.

"That's okay. I like your shortbread and brownies, too."

I laughed and promised to meet her at her house at eight. We'd go over just after sunset. "Wear dark clothes," she reminded me. "And bring a flashlight."

"Anything else?" I grinned.

"I'd say a gun, but neither of us has one," she said, her chipper voice suddenly solemn. "I'll bring my mace, though."

"See you then," I said, giving the streusel a final stir.

———

"What did you tell John?" Charlene asked when I arrived at 8:00. Whereas I had worn dark jeans and a navy windbreaker, she wore a black sweat suit with the words *Maine Squeeze* picked out in rhinestones on the front.

"I didn't," I said sheepishly as I walked into her small but cozy house. "But I left him a note."

"Where is he?"

"Helping out down at Island Artists."

"He's going to kill you, you know," she said, arching a plucked eyebrow. "If whoever killed Derek doesn't get to it first."

I shivered at the thought. "Got a flashlight?"

"Yup. And I decided on a crowbar instead of mace. It's more multi-functional."

"Thinking of prying up a board?"

"Or hitting someone over the head. You never know what you'll need to be prepared to do," she countered. "Ready?"

"I think so."

"Should we take a car, or walk?"

"Let's walk," I suggested. "That way no one will ask why we were parked near the farm." On an island the size of Cranberry Island, any aberration was fodder for gossip.

Despite my nervousness about what we were going to do, it was a lovely evening for a walk. It was cool, but not too cool, and the moon was almost full, illuminating the road so that we didn't need a flashlight. It was almost twenty minutes before we came upon the farm.

"Looks like someone's home," Charlene murmured. The downstairs lights were on in the farmhouse, giving it a cozy, warm glow. "Should we wait?"

I gazed at the house, then looked toward the shadowy hulk I knew was the barn. "It's a pretty long way between the house and the barn. I think we'll be okay."

"Lead on, then," she told me.

Instead of crossing the fields, I moved back to the far edge of the property, near the woods, and skirted the edge of the property, glancing back nervously toward the house as we approached the barn. Fortunately, everything stayed peaceful as we inched up to the big front doors. The padlock gleamed in the moonlight. I reached for it; the door was unlocked, the Yale lock dangling from the latch.

"Now what?" Charlene whispered.

"I'm just going to open the door a crack," I said. "There might be someone in there."

Carefully, I pulled on the handle. It stuck for a moment, and then the door swung out a few inches, spilling bright light out on the grass. A familiar scent wafted out as I pushed it back quickly, my heart pounding, and scuttled to the side of the barn, Charlene on my heels.

"Is someone in there?" Charlene asked in a low voice.

"I don't know," I said, "but I'm not sure I want to risk it." The darkness seemed to fall down on us like a cloak; the thick pines to the side of the building blotted the moonlight.

"Should I turn on the flashlight?" my friend whispered.

"Not yet," I said, squinting up at a slice of light coming from the second story of the barn, illuminating the branches of the pines. "Did you smell anything when the door opened?" I asked.

"I thought I caught a whiff of black pepper," she said.

"Me too." I thought of the pepper in Fred's lobster boat. Another connection. But what kind of connection was it?

"This makes me nervous," my friend confessed, gripping my sleeve with a manicured hand.

"I know, but we've got to find out what's going on. We're here for Tania," I reminded her.

"I know," she said. "But are you sure this barn has anything to do with Derek?"

I was about to answer when I heard voices. Charlene tightened her grip, and we both peered around the corner. The door creaked open, and two people exited.

"Everything's boxed up and ready to go," said one of them. Zeke Forester.

"You're sure nobody's onto us?" It was Evan. "I can't afford to get caught."

"I made sure there was no connection; nobody knows about us. Besides, this is the last time," he said. "Then we won't have to worry."

"You talked with him?"

Zeke's voice was steely. "I've told him my intentions. I won't let threats stop me."

"You didn't tell him I was involved, did you?"

"It's between him and me," Zeke said. "You'll be safe."

"Derek wasn't," Evan said.

It sounded like Zeke sighed. "He brought it on himself. Now, let's get this over with." Together, Zeke and Evan carried four boxes out of the barn, setting them on the ground just outside the door. Zeke reset the padlock, then each of them picked up a box. One of them turned on a flashlight, and both headed toward the woods on the other side of the barn.

"What do we do now?" Charlene asked.

"I'll follow them," I said, watching the bobbing light recede into darkness. "You try and figure out what's in those boxes."

"What if they see you?" She clutched at my arm.

"I'll tell them I was out for a stroll," I said, and before I could talk myself out of it, I shook off her hand and hurried after them.

It was tough going; I was trying to keep up, but without making too much noise or walking into a tree. Although the moon helped, the trees made everything shadowy, and the path was narrow and winding. Thankfully, the light was a good distance ahead of me, and the sound of the water crashing against rocks somewhere not too far in the distance helped mask the crack of twigs as I fumbled through the forest.

The path exited on the shore, and whoever held the flashlight shone it briefly at the dark water; the light illuminated the foam as the waves broke near shore. Seaweed littered the rocks; the tide was low, and the air smelled strongly of fish and brine.

There was a skiff pulled up on the rocky shore. As I watched, the two men loaded the boxes onto the little boat. Evan stayed behind with the boat as Zeke hurried back toward the farm. I hoped Charlene had worked quickly.

It was ten minutes before Zeke arrived carrying the rest of the boxes. He put them in the back of the skiff, then the two men pushed the skiff into the water, with Evan at the rudder. Zeke gave him a quick wave as he motored off into the darkness.

I waited until Zeke was long gone back up the path before I followed.

———

"What did you find?" I hissed when I got back to our hiding spot. Charlene jumped about three feet.

"Don't do that, Nat!"

"Sorry," I mumbled. "So. What was in the boxes?"

"I couldn't tell," she said. "They were taped shut. They smelled like peppercorns, though. It was hard not to sneeze."

"Are they back in the barn?" I asked.

"I don't know about Evan, but Zeke is back at the house. Evan relocked the padlock when he came back for the boxes."

"Did you peek into the barn?"

"I was too scared," she confessed.

I looked up at the window near the peak of the barn. Light still spilled out, illuminating the branches of the trees. If no one was in the barn, I wondered, why was the light still on?

"Let's see if we can peek inside," I told her.

"Are you sure it's okay? Where's Evan?"

"He took off in a skiff," I said. "I think we've got at least a few minutes." Together, we walked around the old building, looking for cracks in the siding or loose boards to pry up, but the barn was sealed tight. "I thought he said this place was falling apart," I murmured to Charlene.

"It's pretty darned tight. Not even a chink for light to come through."

I patted the side of the building. "He's sealed it up tight."

"What's he up to, do you think?"

"I don't know," I said, "but it's not something he wants people to know about."

"Should we call Detective Johnson?" she asked.

"If we do, what are we going to tell him? We have no idea what he's doing in there."

"True. But at least they'll investigate."

"They haven't done a stellar job to date," I said. "That's why I want to call them ... but not yet. If this is connected with what happened to Derek, I want to find out how before they seal it all off."

"What about John?" she asked.

I thought about that for a moment. "I guess I should tell him."

"Aren't you and Eli going to stake out Smuggler's Cove, too?" I'd told her about our plan.

"Wait a moment," I said. "It's low tide right now, isn't it?"

"It is."

"And the next date and time on that page is tomorrow night at low tide. The next high tide is in the middle of the day"

She drew in a breath. "Were they taking those boxes to Smuggler's Cove, do you think?"

"I'll bet they were," I said.

"Do you think we have time to slip in and out tonight?"

"There's no way we'd get back to the inn and out to the cove in time," I said. "But we could make it during low tide tomorrow morning." I shivered at the prospect.

"What are you going to tell John?"

I sighed. "I'll make it up as I go along, I guess," I said as we began heading back to Charlene's.

The walk back seemed longer, somehow, even though Charlene had seemed happier tonight than I'd seen her since Tania was arrested.

"I just wish there were some way to link whatever's going on in that barn to Derek's death," I said as we walked.

"You've got the buoy and the skiff," she pointed out.

"Yes, but we don't know how that's related to what's happening in that barn. Plus, there's no link to Derek."

"Evan said something about a connection, didn't he?"

"Yes, but he didn't say what. Besides, he just thought he suspected. It didn't sound like he knew." I sighed. "Maybe John will be able to come up with something." I'd have to explain what Charlene and I had been up to tonight. Not something I was looking forward to.

"Speaking of John, how are the wedding plans coming?" she asked.

"The resort we were going to have it at went out of business," I told her. "Our deposit's gone."

"Oh, no," she breathed. "What are you going to do?"

"We've got a plan." I told her what John and I had discussed.

"That sounds like a terrific idea," she said.

"I think so too. But it all depends on whether we can get Tania off the hook in time. And to be honest, I don't even want to think about a wedding until I know she's okay."

Charlene reached over and squeezed my hand. "Well, then. We'd better get over to Smuggler's Cove tomorrow!"

We arrived at her house, and as she let herself in the door, I hopped into the van and turned back toward home, my thoughts on Zeke Forester—and that mysterious barn.

———

"You did what?" John blinked at me.

"We walked around the barn and saw them moving boxes," I reiterated. John had gotten the note I'd left him. Since I'd taken the van, he'd been about to ride his bike over to the farm when I'd walked in, and was as angry as I'd ever seen him.

"You didn't tell me?"

"I thought you wouldn't approve," I said.

"You were right," he said. "I also don't approve of you sneaking into murder victims' houses or going places where you could be killed. Nat, think. If Zeke Forester is into something illegal and spotted you, what do you think he might have done?"

"He wouldn't have killed me," I said.

"You have no idea if he would have killed you! For all we know, he put a bullet in Derek Morton's back!"

"But he didn't seem to know about that," I protested.

"That's what he wants Evan to think, anyway," John said. "You have no idea what that man is capable of."

"You don't own me," I said.

"Own you?" He ran a hand through his hair. "You think this is about ownership?" He bridged the gap between us and pulled me into his arms, hugging me tight. "Don't you understand?"

"What?" I mumbled into his chest, inhaling his spicy, woodsy scent.

"I love you," he said, his voice fierce. "If something happened to you, I don't know what I'd do. You are the most precious thing on this earth to me."

My heart melted, and a wave of guilt broke over me. "I'm sorry," I said.

"I'm sorry I was so angry," he answered, still holding me tight. "It's just …" His voice was rough. "It took me my whole life to find you. I couldn't bear to lose you."

"I'm here," I told him. "I'm fine."

"Thank God," he murmured. He gave me a long squeeze and let me go, but still held my hand. "But I think it's time to call Detective Johnson."

"Why?" I asked.

"Because we know Zeke Forester is likely doing something illegal, and it might be connected with Derek's death. They can get a warrant and search the barn."

"That's why I don't want to call him yet," I told him. "Look at what they missed at Derek's house. Besides, the next time and date on that paper is tomorrow night. If Evan did what I think he did tonight, those boxes I saw will still be in Smuggler's Cove tomorrow morning at low tide."

"If you're right," he said. "A big if. And if you are, why the intermediate step?" he asked.

"What do you mean?"

"Forester obviously doesn't want anyone to know about what he's transporting," John said. "Why not just pick it up directly from the farm? Why take the risk of storing things in the cove? Assuming you're right, of course, and that's where it's going."

"Zeke didn't seem to want anyone to know what he was up to. Maybe it's to minimize his involvement."

"But somebody's got to know."

"An middleman, maybe? Somebody he trusts?"

"Maybe," John said.

"Whatever it is, he seems to think it's going to end soon. Maybe the cows he's applied to have here are going to supplement his income enough that he doesn't need to do illegal work anymore."

"If whoever is relying on him knows about that, it might explain why someone set his shed on fire."

"A warning," I suggested. "He talked about that. Said he wouldn't be intimidated."

"Tell me about the barn," John said.

"He says it's derelict, but it's locked up tight, and there aren't any cracks in the boards. And there's a light on even when nobody's there."

"Interesting," he said. "How about those boxes?"

"They smelled like black pepper," I said. "Just like the compartment in Fred's boat."

"Fred's boat?"

"Um, yes." Blushing slightly, I told him about Eli's and my trip to visit the fake *Zephyr*.

"Dear God, Natalie." He stared at me in disbelief. "You snuck onto Fred Penney's boat?"

"Eli was with me," I said. "It was his suggestion that I jump on. And I need to solve this. Tania didn't do it, and the police are doing a shoddy job investigating. We both know that."

He sighed. "I may not let you leave my side again until this is all worked out," he said.

"I think we should visit Smuggler's Cove during low tide tomorrow morning," I said, pressing him. "If we find something, we can alert the authorities, and they can stake the place out tomorrow night."

"I'm not sure I like it," he said.

"We can take two skiffs," I suggested. "Eli offered to help. One of us can stay out and keep watch while the other one goes in and checks it out."

He grimaced. "It's not ideal, but it's a plan. I'm not sure how it's going to help get Tania off the hook, though."

"Derek's mixed up in this somehow. I found the low tide dates in his house, remember?"

"I'd rather not," he said.

"We'll figure it out tomorrow," I said. "In the meantime, I should probably worry about breakfast."

"Low tide is at ten tomorrow, right?" he asked.

I nodded.

"I'll call Eli and set it up," he volunteered.

"Thanks," I said. "I love you, you know."

"I love you too."

———

Despite the fact that both Beryl and Agnes were downstairs at eight, breakfast seemed to take forever the next morning. I had everything cleaned up and had wiped the counters down twice by the time Eli knocked on the kitchen door at 9:30.

226

"I'll take care of the rooms this morning," Catherine told me. She was dressed simply, in linen slacks and a tasteful blue silk top. Must not be a date day.

"Thanks," I said.

"What do you think you'll find?" she asked, sitting down at the kitchen table with a cup of black coffee and smoothing out her slacks.

"I don't know, but I hope it's not a guy with a gun."

"Be careful, Natalie," she said. "I found a terrific Mother of the Groom dress. I'd hate to waste it."

I smiled and gave her a quick hug while Eli snagged a cookie from the jar. "You won't tell Claudette?" he asked as he bit a corner off a Turtle.

"My lips are sealed," I told him as I grabbed my windbreaker from the hook by the door. Biscuit looked up at me from her favorite spot and gave me a sleepy meow. I'd forgotten to feed her, I realized.

"I'll take care of it," Catherine said, as if reading my mind.

I gave her a grateful smile. "Thanks."

"Ready?" he asked.

"As ready as I'll ever be. John's down in his workshop; let's go find him."

"Be careful," Catherine called after us as we stepped through the door.

I turned to smile at her. "We will."

John was already on the path waiting for us. "Fifteen minutes to low tide," he said.

"Let's get moving then," Eli said. John climbed into *Mooncatcher*, and Eli and I hopped into his skiff. The plan was for Eli and me to keep watch while John investigated the cove.

"If there's any funny business outside, just give a yell," John told him before we started the motors.

"I came prepared," Eli said, pulling aside his jacket to show what looked like an antique revolver.

"Does it work?" I asked.

"I don't know, and I hope we don't have to find out," Eli answered.

It seemed like no time at all before we were outside Smuggler's Cove. There were no boats in sight, and as Eli idled his motor, John circled around for a better shot at the entrance.

"Got a flashlight?" I asked.

"Right here," John said, patting his pocket.

"Be quick," I advised him, and held my breath as he gunned the engine and glided into the hole in the cliff, expertly avoiding the rocks I knew lay just under the surface on either side. I caught my breath as he vanished from sight, and turned to Eli. "You don't think anyone's in there, do you?"

"If so, they've been in there all night," he told me. "Tide just got low enough to get in five minutes ago."

We sat quietly, scanning the open water around us, waiting for John to emerge. Eli had to adjust the skiff's position a few times as we waited. No other boats approached, but I felt my blood pressure rise as the minutes passed and there was no sign of John.

When I couldn't stand it any longer, I said to Eli, "Do you think we should go in?"

"Give him another few minutes," he said. "It hasn't been that long."

"Are you kidding me? It's been like half an hour!"

As I spoke, I heard the roar of a boat motor from the cove. My whole body tensed, only to dissolve with relief when *Mooncatcher* emerged a moment later.

"Thank God," I murmured, understanding the feeling of worry John had been describing to me the night before.

"What'd you find?" Eli asked, eyes bright with curiosity.

"I know what Zeke's doing in that barn," John said as he pulled up alongside.

"What?" I asked.

"Growing marijuana," he said.

TWENTY-ONE

"I STILL CAN'T BELIEVE it," I said after John left a message for Detective Johnson to call him back.

"I'm guessing he was growing it in the barn," John said. "That would explain the light you saw last night, and the black pepper to cover the scent. He was probably using grow lights."

"And the fertilizer that came on the mail boat," I said, suddenly remembering. "He'd told me he only used manure for his crops. It was manure from the farm that we found on the floor of the cove last time. And the license he was applying for was probably as a medical marijuana producer."

"Which explains why he told Evan he was finished with the business," John said.

"I hate to turn him in," I told John. "He moved here with his brother so that he could look after him. I think he's a good person."

"Two kids on the island are in jail for drug possession," he reminded me.

I grimaced. "You think that was Zeke?"

"Derek may have sold it to them, but I'm guessing that's where it came from."

I was quiet for a long time, thinking of Brad's happy face as he pulled weeds from the garden. "What's wrong?" John asked when I pulled out a cookbook and began leafing through it.

"I'm feeling conflicted," I said.

My fiancé came up behind me and put his hands on my shoulders. "About what? The fact that we've uncovered a drug ring, but still don't know who killed Derek?"

"Well, that too, of course," I said. "But I'm really worried about turning in Zeke Forester. I think his motives were good, and if something happens to him, I don't know what's going to happen to his brother."

"He still made the decision to get into the business in the first place," John pointed out.

"Yes, but why?" I put down the canister of flour and looked out at the green trees, then told him about what we'd discovered at the old rectory.

"So the priest was a rum runner," he said. "And making his own whiskey, too. Hardly what you expect of a man of the cloth."

"But there was a reason for it," I said. "That's what bothers me. Beryl's grandfather probably got into the business of rum running to help pay for his wife's medical bills," I said, "and he ended up dead. We're planning on turning in Zeke, but I think he only started growing as a way to care for his brother. I'm not a big fan of drug use, but there's a bill up to legalize it right now anyway."

"It's true, it's not like cocaine or methamphetamines."

"What if he was desperate?"

John stopped massaging my shoulders. "Don't tell me you're thinking of asking him."

"I am," I said, then turned to look at him. "Is that wrong?"

"He might alert the people who are doing the pick-up," he said. "And he might be a murderer."

"I don't think he is," I said. "I may be wrong, but my heart tells me he's a good person." I turned around and looked at him. "What do I do?"

He sighed. "Let's wait until Detective Johnson calls. I'll tell him what we found in the cove, but I won't tell him where it came from until we have a chance to talk with Zeke."

My heart swelled, but I was still worried. "Are you sure? Is it obstructing justice not to tell?"

"I didn't say I wouldn't tell," he replied. "I just said we'd talk to Zeke first. If we go together, I can arrest him before he tips anyone off."

"Really?"

"What choice do I have?" he asked, looking grim.

"I love you," I said.

"Good thing."

———

We arrived at the farm just after noon. When John knocked on the door, Brad answered, giving us a beatific smile.

"Hi, Brad. Is your brother here?"

"Hi, John! Hi, Natalie! I'll tell Zekie you're here! He made me cupcakes today. Carrot. My favorite!"

"Who is it, Brad?" Zeke's voice came from somewhere in the house.

"Friends," Brad said, and my stomach twisted with guilt.

Zeke came to the door, patted his brother on the shoulder, then turned to us. "What's up?"

"We need to talk," John said quietly.

"Come in," the farmer said casually.

"Alone," John said, and something in his voice made Zeke pause. His face paled, but his voice was easy as he spoke to Brad. "I'm going to go show Natalie and John the tomatoes. Can you butter the toast when it pops up?"

"Okey dokey, Zeke!"

Zeke exited the house and led us away from it before turning to John. "What's this about?" he asked.

John looked at me. I swallowed hard. "We know what's in the barn," I told him.

He digested that for a moment, and his shoulders slumped. "How?"

"I saw you down at the shore. And John was at the cove this morning."

Zeke looked at the house and ran a hand through his hair. "I was trying to get out of it. It was the only way I could afford to take Brad out here, get him out of the city and into a small community."

"Can we see it?" John asked.

He hesitated for a moment, then said, "Of course." We followed him down the rows of vegetables to the barn. He unlocked the padlock and opened the doors, letting out that strong, sneeze-inducing scent of black pepper—and something else. Something green.

We followed him into the barn and around a partition, and what I saw took my breath away.

Dozens of light fixtures dangled from the ceiling, and the floor of the barn was covered with rows of empty pots. What appeared to be drying racks were toward the back of the barn. It was all empty now.

"Wow. How much were you growing?"

"A lot," he said concisely. "But as you can see, I'm out of business now."

"Who were you working for?" John asked.

"Fred set it all up," he said, surveying the empty barn. "I tried to stay out of it. And when I told him I was quitting, he threatened me."

"He burned your shed down, didn't he?" John asked.

Zeke nodded. "I think it's his only source of income, and he's afraid what would happen if it dried up. I'm applying for a license to grow it medically, but if that doesn't work, I'm hoping I can make up the difference with a dairy." He grimaced. "It's probably too late, though."

"What about Derek?"

"I don't know about Derek," he said. "I don't think Fred is a killer, but I could be wrong." He shook his head. "I knew it was a bad idea, but I couldn't figure out any other way to take care of Brad." He looked haggard. "I quit as soon as I found out Derek was dealing to kids."

"You're sure Derek was dealing?" I asked.

"Yeah. He was hooked up with whoever was organizing everything. I had to cut him loose; he was too dangerous to have around, and I didn't trust him. Plus, he was just a bad business."

"He was taking Adam's boat out," I said. "Do you know why?"

"I think he was taking extra from the barn and selling it himself," he said. "He didn't have a boat of his own, so he used Adam's. The sternman's job was just cover for the money he was making off drugs."

"What did he do when you fired him?"

"He threatened to blackmail me, but when I told him I knew he'd been dealing, he stopped threatening me."

"He had a contact who was providing him money, apparently. Any idea who?"

He shook his head. "As far as I know, once I fired him, he lost his income source, except for what he got helping Fred out."

John gave Zeke a hard look. "Do you think Fred might have killed him?"

"I doubt it," Zeke said. "He set my shed on fire to scare me, but I think he was really scared himself. And as for Derek ..." He shook his head. "It was convenient, in a way, that someone killed him, but it wasn't me."

I thought of Brad, and Zeke's willingness to break the law to protect his brother. Would he kill Derek, too? I wondered.

"Any idea who *did* kill him?" John asked.

"I don't know. It wasn't me, though; I was getting out anyway." He shook his head. "Growing the recreational stuff made enough money to keep Brad comfortable, but I just couldn't handle the fact that children were using it. I don't mind pot, but kids are something different." He looked at John. "Are you going to arrest me?"

"What would happen to Brad if you went to jail?" I asked him quietly.

His face seemed to crumple a bit. "Our parents are dead. I guess ... I guess he'd be a ward of the state." He turned pale at the thought.

John sighed. "If it were up to me, I'd consider staying quiet, but I'm pretty sure Fred will turn you in."

Zeke looked startled. "Have they arrested him yet?"

"Not yet," John said, "but there's a sting operation set up. The police are staking out the cove; the pick-up's tonight, isn't it?"

"Like I said, I don't know." He grimaced. "And I don't even have information to bargain with. The only person I know is Fred."

John sighed. "I wish I had a solution for you."

Zeke stared back at the farmhouse. "Me too," he said, forlornly. "I deserve to go to jail. It's just … I can't bear the thought of Brad being in an institution."

"Why drugs?" I asked.

"I couldn't figure out any other way to make it work," he told me. "I looked at the property, and then I was having a beer down at Spurrell's Lobster Pond, and Fred started talking to me. Said he knew a way I could pay the bills without harming anyone." He sighed. "It seemed too good to be true, and I guess it was."

"I'm sorry, Zeke," I said.

"Me too," he told me, and looked at the barn. "I wish I'd never met Fred Penney."

"If anything happens, we'll do our best to take care of Brad," John told him. "Maybe he can help out at the inn, or something."

"Won't work," Zeke said. "He needs too much care. I couldn't ask you to do that." He sighed. "You know, I've made this mess, I'm going to have to clean it up. Let me make some arrangements for Brad, and I'll turn myself in."

"Are you sure you want to do this?" I asked, worried for his sunny brother.

"I want to clear the air," he said. "This has been heavy on my conscience. I just need some time to arrange things for Brad, if that's okay with you."

"I think we can spare the time," John said.

"I presume you're going to want to wait with me so I don't tip off Fred."

"I'm afraid we'll have to," John said.

"Well, why don't you come in and have a beer. Might as well enjoy my last hour of freedom."

"Thanks," John said. "We'll take you up on that."

TWENTY-TWO

THE AIR IN THE kitchen felt as brittle as hard candy when the phone call came later that evening. Zeke answered, then handed the phone to John.

"What happened?" he asked the moment he picked up the phone.

I watched his face as he listened, but it was unreadable. "Where is he now?" he asked.

She spoke a bit more—it sounded like Catherine—and then he thanked her and hung up.

"Well?" I asked.

"You were right," he said. "Fred turned up in his lobster boat to make a pick-up."

"What happened?"

"He got in, and got back on the boat. There was a long chase, but then…"

Something about the way he trailed off made me fearful. "What?"

"Well, he had a heart attack," he said.

"A heart attack?"

"He lost control of the boat and it ran aground on a rock. They got on and got him off, but he's in bad shape."

"I knew he had a heart condition," I said. "Charlene told me about it. The stress must have brought it on." I looked at John. "Did they find the marijuana?"

He nodded. "They don't know where it came from, though. At least not yet."

"And he hasn't said anything about Derek, either," I guessed.

"He can't speak," John said. "It's a pretty bad attack."

I looked at them both. "Should we just let this go, maybe?"

Zeke stood up. "No," he said, putting an arm around Brad. "I have to confess."

"What about Brad?"

"I won't be gone forever," he said, "and I'll use what money I've earned to find him a good place to stay till I'm back."

"Where you going, Zeke?" The worry on Brad's face made my heart break.

"I don't know yet, Brad." The farmer put a work-roughened hand on his brother's pale one. "I may have to go away for a little while, but I'll come back." My stomach churned. A little while could be decades, I was guessing. "And I'll make sure you're taken care of."

"Are you sure you want to do this?" John asked levelly.

Zeke nodded. "I won't be able to live with myself if I don't take responsibility for my actions. Besides, I might be able to help them clear up this ring. Keep kids from being involved."

"Sleep on it," John said, surprising me.

"No," Zeke said. "I want them to hear it from me first." He looked at me. "I hate to ask this, but could you take Brad back to the inn with you? Just in case…"

"Of course," I said gently. "If you're sure."

"I'm sure," he said, his face grim. "And I'd like to get it over with."

———

As I settled Brad into bed, he looked at me with his trusting eyes. "When will Zeke be back?"

"Soon, I hope," I told him. "Now, why don't you get a good night's sleep, and tomorrow morning I'll make blueberry muffins."

"With sugar on top?"

"With sugar on top," I promised, then plugged in the night light and returned to the kitchen, where Catherine was waiting with a cup of warm milk spiked with rum. John had gone with Zeke to the mainland, to be with him as he made his confession.

"You doing okay?" Catherine asked, compassion in her blue eyes.

"I guess," I said. "I'm worried about Brad, though. If his brother goes to jail, I'd hate to see him institutionalized."

"I'll ask Murray to find him a good attorney," she said. "Maybe if he gives them information to help break up this drug ring John was talking about, they'll give him a reduced sentence."

"I hope so," I said, and the two of us sat and waited.

John called at just before midnight.

"How'd it go?" I asked.

"They took him into custody," he said. "He's doing everything he can to help out, though."

My heart sank. "How about Fred?"

"He's still not able to talk," John said. "He's in the ICU right now."

"Poor man," I said. I didn't like what he'd done, but I still hoped he'd recover.

John sighed. "This whole thing has turned into a giant mess. And we still don't know who killed Derek."

After all the excitement of the day, I'd almost forgotten about Tania's issue. "Zeke didn't think Fred would kill Derek."

"Nope, and he's right."

"What do you mean?"

"They checked on his alibi. Evidently he was in a bar in Bar Harbor when Derek died. Playing in a poker tournament."

"So we're back at square one," I said.

"Looks like it," he said. "I love you."

"I love you too," I said, and hung up the phone feeling empty. Both Tania and Zeke were likely to be convicted and imprisoned. And there was nothing I could do to help them.

"What's going on?" Catherine asked.

I told her what John had shared with me—including Fred's alibi.

"Do you think it could have been someone he was working for?" she suggested.

"Maybe," I said. Something was niggling at me, though. "Or maybe I've been following a false trail all along." I told her about the threatening handwritten note that had turned up in Derek's pocket.

"And there was something Fred said to me," I continued. "He said that Derek was involved with someone on Seal Point Road." All of a sudden I remembered the woman I'd seen crying near the blueberry patch the morning Derek was found ... and the woman I'd seen at his house. I was almost sure it wasn't Tania; and I thought I knew who it was. There was only one piece that didn't fit.

"What time is it?" I asked.

"After eleven," Catherine said.

Too late to confirm it tonight. "If I prepare everything ahead of time, can you serve breakfast tomorrow morning?" I asked.

"I suppose so," she said. "Why?"

"I have an errand to run," I told her. "I won't be long, though."

———

It was raining the next morning when my alarm went off. I leaned over and kissed John, who hadn't gotten in until after two, and padded downstairs to put breakfast together. I had finished my second cup of coffee and slid two pans of blueberry muffins in the oven when the phone rang.

"I heard Zeke Forester got arrested last night," Charlene said without introduction.

"Yeah. He confessed to growing pot in his barn; he's going to try to help the police break up the drug ring."

"What about Brad?"

"He's staying with us for now."

"What happens if Zeke ends up in jail for twenty years?"

"I don't know. I guess we'll cross that bridge when we get to it."

"And no help for Tania, either," she said. "This hasn't been a terrific week."

"No," I agreed, looking out the window at the blue water, which was glittering in the morning sun. I decided to keep my suspicions about Derek's killer to myself; no use getting Charlene's hopes up before I was sure. Ever since that one morning when I'd gone blueberry picking, everything had gone awry.

"There's one good bit of news, though," she told me. "I heard Derek's aunt and uncle are expecting a baby."

"Did they want one?"

"They'd been trying for years," she said. "Jeff came down to the store and bought drinks for everyone yesterday. He's so excited that Turtle's pregnant."

"Who's pregnant?"

"His wife. Her name is Elizabeth, but she used to be called Turtle when she was a kid; she was really shy."

"I don't think I've ever seen her," I said. "She's got a lovely garden, though."

"Anyway, they've been trying for a couple of years. Fertility treatments and everything; they'd just about given up."

"Well, I'm glad there's a bit of good news," I said, trying to sound casual. "Particularly after they lost their nephew. Was he related to him, or her, do you know?"

"Derek was Jeff's sister's son," Charlene said. "Funny how these things happen, isn't it? The doctor said they should give up and adopt. God works in mysterious ways, I suppose."

I pulled the sugar canister out of the pantry. "Let's just hope God manages to get Tania off the hook, too."

"I know," she said. "Well, I've got to run. Let me know if you need help with Brad."

"Thanks, but you've got enough on your plate as it is," I told her.

As I hung up a moment later, my mind was whirling. I was dying to get these muffins finished so I could follow up on my hunch.

A moment later, Catherine appeared in the kitchen, dressed in slim-fitting khaki pants and a cashmere sweater.

"What can I do to help?" she asked.

"I'm so glad you asked. I have a quick errand to run. Muffins are in the oven and fruit salad is in the fridge," I said. "If you could whip up some scrambled eggs and sausage and serve the guests when they come down, that would be terrific."

"I can do that much," she said. "When will you be back?"

"I should be back in time to do the dishes." I grabbed my windbreaker and headed for the door, adrenaline pumping through me.

Catherine's voice had a suspicious edge. "Where are you going?"

I told her.

"Can't John go with you?" she asked, giving me a searching look.

"He's still asleep," I said. "I'm just going to see if I can lay eyes on her."

"Do you want me to join you?"

"No, that's okay. If you'll take care of the guests, that would be great."

"Are you sure this is a good idea?"

"I'm just going to take a look," I said. "If I'm right, I'll come back and tell the cops."

She narrowed her eyes at me. "You're a grown woman, so I can't stop you. But If you're not back in an hour," she said, "I'm waking John and calling the police."

———

I parked the van at the end of Seal Point Road, on the shoulder, and got out into the cool summer morning. The dew glistened on the blueberry bushes on the side of the road, and the breeze off the water was fresh with salt mingled with the scent of pine, but I barely noticed it as I hurried down the road toward my destination.

The little house was as pretty as it had been the day I first saw it. The geraniums still bloomed cheerily in their window boxes, and the roses near the fence bloomed. It looked like a storybook house, but if what I suspected was true, it hid a darker tale.

I turned off the road and plunged into the damp bushes, my eyes trained on the house. There was a light on toward the back. I pushed through the bushes toward the back yard, which was fenced in with a white picket fence and lined with roses. As I peered over the fence into the lit room—the kitchen—I hoped I was right. If I was able to confirm my suspicion, I'd hurry back home and tell John everything, and the police could take it from there.

The thought that I could be wrong flitted into my head, but I decided to banish that until I knew one way or the other.

There was a person in the kitchen, but the leaves of the rose bushes obscured my view. I moved around a bit, hoping to get a better view, but between the filmy lace curtains and the roses, I couldn't get a clear line of sight.

There was a garden gate, though, flanked by hydrangeas and white roses. If I could get a little way farther into the yard—I spotted a rose bush that would make a good vantage point—I'd get a better look.

I crept up to the gate and pushed it open. There was a small beeping sound, like a cardinal chirping, as I closed it behind me and scuttled into the yard, positioning myself behind a rose bush. The person in the kitchen disappeared for a moment. Then there was the squeak of a door, and a woman's voice said, "I don't know who you are, but I've got a gun."

TWENTY-THREE

I RECOGNIZED HER IMMEDIATELY. Elizabeth Abingdon—Turtle, to her friends. The woman I had seen crying by the blueberry patch the morning Derek Morton turned up dead. The woman who had been in Derek's house the day I was there. The woman who had been seeing Derek secretly—and possibly gotten pregnant by him. She held what looked like a shotgun in her hands and was staring at me from wide brown eyes. She was a pretty woman—or would have been, in different circumstances.

"Sorry to bother you," I said lightly. "Your roses were so beautiful, I thought I'd take a closer look." Lame, I know. But it's tough coming up with reasonable excuses on short notice. Particularly when someone's pointing a shotgun at you. "Would you mind, uh, putting away the gun?"

She didn't lower it a millimeter. "That's not why you're here."

I pasted on a quizzical look. "What do you mean?"

She didn't answer.

"Did I set off some kind of motion detector?" I asked, still trying to sound casual.

She didn't answer.

I struggled to keep my voice conversational, which was a challenge with a gun pointing at my head. "I hear you're expecting your first child. I can understand your desire to be safe. Your garden is gorgeous, by the way."

"What do you know about Derek and me?" Her voice quivered, and she bent over a little bit, as if the name hurt her.

"He's your nephew."

"He was." She narrowed her eyes at me. "You saw me that morning. You were out with a coffee can."

"What morning?" I swallowed. "Oh. The other day, when I was picking berries?"

"You know what morning," she said, looking scared. "When he died." She glanced around the back yard. "In the house. Now."

With my hands still up, I walked up the path to the back of the house and into the kitchen, with Elizabeth behind me. The door shutting behind me reminded me of a coffin lid slamming shut. Thank God, Catherine had told me she'd call the police. I glanced at the clock on the wall; I had thirty minutes to stall. Why had I been such an idiot and gone through the stupid gate?

"Sit down," she said, pointing me toward a white painted chair. It was stenciled with blue and red designs that went well with the tile backsplash, which was white with blue windmills. It was not what you'd expect from a murderer's kitchen. "How did you figure it out?"

I glanced at the clock. Twenty-nine minutes to go. "You must have had a challenging relationship with your nephew," I said slowly. "His death must be very upsetting to you."

She sank down into a chair across from me. She was still holding the gun in one hand, but the barrel pointed toward the floor now. The other arm curled around her stomach. "Yes," she said in a hollow voice. Her eyes were ringed with shadows. "He was a bad man. That's why Jeff sent him away the first time. I didn't understand it then … but he was right."

"Did your husband find out that you and Derek were lovers?"

She was silent for a moment, as if she were wavering. Finally, she nodded. "He suspected, but he didn't know." She looked at the floor.

"And Derek came back to be with you," I said. "He must have really cared for you."

"I thought so," she said, eyes welling up with tears. She dabbed at them with her apron, but still kept one hand on the gun. "But he was seeing that other girl. And then …" She took a gasping sob. "He turned on me."

"He's the father of your baby, isn't he?" I asked gently.

"Yes." Her voice was soft and ragged.

"And he was threatening to tell your husband," I guessed. When she didn't contradict me, I continued. "Was he blackmailing you?"

"Yes." The words sounded like they'd been torn out of her, and her hand went to her stomach as if she were in pain. "He told me he'd tell Jeff everything about us. Tell him he was the father of the baby." Tears streaked down her face as she clutched at her stomach. "It would have killed Jeff. He would have killed me, maybe." She glanced over her shoulder. There was a gun cabinet in the mudroom, right behind the kitchen.

"You asked to meet him, didn't you?" I asked. "Where was your special place?"

"By the blueberry field," she said. "There was an old house back in there." She sniffed. "His house was too close to the pier. I was afraid Jeff would find us here, so we had another place."

"Did you plan to kill him?"

She shook her head. "I don't know why I took the gun. I guess maybe I had a feeling I might need it, but I thought I could talk sense into him. I thought he'd care enough about me to let me go." Her eyes filled with tears.

"He wanted more money, didn't he?"

"Yes." It was a whisper. "And if I gave it to him, we'd be broke. Jeff would find out. I'd have to tell him. And then I'd lose everything. My husband, my baby's future … my home." She burst into tears.

"How did it happen?" I asked gently.

"He started toward me. He was angry. Called me a … a stupid bitch. And I just … the gun went off in my hand, and he was dead."

"Why did you put him in the skiff?"

"I was afraid," she said in a small voice. "I was hoping it would drift out to sea, and no one would find him."

"Why Adam's skiff?"

"I knew where it was," she said. "And Derek had the key with him still; he had a copy made. I went and got the skiff and then put him in it. I didn't know what else to do."

"And the gun?"

"I put it in that slut's trash can," she said, her voice sharp for the first time.

"Tania's, you mean," I clarified. She nodded. "Did you call in the tip, too?"

Her brows knitted in confusion. "What tip?"

"Someone called and said she had drugs. That wasn't you?"

"No," she said, shaking her head. Then she seemed to take stock of the situation, and raised the gun. "Now you know everything," she said. "But you're going to tell." She bent over again, as if she were in pain. She cried out and doubled over, and the gun dropped to the floor.

Her dress was stained with blood, and a small puddle was forming at the bottom of the chair.

"Elizabeth," I said, leaping up from my chair to catch her before she keeled over.

"The baby," she wailed.

"Lie down," I said, easing her to the floor. "I'm going to call emergency services." I pushed the gun away with my toe, sending it skittering across the kitchen floor.

"But if Jeff finds out…"

"All that matters right now is that you're okay," I said, tucking a chair pillow under her head and then reaching for the phone.

———

I'd been sitting beside Elizabeth for fifteen minutes, holding her hand and stroking her forehead, when the front door opened. A man's voice called out, "Turtle?"

"In here," I called.

He stopped short in the doorway to the kitchen, and his ruddy face paled. "Oh, Turtle…" He crossed the kitchen floor in three short steps. "What's wrong with her?" he asked.

"I'm afraid it may be a miscarriage," I said, and he looked as if I'd punched him. "Emergency services are on their way."

"What are you doing here?" he asked. "And why is the shotgun out?"

"It's not important now," I said.

"Jeff," Elizabeth said. "I'm a terrible wife. You never should have married me."

"Hush now," he told her. "Don't say another word. Just take care of our baby."

She convulsed again at his words, and he looked at me helplessly.

"All we can do is keep her calm," I said. "They're on their way."

We sat on the kitchen floor together, Elizabeth sobbing, Jeff stroking her head and comforting her, until the paramedics arrived.

———

"They found an empty spot in one of the gun cases," John said, "and Jeff Abingdon identified the gun."

"So Tania's free to go?"

"She will be shortly," he said. Charlene slumped into one of my kitchen chairs, relieved. "I'd say that calls for a brownie." The sun shone through the windowpanes, making her caramel-streaked hair glow.

I'd called Catherine while we were waiting for the paramedics to come, and John had raced home as soon as his mother had gotten in touch with him. Charlene had come over shortly afterward, and we'd sat in the kitchen, eating muffins and waiting for news ever since. Brad had popped in from time to time, but Catherine had asked him to water the flowers in the back yard, and we could see him happily filling the watering can and taking it from window box to window box.

"What about the baby?" I asked.

John shook his head. "I'm afraid she's lost it."

"Poor thing." I looked out the window toward the mainland. "Does Jeff know it's not his yet?"

"I think so," he told me. "It's got to be a terrible day for him."

I sighed. "You were right, Charlene. Derek really was bad news. He got his aunt pregnant, and then blackmailed her to keep it quiet."

"Very chivalrous," Catherine observed, adjusting her pearls around her neck. "Murray would never do that."

Charlene licked a crumb from her finger. "Thank God Tania didn't get pregnant. It's bad enough that she's in jail." She looked at John. "When can I go and get her?"

"They'll call as soon as she's cleared," he told her. "I'll go over with you; I'm so relieved she's going to be freed."

"Will she be? Elizabeth—Turtle—confessed to me, but what do they have for evidence?"

"She might confess on her own," John told me. "And there's a good chance we'll find her fingerprints at Derek's house—and on Adam's dinghy. Why did she take Adam's dinghy, anyway?"

"Because Derek had a copy of the key," I said.

"That makes sense. There's one more outstanding question, though."

Charlene looked up at him. "What?"

"Who called in the tip on Tania? I mean, if it wasn't Turtle, who was it?"

John leaned back in his chair. "Someone else who had a grudge against her?"

A light clicked on in my head. "I know who had a grudge against her. I'll bet you dollars to donuts it was Ingrid who made that call. I heard her telling Evan she was a bad influence, and I think she wanted to get rid of her."

Charlene perked up. "That makes sense. And it was just bad luck that the gun was there."

"Not entirely bad luck," I pointed out. "I think Turtle was jealous of Tania."

"Jealous because Tania was dating her bum of a nephew?"

"Love makes people do strange things," I said.

"But she didn't want to leave her husband," John said. "She was willing to kill Derek to keep that from happening." He shook his head. "She must have loved them both, somehow."

"I hope he's able to forgive her." I took a bite of muffin. "He was the one who wrote the note threatening Derek. He told me that was what he and Derek had an argument about."

"So it wasn't just about a lobster license."

"Apparently not. I wonder about Evan, though. He's got prior convictions for drugs." I took a bite of muffin. "Did Zeke turn him in?"

John shook his head. "He said he just worked around the farm. It depends on whether or not Fred decides to give him away. I haven't heard anything about it yet."

Catherine crossed her legs and brushed a crumb off of her pants leg. "Fred? I thought he'd had a heart attack and couldn't speak."

"He came to this morning," John said. "The police offered to reduce his sentence if he'll help them crack the drug ring, and he agreed. They found the skiff that rammed yours at his property, by the way."

"Good," I said.

"I'm hoping he'll be the key they need to break up the ring. Marijuana's one thing, but they were transporting some dangerous drugs like heroin and cocaine." John sighed. "He confirmed that Derek's the one who was dealing to kids at the school."

"I figured as much." I glanced at my watch. "I hope they let Tania out this afternoon."

"She'll still have to answer to the drug charge," John warned me, "but it shouldn't be too serious, and I hope it will teach her a lesson."

I sighed. "I hope she's back for tomorrow, at least. Adam's picking Gwen up in a few hours; she'll be here for dinner." I looked at John. "Any word on Zeke?"

"He was cooperating with the police. He may be able to get a reduced sentence if he testifies."

"What's he looking at, anyway?"

"Maximum sentence is ten years and $20,000," he said.

"Better than I expected, but it won't help Brad." I tucked two muffin pans into the oven. "If you get a chance to talk to him, tell him we'll take care of Brad until he has things figured out, okay?"

"Of course," John said.

Catherine took a sip of tea. "I'm so glad all this got wrapped up before Gwen arrived," she said. "Are your plans still a go for the weekend?"

I was about to answer her when there was a knock at the kitchen door, and Beryl peeked through.

"Hi, Beryl. Everything okay?" I asked.

"I'm sorry to interrupt, but we just got back from talking with Matilda, and she's got the most exciting news," Beryl said. "We were going to wait until dinner to share, but we decided we just couldn't."

"Come on in," I offered, and she and Agnes trooped into the kitchen. "Have a muffin and join us."

"Oh, thanks so much," Agnes said, reaching for the plate.

"What did you find out?" I asked.

"Well," Beryl said, "Matilda has a friend who specializes in the Prohibition era, and she just called her this morning." Her eyes sparkled with excitement. "It turns out there was a rum runner in Nova Scotia who was known for transporting whiskey over the border to Maine. He had a whole network of people to smuggle his wares, and was ruthless with people who tried to cut him out of their distribution networks."

"She thinks that's who your grandfather's contact was??" I asked.

Beryl nodded. "Guess what his nickname was?"

"What?"

"The Bishop," Agnes said.

TWENTY-FOUR

SATURDAY DAWNED CLEAR AND bright, and I felt a frisson of excitement as I leaned over and kissed John. "You ready?" I asked.

"I've been waiting for this moment for years," he said, kissing me back. He released me and gazed at me. "I guess you're going to want me to head down to the carriage house for a while, aren't you?"

I nodded. "It won't be long, though."

He glanced at the clock. "Four hours." He kissed me again, then said, "I don't know if I can wait that long."

I shooed him out anyway, and headed downstairs for a cup of coffee and a piece of toast. My stomach was too jittery to eat anything else.

Charlene arrived just as I finished the last swig of my coffee, bumping down the drive in her old truck. "Where's Gwen?" she asked as she swept into the kitchen on a cloud of orange blossom perfume.

"Still asleep, I'm guessing," I said.

She rolled her eyes and set her makeup bag on the counter. "If she's not up in an hour, I'm going in and getting her. Now, before I begin; do you have coffee, and maybe something to nosh on?"

I laughed and pointed her in the direction of the apple dumplings I'd made for Gwen as I poured her a cup of coffee. When she was armed with a dumpling in each hand, she looked at me. "Time to head upstairs," she announced. "We've got work to do."

———

It was eleven o'clock by the time Charlene was finished with me, and when I looked in the mirror, I barely recognized myself. My bobbed hair had been smoothed and sleeked, my eyes seemed bigger, and my face somehow... more sculpted. The dress, a simple silk gown, still fit. It was a far cry from my normal T-shirt and jeans.

"Wow," I said.

Charlene grinned. "You clean up pretty well, my dear. I can't wait to see the look on John's face!" She glanced at her watch. "Ready?"

"I think I am, but I'm worried. Did Emmeline get the cake together?"

"I talked with her this morning, and she was on her way to the church. I think everyone on the island has made something for the reception, and the band stayed at Tom's last night." She glanced down at my shoes. "I hope you can dance in those!"

I laughed. "What about the flowers?"

"Everyone's brought what the goats haven't eaten, and Claudette's been making arrangements in the Fellowship Hall. Your bouquet will be waiting at the church, and one of the photographers from the

Daily Mail will be recording it all for posterity." She grinned. "Welcome to weddings island style."

"I can't believe I'm saying this, but I think I'm glad the Florida thing fell through," I said, feeling a warm glow at the generosity of my island community. As I headed downstairs, holding up my dress so I didn't trip, I felt a swell of gratitude, not just for the wonderful man I was marrying, but for the islanders who had opened their arms and adopted me as one of their own.

The sun was high in the sky and the breeze was cool, but light. It was a short drive to the church, and we passed several islanders walking in their Sunday best as we got closer. They waved, smiling, and my stomach fluttered. "I can't believe I'm getting married," I told Charlene.

"It's about darned time," she said as she pulled the van into a parking space behind the church.

"Are you sure I look okay?"

Charlene, who was dressed in a green taffeta number that accentuated her hourglass figure, gave me an appraising look. "We'll touch up your lipstick and dust on a bit more powder before you walk down the aisle, but you look amazing." She gave my arm a squeeze. "Now, let's get you in there; the ceremony starts in fifteen minutes!"

Gwen was already waiting for me, her face glowing. She wore a gorgeous red dress that highlighted her creamy skin and dark hair beautifully. I was so glad to have her back; I hadn't realized how much I'd missed her. "Aunt Nat, you look beautiful," she said. "That dress is amazing, and your hair ..."

"Thanks," I said, feeling my face heat.

She shook her head. "I can't believe you're getting married. And on such short notice!"

"Me neither," I said. "But when the resort in Florida went out of business, we just decided we'd rather celebrate with all the people we love."

"I think it's wonderful. Thank you so much for waiting until I could be here. I wouldn't have missed it for anything!" She grinned. "And I think you've inspired Adam."

"What do you mean?"

She held out her left hand. A small diamond sparkled on her ring finger.

Even though I'd been expecting it, my heart swelled. "Oh, Gwen . . ."

"He asked me last night," she said, beaming.

"I'm so happy for you," I said, pulling her into a big hug. "How did he propose?"

"I'll tell you after the wedding," she said. "Aunt Nat, I think it's time!"

Charlene rummaged in her bag. "Let me do one more check on your lipstick." She fiddled with my face for a moment, adjusted my hair, and nodded. "You're ready."

———

It was a wonderful ceremony. John stole my heart all over again, looking dashing in a crisp black suit, and the pews were overflowing with the faces of people I cared about. Even Beryl and Agnes were there, grinning and waving from a pew near the back. Catherine, who was holding hands with Murray, smiled and nodded at me as I made my way up the aisle, and as John and I exchanged the vows that would bind us forever, the loving expression in his green eyes made something inside me crack open. I never believed it would be possible to be so happy.

Every person on the island seemed to have brought a tablecloth and a mason jar or vase filled with flowers from their gardens, and the array of dishes—from lobster casserole to mussels to hot dogs with pickle relish—was bountiful and delicious. There were two cakes: one with mounds of buttercream frosting and decorated with delicate candied violets, and one that was dark devil's food with a decadent chocolate frosting, decorated with sugared strawberries.

"So," John said when the festivities finally ended—there had been hours of dancing, and the cases of champagne John had delivered to the church were long gone—"how does it feel to be married?"

I fingered the gold ring on my hand. "Amazing," I said. "I'm so glad we had the ceremony here, where all of our friends could share it with us."

"Me too," he said. "And I hear we've got another wedding coming," he added as Gwen walked by carrying a tray full of dishes to the kitchen.

She smiled. "As soon as I'm finished with my degree, I'm coming back. You're stuck with me, I'm afraid!"

"We wouldn't have it any other way," John said.

Charlene walked up to us with the remains of a piece of chocolate cake, licking frosting from a fork. "Isn't it time you two went off for your honeymoon?"

"We have to help clean up," I said.

"Nonsense. Emmeline is taking over the cooking for the next few days, and Catherine will do the cleaning. We've done up the Lockharts' rental cottage at the end of the island for you, so you can have a bit of time to yourselves."

"But Gwen's in town …"

"And will be spending most of her time with her new fiancé, I suspect," she grinned. "Now, the two of you skedaddle. You've got a weekend to yourselves; go take it!"

"Thank you so much for helping arrange everything," I said, giving Charlene a big hug.

"That's what friends are for. I hope you'll do the same for me someday. Although you've already helped me out enough by springing Tania," she said, nodding toward her niece, who was in the corner talking with Evan Sorenson. Neither would be spending much time in jail, it appeared, and despite her harrowing experience, Tania looked better than I'd seen her in months.

"I'm glad that all worked out okay."

"The school did, too," Charlene said. "Catherine talked Murray into supporting its continuation!"

I smiled at Catherine, who raised a glass of wine to me from across the room and winked. Murray had a protective arm around her, and looked completely and totally enamored of her. I winked back and gave her a thumbs-up. She was evidently an excellent influence on him.

"How did all that happen?" I asked.

"We can talk about it Monday," she said. "Now let us all wish you well and toss birdseed at you!" She hustled me to the front of the church, where John was waiting for me. His green eyes crinkled when he smiled, and despite the suit, the familiar and comforting smell of fresh sawdust hung around him.

"Ready?" he asked once Charlene had arranged almost the entire population of the island outside the church.

"Absolutely," I said as we marched out of the church arm and arm, and into our new lives together.

RECIPES

ZESTY LEMON SQUARES

Ingredients:

½ pound unsalted butter, at room temperature
½ cup granulated sugar
2 cups flour
⅛ tsp kosher salt
6 eggs at room temperature
3 cups granulated sugar
2 Tbsp grated lemon zest (4 to 6 lemons)
1 cup freshly squeezed lemon juice
1 cup flour
Confectioners' sugar, for dusting

Directions:

Preheat the oven to 350 degrees. For the crust, cream the butter and sugar until light in the bowl of an electric mixer fitted with the paddle attachment. Combine the flour and salt and, with the mixer on low, add to the butter/sugar mixture until just mixed. Dump the dough onto a well-floured board and gather into a ball. Flatten the dough with floured hands and press it into a 9x13x2-inch baking sheet, building up a ½-inch edge on all sides. Chill.

Bake the crust for 15 to 20 minutes, until very lightly browned. Let cool on a wire rack. Leave the oven on. For the filling, whisk together the eggs, sugar, lemon zest, lemon juice, and flour. Pour over the crust and bake for 30 to 35 minutes, until the filling is set. Let cool to room temperature. Cut into squares and dust with confectioners' sugar.

STEAMED BLUEBERRY PUDDING

Ingredients:

    2 cups all-purpose flour

    4 tsp baking powder

    ½ tsp salt

    2 Tbsp sugar

    2 Tbsp butter

    1 cup milk

    2 Tbsp molasses

    1 cup blueberries

    Enough flour to coat the blueberries

Directions:

Sift together the flour and baking powder, mix in the salt and sugar. Cut in the butter. Mix in the milk and molasses. Coat the blueberries lightly with flour and add to the mixture. Pour the pudding into a lightly greased 1-quart pudding mold and put on lid (or cover with aluminum foil). Set on rack in a pot and add hot water to about halfway up the sides. Simmer on low heat for 1½ hours or until pudding has set, and unmold. Serve warm with Lyle's Golden Syrup or Foamy Sauce.

FOAMY SAUCE

Ingredients:

    3 Tbsp butter

    1 cup powdered sugar

    2 eggs, separated and well-beaten

    ½ tsp vanilla

    ½ cup cream, whipped

Directions:

Cream the butter and sugar together. Add the well-beaten egg yolks and beat thoroughly over hot water in a double boiler. Remove from the heat and fold in the stiffly beaten egg whites, then vanilla and whipped cream, and pour over pudding.

TEXAS RANGER COOKIES

Ingredients:

1 cup butter

1 cup sugar

1 cup brown sugar

2 eggs

2 tsp vanilla extract

2 cups flour

Pinch of salt

2 tsp baking soda

1 tsp baking powder

2 cups Rice Krispies

2 cups oats

1 cup coconut

½ cup butterscotch chips

½ cup chocolate chips

1 cup chopped pecans

1 cup toffee pieces

Directions:

Preheat oven to 350 degrees and lightly grease cookie sheets. Cream butter and sugars until light and fluffy, then add eggs one at a time, beating well after each, and add vanilla. Whisk together flour, salt, baking soda, and baking powder. Add to butter mixture and fold in remaining ingredients. Drop by tablespoons full onto baking sheet. Bake for 8–10 minutes or 10–12 minutes for crispier cookies. Remove from oven and allow to firm up on cookie sheet about 5 minutes. Cool completely. Makes four dozen cookies.

JOHN'S SHRIMP AND PASTA ALFREDO

(With thanks to Bethann Eccles)

ALFREDO SAUCE

Ingredients:

½ cup butter
8 oz. cream cheese
2 tsp garlic powder
2 cups milk
6 oz. grated Parmesan cheese
Pepper to taste

Directions:

Melt butter in a saucepan over medium heat. When melted, add cream cheese and garlic powder. Stir near-continuously with a whisk until the cream cheese is fully melted. Gradually add milk (any variety—even skim will thicken), a little at a time, continually whisking, until smooth. Stir in grated Parmesan. Keep it on the heat until the cheese melts fully. This may take a while.

Add pepper to taste. No additional salt should be needed. Remove from heat when the Parmesan is fully melted, and the sauce reaches your desired consistency. If your sauce cooks too long and is too thick, it can be thinned with more milk. Toss with hot pasta to serve.

SAUTÉED SHRIMP

Ingredients:

    3 Tbsp butter, separated

    1–2 tsp minced garlic

    1 pound uncooked, peeled shrimp

Directions:

Melt butter in a frying pan over medium heat. When melted, add garlic and sauté until soft, but not browned. Then add shrimp and an additional tablespoon of butter. Stir often until shrimp are cooked through. Remove from heat and, using tongs, place the shrimp on top of the prepared pasta.

CHOCOLATE EXPRESS MUFFINS

Ingredients:

4 cups all-purpose flour

1½ cups sugar

5 tsp baking powder

2 tsp ground cinnamon

1 tsp salt

2 cups milk

4 Tbsp instant coffee granules

1 cup melted butter

2 eggs

2 tsp vanilla extract

1 cup bittersweet chocolate chips

1 cup milk chocolate chips

Directions:

Preheat oven to 375 degrees. In a large bowl, combine the flour, sugar, baking powder, cinnamon, and salt. In another bowl, combine milk and coffee granules until coffee is dissolved. Add the butter, eggs, and vanilla. Stir into dry ingredients just until moistened, and fold in chocolate chips.

Fill prepared muffin cups two-thirds full. Bake for 17–20 minutes or until a toothpick inserted near the center comes out clean. Cool for 5 minutes before removing from pans to wire racks. Serve warm. Makes about 24 muffins.

TURTLE BARS

Ingredients:

    2 cups all-purpose flour

    1 cup firmly packed brown sugar

    ½ cup butter

    1 cup pecan halves

    ⅔ cup butter

    ½ cup firmly packed brown sugar

    1 cup good quality milk chocolate chips

Directions:

Preheat oven to 350 degrees. For the crust, combine the first three ingredients. Beat at medium speed until mixture resembles fine crumbs. Press onto bottom of ungreased 13x9 inch baking pan. Place pecans evenly over unbaked crust. Combine the ⅔ cup butter and ½ cup brown sugar in 1-quart saucepan. Cook over medium heat, stirring constantly, until entire surface of mixture comes to a boil. Boil 1 minute, stirring constantly. Pour evenly over pecans and crust.

Bake for 18 to 22 minutes, or until entire caramel layer is bubbly (do not overbake). Remove from oven and immediately sprinkle with chips. Allow to melt slightly (2 to 3 minutes). Swirl chips, leaving some whole for a marbled effect. Cool completely, then cut into bars. Makes about 24 bars.

KAT'S STUFFED FRENCH TOAST

(With thanks to Kathleen Kramr of the Country Place Hotel)

Ingredients:

    1 8-oz. pkg. cream cheese
    ½ cup chopped walnuts
    1 tsp vanilla extract
    12 slices white bread
    4 eggs, beaten
    ¾ cup cream
    1 tsp vanilla extract
    dash nutmeg
    Butter for the pan
    1 12-oz. jar apricot jam
    ½ cup orange juice
    Sliced bananas

Directions:

Combine the cream cheese, walnuts, and vanilla. Spread on six slices of bread, and top with the remaining six slices to form sandwiches. Combine the eggs, cream, vanilla, and nutmeg. Dip each sandwich into the mixture and cook in butter in a skillet as for French toast. Combine the jam and orange juice. Garnish the top of the diagonally cut toast with bananas and serve with apricot sauce.

kennethgall.com

ABOUT THE AUTHOR

Although she currently lives in Texas with her husband and two children, Agatha-nominated author Karen MacInerney was born and bred in the Northeast, and she escapes there as often as possible. When she isn't in Maine eating lobster, she spends her time in Austin with her cookbooks, her family, her computer, and the local walking trail (not necessarily in that order).

In addition to writing the Gray Whale Inn mysteries, Karen is the author of the Tales of an Urban Werewolf series. You can visit her online at www.karenmacinerney.com.

WWW.MIDNIGHTINKBOOKS.COM

From the gritty streets of New York City to sacred tombs in the Middle East, it's always midnight somewhere. Join us online at any hour for fresh new voices in mystery fiction.

At midnightinkbooks.com you'll also find our author blog, new and upcoming books, events, book club questions, excerpts, mystery resources, and more.

MIDNIGHT INK ORDERING INFORMATION

Order Online:
• Visit our website *www.midnightinkbooks.com*, select your books, and order them on our secure server.

Order by Phone:
• Call toll-free within the U.S. and Canada at 1-888-NITE-INK (1-888-648-3465)
• We accept VISA, MasterCard, and American Express

Order by Mail:
Send the full price of your order (MN residents add 6.875% sales tax) in U.S. funds, plus postage & handling to:

Midnight Ink
2143 Wooddale Drive
Woodbury, MN 55125-2989

Postage & Handling:
Standard (U.S. & Canada). If your order is:
$25.00 and under, add $4.00
$25.01 and over, FREE STANDARD SHIPPING

AK, HI, PR: $16.00 for one book plus $2.00 for each additional book.

International Orders (airmail only):
$16.00 for one book plus $3.00 for each additional book

Orders are processed within 12 business days. Please allow for normal shipping time.
Postage and handling rates subject to change.

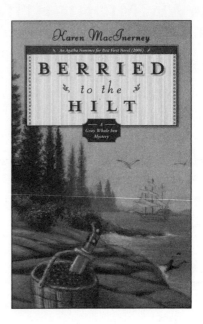

Berried to the Hilt

Karen MacInerney

When a lobsterman pulls up a 200-year-old anchor, Cranberry Island is abuzz with excitement. Is it from the elusive Santa Elena, a famous eighteenth century pirate ship? Soon the island is swarming with marine archaeologists, treasure seekers, and ghost-hunters. It's good news for Natalie—and the Gray Whale Inn—until one of her guests turns up dead. Will Natalie find the killer? Or will she be joining the lost ship's crew, down in Davy Jones' Locker?

978-0-7387-1966-5   **$14.95**

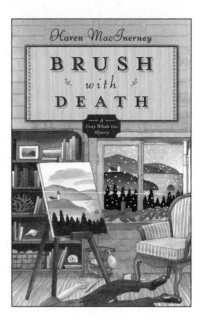

Brush with Death

Karen MacInerney

**Midnight Ink's top-selling,
Agatha Award-nominated
series continues**

With an upcoming gallery show and a popular artist visiting Cranberry Island, art is on everyone's minds—especially innkeeper Natalie Barnes. When Gwen, Natalie's niece, is invited to present her paintings at the art show, Natalie is torn between worrying about stressed out Gwen, the arrival of her future mother-in-law, and the threat of foreclosure on the Gray Whale Inn. But then Natalie finds Gwen's mentor dead. Will she uncover the truth behind this murder masterpiece?

978-0-7387-3459-0 $14.99